THE
AZTEC
CODE

THE AZTEC CODE

STEPHEN COLE

BLOOMSBURY

First published in Great Britain in 2007 by Bloomsbury Publishing Plc
36 Soho Square, London, W1D 3QY

A CIP catalogue record of this book is available from the British Library

ISBN 978 0 7475 8427 8

All papers used by Bloomsbury Publishing are natural, recyclable products made
from wood grown in well-managed forests. The manufacturing processes
conform to the environmental regulations of the country of origin.

Typeset by Dorchester Typesetting Group Ltd
Printed in Great Britain by Clays Ltd, St Ives Plc

1 3 5 7 9 10 8 6 4 2

www.bloomsbury.com

To Linda Chapman,
for sharing all the madness

CHAPTER ONE

They came like shadows out of the warm, wet night. Three of them in black, moving swiftly and quietly through the long grass beside the winding dirt track. Their destination loomed up ahead of them: a sprawling complex of stained concrete, serene in the moon's silver light.

Jonah Wish stared at it with foreboding, rubbing the stitch in his side while his friends pushed on ahead. It was late Saturday night and what was he doing – partying hard? Clubbing all night? Getting trashed with his mates?

No. He was breaking into a nuclear power station in the wilds of Guatemala.

He pushed his damp blond hair up from his forehead. *Same old, same old.*

However weird it might seem, this was his life now. A few months ago he'd been stuck in a Young Offenders Institution: a loser with no friends and family, better with codes and computers than with people. It was cyber-fraud that had got him locked up in the first place – but it had also brought him to the attention of a powerful and most unusual man . . .

'Great place to stop, geek!' Motti's angry hiss cut

through the muggy night from behind a dense tropical thicket. 'You're in plain view! Get your ass over here before I kick it clear over the perimeter fence.'

'S'pose that's one sure way of getting inside,' Jonah muttered as he ran to catch up.

Motti was a tall, rangy American guy, all glower and goatee, with black hair tied back in a ponytail. 'About time.' He squinted at some high-tech gadget through his round-rimmed glasses. 'Thought you'd stopped to take a leak or something.'

'Nope. I'm keeping a full bladder so I can wet myself properly when we tackle the main security systems.'

Motti cracked the tiniest smile. 'That I can believe.'

'Oi, stop picking on Jonah,' came a rough, south London accent from deeper in the thicket.

'He's eighteen, Patch. He don't need no scrawny kid cyclops sticking up for him.'

'He don't need some gangly bearded tit on his backside either.' Patch's thin, freckled face pushed out from the fleshy leaves. In the moonlight, the square of leather over his missing left eye looked creepily like a gaping socket. 'Actually, I s'pose no one needs a tit on their backside. How would you ever sit down?'

'Carefully,' Motti suggested, still scrutinising his gadget. They all sniggered, but then a red light started flashing. 'OK, we got a signal. Power supply for the electric fence is thirty metres north.'

Patch was suddenly dead serious too; like Motti, he knew when it was time to stop clowning. 'Reckon you can bust it?'

''Course I can bust it,' said Motti, calibrating

something on his box of tricks. 'And those dummies in security control will have no idea. Provided Tye and Con stay on the ball.'

'I hope they're OK,' muttered Jonah.

They waited edgily in silence – although 'silence' was hardly the word. The cicadas all around them sounded like some freaky giant generator. Night sounds carried eerily from the dark and distant rainforest, the howls and screeches of creatures unknown. But Jonah thought the loudest thing had to be the thrum of his racing heart.

He bit his lip and tried to think of all the perks of his new lifestyle – the travel, the money, the freedom, the feeling of belonging somewhere after all these years. But right now he could only see the downside. OK, so they only ripped off people who *deserved* ripping off – shady, super-rich types who stood to lose a whole lot more by going to the cops. But in the long, nerve-twisting build-up to a job, with the iron taste of fear in the back of his throat, Jonah couldn't help thinking: *Someone get me out of here. I'm not cut out to be a thief.*

Especially not the creepy, freaky brand of thievery the boss man specialised in.

'You know,' Patch breathed, 'I think I'd feel a whole lot happier if this place really *was* just a nuclear power station.'

'Me too,' said Jonah. 'Which is saying something.'

'OK, keep it down, we're ready to go,' said Motti. 'And remember, we got a job to do. If we mess up . . .'

He mimed a knife moving slowly across his throat. Then he moved off quietly into the undergrowth.

Patch rubbed nervously at the leather over his eye, and scrambled after him.

'Roll on Sunday morning,' Jonah muttered, following close behind.

Another day, another job, Tye told herself. Only this one was a little too close to home for her liking. She was born and raised in Haiti, and from the age of eleven had spent five years smuggling contraband all across the Caribbean and South America. She'd almost got herself killed in Guatemala a couple of times, crossing the border to Honduras. Making it three times unlucky was not high on her 'to do' list.

Yet here she was, crouching close to the main gates of the apparently deserted complex. Beside her stood a rusted sign advertising clean, cheap nuclear energy for all.

But Tye knew what the place was *really* for. And just how dangerous this heist would be. The sweat soaking her back wasn't only down to the humid night.

She looked at Con, her companion and colleague, wishing she could share her fears with a friend. But Con didn't do friendship – *alliances* were more her thing. Platinum blonde and striking, the only thing she allowed close to her was money.

Con raised a perfectly plucked eyebrow. 'Everything is all right?' Her voice held a trace of European accent, and was like a cool breath in the heat.

'I'm fine.' Tye straightened, smoothed out the clinging pink top Con assured her looked great against her dark skin. 'You really think this will work?'

'The men guarding this place are lonely and bored.' Con undid the top few buttons of her lacy blouse. 'They will not turn down the chance of some female company while the boss is away.'

'You're sure of that?'

Con smiled, hitching up her short black skirt a fraction. 'We'll have them eating out of our hands, yes?'

Tye nodded unhappily. 'They'll be eating out of my fist if they try to lay a finger on me.'

'It will be OK.' Con strutted up to the main gates. 'We must give our boys their distraction.'

Distracting boys comes easy to you, Tye thought. *When you're around I just fade into the background.*

And that had never once bothered her, until Jonah Wish had showed up in her life.

It wasn't so much his looks, though they were just fine – scruffy blond hair, serious eyes, a smile that suggested he knew stuff he wasn't meant to tell. It was more about the person he was. Tye had a gift for reading people – it had helped her stay alive in her smuggling days, and she'd known from the first time they'd met that if she was ever to really open up to someone, it would be Jonah.

Yeah. If.

'Come *on*,' Con urged her. 'It's time.' She jabbed a buzzer on the entryphone beside the gates and looked up nonchalantly into the security camera.

Tye took a deep breath and crossed to join her.

A squawk of static and Spanish erupted from the entryphone. The man's voice sounded gruff and threatening, but Con gabbled back at him, all smiles.

She was fluent in eight languages and could get by in eleven more. It was just a shame you could barely believe a word she said in any of them.

Tye spoke enough Spanish to understand the gist of the conversation. As rehearsed, Con was explaining they were backpackers fooled into coming out here by a couple of *bastardos* with more on their minds than a moonlit walk. They had run for it – but now didn't have a clue where they were. Could anyone in there help?

The voice told Con to wait.

Tye looked up at the camera and tried to do 'pleading'.

The entryphone squawked back into life a minute later. A different man's voice gave instructions to wait by the gate until someone came to fetch them.

'They want us,' Con murmured through her grateful camera-smile.

Tye allowed her eyelids a token flutter. Already she could hear the distant roar of an engine approaching. Yellow headlights rushed to meet them from the shadowy buildings of the main complex. The gates rattled as some invisible bolt was released, and they started to swing inwards.

'Get going, Motti,' Tye breathed.

Then floodlights snapped on. Tye shielded her eyes as three black men in a battered open-top jeep pulled up beside them. Automatic weapons were slung carelessly from their shoulders. They looked over at Tye and Con, sweaty and severe.

Then the driver slowly smiled, showing teeth as rotten as he smelled. 'Get in,' he told Con, patting the seat beside him. Which left Tye the tiny space between his pet thugs in the back. She clambered in. They stank of BO and garlic, and made no effort to help her or to move out of the way. They must really believe they were dealing with a couple of helpless girls they could intimidate.

Tye squeezed in between them and allowed herself the tiniest of smiles. *You have no idea*, she thought.

Motti heard the low electric hum carry through the drowsy night.

'Main gate's opening,' Jonah hissed beside him.

'I ain't deaf,' Motti growled. *Ain't blind, neither*, he thought as floodlights flicked on, sending long shadows streaking from the sprawl of buildings towards the electrified perimeter fence – a standard twenty-one-wire job on three-metre posts. Luckily, this far round from the entrance, the floodlights stopped short of him and the guys as they crouched down in their muddy trench. They had dug down to expose the power spur feeding the complex's systems without tripping an alarm. Given the crappy state of repair of the place – weeds and shit all up the fence, kinks in the wire and worse – Motti wasn't really surprised. But he was sure as hell relieved.

So far so good.

Patch trained a torch on the spaghetti-wiring inside the spur, while Jonah heaved a heavy-duty black box crammed with capacitors into position beside it. Expertly Motti hooked up jump-leads from his home-made device to the right terminals.

'OK. As of now, all the charge in this part of the

fence is being absorbed by the Motti-box. That's 10,000 volts.'

'Glad it's running into there and not into us,' said Patch.

'It will do if you don't get over that fence in sixty seconds,' Motti told him, crossing to the fence and starting to climb. 'That's about how long we got before the box fills to capacity and the current flows back to the fence circuit.'

Jonah and Patch hurled themselves at the chain-link and clambered up after him. 'You *sure* the guards won't notice the power's been bled from this section?' said Jonah as he climbed. 'You said yourself there were anti-tamper devices –'

'Computers and ciphers are your shit, security's mine, OK?' Motti swung himself over the top, counting in his head. *Thirty-five seconds left.* 'Point one, all fence control comes from the monitoring station – the guard house, right? From there they can activate or isolate the entire fence or any individual sector.'

'Like the way they just cut the charge around the entrance,' panted Patch, close behind him.

'Uh-huh, and when they do that, this little surge goes through the whole system. That's why I waited till then before hooking up.' *Twenty-five seconds.* 'It causes a spike in the current – but since a single mom in a trailer park sees more maintenance than this fence system, if they notice they should put it down to wear and tear.'

'Let's hope so,' said Jonah, last to haul himself over.

'Ten seconds, geek!' hissed Motti. 'C'mon, move it!'

Jonah hit the ground and flattened himself against it.

'Main gates should be closing any moment,' whispered Motti. Sure enough, a rattling clang sounded from the entrance. The floodlights died, plunging the periphery of the complex back into moonlit shadow. 'And the power's running back into the fence any time . . .'

'. . . Now!' Patch concluded, as the ominous hum of the electric fence resumed.

'Nice work, Motti,' breathed Jonah.

'Whatever,' he said gruffly. 'The fence may have been left to rot, but getting inside the containment vessel's gonna be way harder.'

'You don't say.' Patch sighed and shook his head. 'I can't believe we're raiding the core of a nuclear reactor.'

'It ain't been used for years,' Motti pointed out.

'But it could still be radioactive! Our bums could be glowing bright green by the time we get out of here!'

'Cool. Yours'll be easier to kick in the dark.' Motti booted it now for good measure. 'Now get us inside that containment vessel.'

Jonah had raised his head and was looking all around. 'Coast seems to be clear.'

Motti nodded. 'With any luck, the guards'll go check out those two babes who just showed out of nowhere.'

'Good for us,' Jonah agreed grimly. 'Bad for Tye and Con.'

The bone-rattling ride to the guardhouse seemed to

take for ever, but at least conversation was impossible over the jeep's spluttering engine. In the headlights' glare, Con could see the whole complex was decaying like some vast industrial corpse. Long grass was growing up through the cracked asphalt. Rusting forklifts and rotting pallets littered empty yards. Abandoned buildings were falling into disrepair.

The jeep pulled up at the guardhouse that adjoined the main reception. Once it must have looked impressive, but the mirrored glass was now cracked and cobwebbed, divided by rusting steel strips. Con supposed only one area would be well maintained – the containment vessels that had once enclosed the reactor core.

Now they held a secret treasure. The thought of the cash it could earn her was making her heart race. It was worth the danger. It was worth anything.

She checked out the guards and was unimpressed. If you could scrub away the dirt, sweat and tattoos you'd find 'mercenary' written all over them. There was nothing wrong with that, of course – Con would hardly be here herself if not for the hard-cash incentive – but this lot must be pretty low-grade if they were stuck on guard duty in a place already so well defended. The owner must know that any self-respecting thieves would be mad to enter here.

Unless they're thieves like us, thought Con.

'Get inside,' the driver told her in Spanish.

'May we use your phone?' she asked. He just laughed in her face, his breath stale and spicy, and shoved her out of the jeep. Tye had already been bundled out by her two towering escorts.

'Not very friendly, are they?' whispered Tye. 'Can't you turn up the charm a bit?'

'Please, we've been walking for hours,' Con told the driver meekly. 'All we want to do is rest and then –'

'Inside,' the driver insisted, opening the door to the guardhouse.

What had once been the gleaming hub of security here was now a large, grotty living space, hazy with cigarette smoke. The stained floor was strewn with litter. Few of the spotlights in the ceiling still worked; more light came from the CCTV screens showing views of the complex in flickering black and white. A poker table had been squeezed into one corner, cards and chips scattered round half-empty bottles of tequila and whisky.

A wiry white man in a swivel chair spun round from the monitors to size up the newcomers. Con nodded to him politely. He looked greedily between her and Tye like a kid trying to decide which present to tear open first.

The two big black men from the jeep stood blocking the way out behind them, and the driver barred the way ahead. Intimidating assholes. Con did her best to look scared, watched them get off on it with quiet loathing.

'Take off your shoes,' said the driver quietly.

She looked at him blankly. 'Why?'

'You've been walking for hours, you say? Let's see your feet!'

Not so stupid, then. Con shrugged over at Tye and did as she was asked. Luckily, they *had* been tramping for some time through the rough terrain beyond the complex, so as not to be observed. Her feet were chafed and red, almost as blistered as Tye's. She promised herself a pedicure the second she got back to base.

The driver peered down at their feet, then seemed to relax a little. 'So, the two of you just happened to find your way here, huh?'

'We saw your lights from the hillside,' said Tye in halting Spanish. 'These guys picked us up on the main road, said they would give us a ride to Livingston.'

'Is that so?' the driver sneered. He turned to his bozo buddies guarding the door. 'Take Samuel and Kristian and search outside the grounds. Start with the main track. If you find anyone hanging around, bring them here. In one piece or several – Kabacra won't care.'

'Who are you people?' Con affected horror, though there had always been a chance this would happen. At least Motti and the others would have fewer guards patrolling *inside* the complex to worry about. 'What is this place?'

'And who's Kabacra?' Tye added, glancing round as the men disappeared back through the doorway.

'You want us to let you go, right?' The driver showed his broken teeth in an unpleasant leer. 'So just shut up till you're spoken to.' He poured some tequila into a filthy glass. 'José, watch them.'

The man in the chair gave a dirty chuckle. 'Man, I *am* watching them.'

Be my guest, thought Con coldly, as behind him on one of the fuzzy grey monitors three dark figures flitted past.

12

Patch skidded to a halt at the sound of deep voices calling to each other in some foreign language. He dropped swiftly to the ground and Motti and Jonah followed suit. They held themselves still as stone till the voices moved away.

'What was that about?' Patch wondered.

'The guards may not believe the girls came alone,' Motti hissed in his ear. 'If they've figured it's a distraction tactic, they'll be looking for trouble.'

Jonah swore under his breath. 'But if they find your box hooked up to the power supply –'

'So let's get going, huh? Patch, the door we need open is right across the courtyard.' Motti gestured to a dark, towering building that kept a vast swathe of stars from sight. 'The door recess ain't well lit, so chances are the CCTV won't catch you. You just gotta get there quick, don't make no sudden moves, and get us inside.'

Patch glared at him. 'You don't have to treat me like a kid.'

'You're fourteen, you *are* a kid.'

'Technically, maybe.'

'So go get technical before I poke you in the eye.'

Patch flipped up his leather patch, reached under his eyelid and plucked out his glass eyeball with a soft sucking noise. To his delight, Motti cringed and nearly gagged.

'God damn it, you cyclops freak,' he gasped. 'Will you quit with the "utility eye" crap!'

'Jonah thinks it's cool, don't you, mate?' Patch unscrewed the top half of the false eyeball to reveal a soft squishy blob inside.

'Plastic explosive?' asked Jonah.

'Play-Doh,' Patch replied. Then he flipped down his eyepatch and sprinted for the doorway. His nerves ebbed away as he studied the barriers to opening the door. Fingerprint scanner – from the make and model, Patch guessed it was maybe two years old – linked to an older numeric keypad with eight-character capacity.

Piece of cake.

He pressed the Play-Doh against the 1 key on the keypad. Bound to be an impression there, it hadn't been cleaned since for ever. He daubed the squashy blob against the scanner plate. OK, so the match might be muddy, but after so long exposed to the elements the plate would be less sensitive and –

A green light winked on as the fingerprint was accepted. 'Bob's your auntie,' Patch muttered to himself, sticking the squishy blob back in his false eye. 'Now for the keycode.'

'C'mon, cyclops!' Motti hissed from across the overgrown courtyard.

'Gonna have to use the bit-buster.' So saying, Patch pulled a little gadget the size of a TV remote from his back pocket, raised its little backlit screen, and attached it to the keypad. Numbers streamed across the display in blurring columns. The bit-buster used a wireless link to interrogate the keypad's chip and find the last successfully input code. Sometimes it took a while for the two little computers to hook up, but –

With a beep of quiet pride, the bit-buster finished its digital chat. Now its screen displayed eight numbers. But were they the right numbers?

Holding his breath, Patch tapped in the sequence: 1-5-3-0-9-0-1-5.

The door clicked loudly as it unlocked and opened, but still Patch held his breath, staring warily into the pitch darkness beyond.

What was waiting for them in there?

CHAPTER TWO

A smear of dark movement on the screen told Tye that Patch was going to work on the door to the containment vessel. Con had seen it too and was holding eye contact with José, smiling coyly, making sure he kept his attention only on her.

Tye decided to play a game she was better equipped for. She cleared her throat and once she had the driver's attention she tilted her head to one side. 'Look, we're sorry if we trespassed. We honestly didn't know. You do believe us, right? You will let us go?'

He hesitated for less than a second. But Tye could read body language like Patch could read comics, and this doofus had licked his lips, glanced over at his friend and shifted on the balls of his feet before he'd even drawn breath – classic signals that he was about to tell a point-blank lie. 'Sure. I'm just taking precautions. Whatever happens, you'll be OK.'

Uh-huh. Right. 'Thank you.'

'Keep watching them, José. I gotta pee.'

Yes. Go on, go. Tye willed the driver not to look back round at the screens before he left. Luckily he was too busy scratching his crotch. Once he'd gone, she spoke to Con quietly in English. 'He's lying, and he's pretty sure that we are too. We're dead if we hang around here for too long.'

'Or sooner if he sees that the door's been opened,' Con murmured.

Tye glanced up to see a dark figure – it looked like Patch – move cautiously through the now-open doorway.

Con smiled. 'I'd better get to work.'

'What're you saying?' asked José, suddenly suspicious.

'My friend was wondering which of us you like best. I think you like *me*. Look into my eyes, José. Into my eyes.'

'No tricks,' he warned. 'Not from either of you.'

'No tricks,' Con agreed in a lower voice, soothing and exotic. 'Just look into my eyes, José, and forget about her. Forget about anything else.'

Tye caught a flicker of movement on the screen. Another figure had come into shot and glanced nervously up at the security camera. Through the fuzz she saw Jonah's sweet face, lined with worry.

The same second, some instinct made José break eye contact with Con, turn in the chair and spy Jonah too.

With a roar he leaped up from the chair and pointed a handgun at Con. She threw herself aside as he fired. Tye picked up one of her walking boots and hurled it like a missile. The steel toecap cracked into the man's forehead and he fell backwards over his swivel chair. He didn't get back up.

'Thanks, sweets,' Con said shakily, picking herself up from the filthy floor. But Tye could hear running footsteps. The driver returned, face twisted in anger, his flies gaping open. Leaping forwards, Con landed a karate kick there with vicious satisfaction. He doubled up with a hoarse squeak. Tye punched him in the jaw and sent him crashing back into the poker table, which collapsed under his weight.

Con crouched beside the driver and slapped his face lightly to try and revive him. 'God, Tye, did you have to hit him so hard?'

'Can you put the 'fluence on him?' Tye asked anxiously.

'It's not voodoo magic, Tye,' said Con curtly. 'It's *mesmerism*. And I can't work it when the subject is out cold.'

Tye bit her lip. The way Con could hypnotise just about anyone into doing just about anything *was* magical to her. And the plan had been to get at least one of these guys under Con's 'fluence so he could steer the rest of security well away from the thieves' planned exit. Now, when the mercenaries in the grounds radioed back in, there would be no one to answer them – and something very nasty would hit the fan.

Con pulled out her mobile phone and hit the speed-dial. 'Motti? You'd better move things along in there, yes?'

Jonah followed Patch up a flight of concrete steps that led to a blast door. Predictably it was locked – another fingerprint scanner.

Patch was already getting busy with his Play-Doh. 'Where's Motti?'

Jonah looked behind him nervously. 'Mot?'

'Right here,' he hissed, scaling the steps soundlessly. 'Con just called. We don't got long.'

'Then it's lucky this old relic's as crap as its twin outside,' said Patch, as the lifted fingerprint did the job again. The blast door slid open to reveal an antechamber of mouldering concrete, empty save for a high-spec PC perched on a rickety camping table. Thick snaking cables connected it to an uninterruptible power supply. A high-res webcam was fixed to the top of the monitor with a blob of plasticine.

'This place is a real lash-up, isn't it,' said Jonah.

'Could be what the owner wants you to think,' Motti warned him, 'trying to catch you off-guard.' He pointed to another set of blast doors. 'The main containment vessel should be just through there. Which makes this the last line of defence.'

Jonah kneeled down in front of the PC, which was quietly humming to itself, and nudged the mouse to wake the display. A box appeared at once, prompting for a password. He pulled a CD from the inner pocket of his lightweight jacket and loaded it up. It was crammed with enough hack 'n' crack software to break the toughest encryption algorithms.

He hoped.

Slowly, as he worked, pitting his wits and his code against the computer, he became totally immersed in the challenge. He could have been anywhere: in the dark bedroom of one of his many past foster homes, or in the computer lab of one of his endless dreary new schools. It was like the monitor was a window on another world, one he could retreat to. An orderly world that made beautiful, crystal-clear sense if you could only see it in just the right way. And right through his teens, the sorrier his circumstances became, the stronger the urge inside him had grown to crack ever greater codes.

Compared to cracking real life, it was a cinch.

'I'm into the security systems,' he announced, checking his watch. Three minutes. Not bad.

Patch and Motti were studying the double doors. 'Can you get these open, geek?' Motti demanded. 'There's no entry-coder, nothing to override.'

Jonah double-clicked on folders, sifted through directories. 'Can't see anything relating to . . . Wait.' By opening a folder he had triggered a software program; his heart did a flip. 'Uh, guys? This could screw us.'

'What?' Motti and Patch stalked over.

'I've found the key to those doors.' He gestured to the screen, where a wireframe map of a human face was picked out in vivid blue and green. 'Facial recognition scan, hooked up to the webcam. And from the look of things, designed to recognise one face only.'

'Whose?' asked Patch.

Motti shoved him. 'The guy who owns the place, dumb-ass.'

'This is the mapped image. Let's take a look.' Jonah double-clicked it: *Kabacra.jpg*. 'You never know, maybe he looks like one of us.'

He didn't.

A gaunt Hispanic face glared out at them through hard, feral eyes. His features were narrow and angular, and livid scars criss-crossed the skin in all directions.

'Jeez!' said Patch. 'Looks like someone tried to cross out his face with a Stanley knife!'

'Son of a bitch ain't beaten us yet,' said Motti darkly. 'That PC got Bluetooth, Jonah?'

'Yeah, but –'

'Well, so's my cell phone, as well as a high-res camera. So one of us smiles for the camera, we Bluetooth it across to the PC, you dump it in that folder, and –'

'It's gonna take too long,' said Patch nervously. 'These systems make a map of every detail on your face – distance between your eyes, length of your nose, all of that.'

'He's right,' Jonah agreed. 'Converting that info into code for the Local Feature Analysis could take ages.'

Motti swore. 'OK, plan B. Patch, drop your trousers and bend over.'

Patch frowned. 'You could buy me a drink first!'

'We need something with less local features – I'm guessing it's quicker to map an ass than a face. Am I right, geek?'

'That's thinking outside the box. Or outside the pants anyway.' Jonah was impressed. 'I suppose with a bit of reprogramming it could work.'

'Why not my back or something?' Patch protested. 'Or my arm?'

Jonah was already calling up the code. 'Less reprogramming if it's something round.'

'Your ass, your face, same difference,' Motti agreed.

Patch sighed and undid his belt. 'If my pants have got skids, promise you won't tell Con?'

Motti grimly angled the phone. 'Man, I ain't telling a soul.'

Tye straightened up from the security console. She had mashed up the wiring so none of the surveillance cameras worked – that might delay the mercenaries upon their return. And Con had tied up both men with some nylon twine she'd found out the back.

Suddenly the driver's RT belched into life. Tye didn't catch the urgent flurry of Spanish, but Con did, and at once she started trying to shake the driver awake. 'They've found where we hid the 4x4. They want further instructions. We need this jerk to talk to them.'

The driver stirred groggily. 'Go to hell,' he hissed.

'I don't have time to mesmerise him now,' Con said with a pointed look at Tye.

'Then we'll try the blunt approach.' Tye grabbed Jose's fallen handgun and jammed it up against the driver's collarbone. Of course, no way would she ever use a gun for real – but *he* didn't know that.

Con nodded, her eyes hard and arctic pale. 'Tell Kristian to bring the car up to the main entrance. Tell him to wait there while the others keep looking.'

The man glared at her, said nothing.

The RT squawked again irately. Con grabbed it and shoved it in his face. 'You heard me. Do it *now*.'

Through gritted teeth, the driver did as he was told. When he was through, Con blew him a kiss.

'I'll open the main gates,' said Tye, throwing the switch.

Con nodded. 'Make sure they stay open, yes?'

Tye brought the butt of the gun down hard on the controls, smashing them.

'You'll never get away with this, even if you get past my boys,' snarled the driver. 'Wherever you run, Kabacra will find you.'

The conviction in his voice sent a small shiver through Tye. She knew he meant what he said. But Con ignored him and switched back into low, soothing Spanish. 'Shh, little man. Look into my eyes. See how they glitter? You are feeling tired, I think. Relax a little . . . If anyone else calls you on the radio, you tell them to stay out there searching the woods. They are not to return. You don't want to be disturbed when you're feeling so tired, do you? So listen to what I say . . .'

The driver's eyes were slowly glazing over. It was uncanny, the way Con could put just about anyone into a trance, given enough time. But Tye had the uneasy feeling that their time, like their luck, was close to running out.

'Sorted,' said Jonah. 'Patch's bum is now access-all-areas. Let's see if the computer can recognise the real thing.'

Patch dropped his trousers again and mooned the webcam. His buttocks graced the screen in stereo as the software began cross-referencing the new image against the stored photo. It had mapped just eleven nodal points, so fingers crossed it wouldn't take too –

The computer bleeped. ACCESS GRANTED.

'Yes!' hissed Jonah.

Patch planted a smacker on the monitor screen.

'Kiss my ass!'

Jonah grimaced. 'I'm not even going to shake its hand.'

Motti took no part in the celebrations, crossing at once to the containment vessel's blast doors. They opened smoothly and he hesitated in the dark doorway. 'Let's spill some light in here,' he said, groping for a switch. 'See what we're stealing.'

The lights faded up, and he walked purposefully inside. Jonah stood in the doorway with Patch as the nerves crawled back into his stomach. He had never seen inside a nuclear reactor before, but he imagined that not many looked like this.

The vast, square concrete chamber had been turned into a secret museum. Mounted around the walls were precious antique weapons – swords and scimitars, rapiers and daggers. They ranged from crude, primitive knives to cavalry swords with exquisitely designed hilts and jewel-encrusted scabbards. But, beautiful as they were, they sent a shiver through Jonah. He had the feeling these were swords that had been used, and used often.

'Looks like there's pistols and rifles and stuff downstairs,' Patch observed, pointing to a spiral staircase in the corner that led down to the next level of the containment chamber.

'We ain't here for pistols and rifles and stuff,' said Motti, moving from sword to sword, peering at each intently.

'So come on, then,' Jonah said impatiently. 'You're our designated treasure-finder, we're only here to help you get access . . . Where is it? Where's Cortes's sword?'

Hernando Cortes.

It was a name that until recently had meant nothing to Jonah, though it was written big in the history books. In 1519, with only six hundred men, twenty horses and ten small cannons he sailed from Spain, arrived in Mexico and conquered the entire Aztec empire of more than five million people. Never before had such a massive and wealthy region been taken by such a small force. So all in all, Jonah guessed it was fair enough that the very sword Cortes used when he took the capital city and imprisoned the rightful Aztec ruler would be worth a few quid and be a tempting target for thieves. But was it really worth him and the others risking their lives for?

Do we work for the boss, or does he own us?

'It ain't here.' Motti was staring round the room, confusion on his face hardening to anger. 'After all that, the goddamned thing ain't here!' He bunched his fists, punched the wall in frustration. 'Coldhardt's fouled up, he gave us dud info! Jesus, what a f—'

'Look at this space.' Patch was pointing to an area of bare wall. 'Maybe the special sword *was* here.'

'Well, it ain't now.' Motti started setting about random swords, impatiently unhooking them from their mountings. 'I'm damned if we're not taking *something* away with us. This crap's gotta be worth a fortune to some dumb-ass collector. Give me a hand.'

'Shouldn't we just get the hell out of here?' Jonah worried.

Motti ignored him and hurled a sword in his direction. Jonah caught it awkwardly and thanked God it was still in its scabbard.

'Hang on,' said Patch, waving a hand frantically for silence. 'I think I heard something.'

He was right. Jonah could hear the stealthy tread of someone on the concrete steps. He gripped hold of the sheathed sword tightly and turned to Patch and Motti. 'Do we hide or fight?'

'Neither,' came a familiar voice behind him. 'You come with us.'

'Tye!' Jonah felt weak with relief. 'God, it's good to see you.'

She opened her mouth to reply, but it was Con who spoke, running up behind her. 'We've got to get out of here,' she said. 'Now.'

'Situation?' snapped Motti, helping himself to more antique silverware.

'The car's been parked at the main exit,' said Con. 'Gates are open, one guard to take care of.'

'What about the others?'

'Still searching the grounds, but could come back any time. If they do, their leader will detail them to the turbine end of the complex, nicely out the way.'

'But it won't take them long to find there's no intruders there,' Tye added. 'Have you got what Coldhardt wanted?'

'It's not here,' said Patch miserably.

'So we're taking the other swords,' added Motti. 'C'mon.'

Tye started forwards, but Con didn't move. She was too busy staring at the computer screen, her striking face caught somewhere between horror and amusement. 'Ugh! Whose spotty butt is that?'

'Even my virtual bum gets kicked,' Patch muttered,

his cheeks glowing crimson, crossly snatching daggers from the wall.

Tye led the way as they moved out, weighed down with their antique trophies, and stole across the moon-lit compound. She signalled the others to stop as they came into view of the car. It was parked facing the open exit, thoughtfully pointing the way they wanted to go. The guard was sat at the wheel, listening quietly to the radio, having a smoke.

'A rare moment of peaceful reflection in the life of a low-rent mercenary,' Jonah observed.

'Almost a shame to disturb him, isn't it?' Tye agreed.

'Let's just nail the sucker and get out of here,' said Motti.

'Nail him how?' asked Con practically.

Motti hefted the stack of steel in his arms. 'Biggest damn nails *I* ever saw.'

'You're not seriously thinking of using one of those things?' Tye hissed, swapping a worried look with Jonah. But Motti only winked at her, crouched down and swiftly sidled towards the 4x4, clanking a little as he went. Stealthily he crept towards the passenger door . . .

'What the hell is he up to?' Jonah muttered.

Motti dumped the swords down on the concrete as hard as he could. The sudden noise was deafening. Even at this distance Tye saw the guard jump so high in the driver's seat he must have whumped his head on the roof. And before he could recover his wits, Motti threw open the passenger door and socked him with a scabbard.

'He's crazy!' hissed Jonah. 'A noise like that will have carried for miles!'

'So let's move it!' said Patch.

Tye led the charge over to the car. Motti was already throwing the back doors open for the others to dump their stolen arsenal inside. Tye got rid of her bundle, flexed her aching arms and opened the driver's door. The guard flopped out to the ground, bloody mouthed – she stepped over him and jumped inside. The key was in the ignition and she clutched for it; the engine turned over with a rich growl.

The car lurched as the others finished loading up and launched themselves inside, Motti, Patch and Jonah in the back and finally Con in the front.

'Great plan, Mot,' said Jonah coldly. 'Wake up the whole neighbourhood, why don't you –'

'I think we've got company,' Con shouted, checking the wing mirror. Then she swore as the back of the car took a fierce smack of bullets. The rear windows shattered under the onslaught.

'Jesus, Tye, get us out of here!' Motti yelled, as Jonah roughly bundled him and Patch forwards to the floor before they got their heads blown off.

'Guess they worked out we weren't hiding in the turbine block, then,' called Patch weakly.

Tye stamped down on the accelerator as she eased up on the clutch, and with a screech of tyres the car sped away. She steered in a crazy zigzag, felt the bullets pumping into the bodywork, the steering wheel twitching with each hit. If just one of the tyres burst . . .

But the car held it together as she steered out on to the bumpy dirt road that would take them back to the highway. She was about to let out a cry of relief when two more guards came sprinting out of the thick foliage ahead of them, raising their automatic weapons. 'Hang on,' Tye shouted, yanked up the handbrake and tugged the wheel round hard left. The car tore into a screeching 360-degree spin, and its rear end broadsided the guards before they could open fire. Sticking the gearstick into first, Tye pumped the accelerator and they lurched off again, careering down the track, bumping round the bends, until finally the broad grey strip of the highway came into sight and they roared away into the night's thin traffic.

They'd gone a full half-mile before Tye realised she was gripping the wheel so tight she had lost all sensation in her fingers.

'Am I still alive?' Patch wondered weakly.

'You feel this?' Motti pinched his arm.

'Ow! Yeah!'

'Then you're still alive.'

'No thanks to you,' snapped Jonah. 'That drop-the-swords trick was stupid.'

Motti climbed shakily back into his seat. His long dark hair had scraped loose from its habitual ponytail and gusted in the wind through the broken windows. 'Got the armed hood out of our transport, didn't it?'

'And brought another three running!' Jonah stared at him angrily. 'You could have got us all killed!'

'Oh, get the new boy, ticking me off like he knows it all!'

'I'm just saying maybe you should have told us what you were –'

Motti leaned forwards and shouted in Jonah's face.

'There wasn't time for a debate!'

'The important thing is, we got out unharmed,' said Con diplomatically. 'We may not have got the main prize, but I think Coldhardt will be very happy with the rest of our little haul, yes?'

'Quantity, not quality,' said Patch with a sigh.

'Just pray those jokers didn't hole the fuel tank,' said Tye. 'Or we'll be carrying that "little haul" on foot, fifty miles cross-country.'

'Maybe we'd better stop at a drive-through on the way, then,' Patch suggested. 'They gotta have 'em even in Guatemala, right? A Big Mac might help keep our strength up.'

'Filet-o-Fish,' Con corrected him. 'And I'm having two.'

'Beanburger, Jonah?' Tye asked lightly.

He forced a small smile. 'Sure. Nothing like dodging bullets to give you an appetite.'

Tye kept glancing expectantly at Motti, hoping he would join in the banter and the bickering and make things more normal. But he just sat there brooding, the moody look only let down a little by the way his glasses were perched wonkily on his nose.

CHAPTER THREE

It was ten in the morning when Jonah dumped his heavy holdall on the spotless marble floor of Livingston's finest hotel. He rubbed his gritty eyes and wished he could just keep them closed. Tye was on the phone, bypassing the posh receptionists, trying to get through to Coldhardt to see if a) the big man was up and b) he was ready for an audience with his employees.

The luxury resort certainly seemed a million miles from the filthy, impoverished town where they'd dumped the 4x4. Seeing just how many bullets had churned up the bodywork made him feel sick, and the others had looked pretty shaky too. Even Motti had kept his usual smart comments to himself.

While Patch had gone scouring the town for rucksacks so they could shift the swords a little more discreetly, Tye had bought them a battered Subaru from a dealership – refusing to let Con 'persuade' the owner to give them one for nothing. 'She has no idea what it's like, living some place like this,' she'd said. 'To be so trapped.'

Jonah hadn't answered. Sure, Con had been educated in the best schools all over Europe, but only because she'd been shunted round from relative to uncaring relative after her mum and dad died in a car crash. Maybe she'd felt just as trapped in her own way. Why else would she have split at fifteen and turned to conning dirty old men out of their cash to survive?

He watched Con now, taking a long swig from a can of Seven Up. She glanced at Motti, who was slumped against an ornate pillar beside her, and offered him the can. He just shook his head. He'd barely said a word since they'd got away, and Jonah found himself feeling bad for bawling him out. God knew Motti had been ready enough to forgive in the past when Jonah messed up. And despite the brown-trousers getaway, things had worked out. Hadn't they?

It was funny. Jonah knew that Patch had lived rough round London from the age of nine when his mum had finally flipped out for good, knew that Tye had been forced into smuggling as a kid to support her drunken father. Their stories made Jonah's spur-of-the-moment decision to divert funds to his foster mum's bank account so they could escape her cheating, manipulative husband seem a bit lame. But Motti's hard-luck story was a little different. He used to design elite security systems for different companies in his native Minnesota – until he was caught exploiting hidden weaknesses he'd built in so he could rip them off himself. Was it greed or boredom that had driven him to steal and first brought him to Coldhardt's attention? Or something more?

'Coldhardt will see us now,' Tye announced, jolting

him from his thoughts. She slipped her mobile back into her jeans pocket and led the way over to the lifts.

Hastily Jonah picked up the holdall and fell into step with Motti, who was last in line. 'Hey. I'm sorry about having a go, before,' he said.

'S'OK,' said Motti, looking straight ahead. 'I'm sorry you're a pussy.'

Jonah decided to leave it there.

The lift whooshed them up to, where else, the penthouse. The doors opened on to a large air-conditioned room, done out in black suede and calico. The sudden dip in temperature brought Jonah's skin out in gooseflesh.

Who was he kidding? He got shivers every time he was summoned to the presence of Nathaniel Coldhardt.

The boss man was maybe in his early sixties. He sat in the dead centre of the room in a high-backed chair, watching as they filed in to face him, deathly pale in a dark, tailored suit. A mane of white hair framed the craggy features, lined more with experience than the years. And age had done nothing to diminish the rogue's sparkle in his piercing blue eyes.

Coldhardt sat and watched them, as if daring them to fill the chilly silence. He could easily be taken for a big businessman, Jonah decided, a mover and shaker. You might put his arrogant half-smile down to decades of deal clinching, or assume his easy confidence and charm was simply the badge of someone at the top of his game.

And in a way, you'd be right.

Coldhardt was a crook. A master-planner. Getting

too old to pull off heists himself, he'd recruited kids to act for him, all from the wrong side of the tracks and all experts in the fields he needed. One by one Coldhardt's ageing hands had scooped them out from their dead-end situations and into a life their peers could only dream about: luxurious homes, the coolest creature comforts, fast cars, bikes, yachts, even a plane, for God's sake . . . Pools, gyms, amusement arcades, they had them all in half a dozen homes all around the world.

The only thing they didn't have was the option to turn him down. Whatever they were told to do, they did, trading their lives and skills for 10 per cent of Coldhardt's net profits. And with the kind of capers the boss man set up, those profits could easily roll into millions.

'I understand from Tye you encountered trouble.' The Irish lilt in Coldhardt's deep voice held a gently mocking edge.

'We encountered guards armed with automatic weapons,' said Con coolly.

'AK74s by the looks of it,' Motti added. 'That's Russian issue, right?'

'Kabacra's an arms dealer who operates all over the world,' said Coldhardt, rising to his full imposing height of well over six feet. 'He'll locate, acquire and sell on anything to anyone, from a crate of assault rifles to weapons-grade plutonium.'

Patch piped up, 'But not made at *that* nuclear power plant, right?'

Coldhardt shook his head. 'He bought the Guatemalan complex when it was decommissioned fifteen years ago, stripped it bare and made it into a strongroom to hold his personal collection of weapons. Weapons that are allegedly *not* for sale at any price.'

'Well, Cortes's sword ain't there, man,' said Motti sourly. 'May have been once, but not now.'

Coldhardt stared hard at him. 'You're certain?'

'You told me what to look for. There was a whole lot of metal in that containment chamber, but not the blade you want.'

'The information came from a most reliable source.' Coldhardt took a thoughtful sip of his drink. 'An unknown collector has recently made it known that he – or she – is willing to pay an incredible sum for Cortes's sword, and I had reason to believe it might be found in Kabacra's collection.'

'Which is why you decided to rip him off before he could flog it to them,' Jonah realised.

'There was this space on the wall,' said Patch cautiously. 'The mounting screws were there, but . . . Well, maybe that was where this Cortes geezer's sword used to hang, and Kabacra's already got rid.'

Jonah tapped his holdall with his foot. 'We brought most of his collection back with us if you want to check it for anything else you might like.'

An unfathomable look came into the old man's eyes and he slowly shook his head. 'It must be Cortes's,' he said quietly, and a faint chill ran down Jonah's spine. Coldhardt specialised in the theft of artefacts, both ancient and arcane – fabled relics that were near priceless on their own, but which more often than not held the key to secret, spooky mysteries smothered by the centuries. And Jonah got the feeling that *this* was the real treasure in Coldhardt's eyes. Not just acquiring dark knowledge for its own sake, but because he knew of some way to use it. Though to what end Jonah didn't like to think about.

Abruptly Coldhardt chuckled out loud. 'I shall enjoy going through your little haul,' he told them, like an indulgent uncle, 'and I believe it will prove most valuable to us.'

Con's eyes brightened. 'You are going to sell the swords, yes?'

'No.' That cryptic half-smile was back on his lips. 'I am going to give them right back.'

Jonah lay down on a sunlounger, cradling a beer. The job was done; typically that was the cue to relax and party. But there was an air of unease about the guys as they gathered by the hotel's private pool. *Glad it's not just me*, he thought.

'Thank God we're out of there,' said Tye quietly, angling a parasol to keep the sun out of her eyes.

Patch nodded, rocking back in his chair. 'We nearly got ourselves killed to get those swords, and now Coldhardt's just gonna . . .' He trailed off as Con undid her towelling robe to reveal a tiny blue bikini. 'Hey. That's new.'

She glared at him. 'Someone stole my red one.'

Patch grinned. 'Who would do a thing like that?'

'Someone who's gonna go blind in his other eye if he don't watch out,' said Motti. As usual he was making no concession to the sunshine, lying on a lounger in black grungy gear and flicking through Manga.

36

'Told you before, Con, you wanna pay me to secure your pantie drawer, I'm open to offers.'

'I'll pay you to take pictures while you're in there, Mot,' Patch suggested.

Con walked slowly up to him, slipped her hand around the back of his neck and pulled him to his feet. But his dreamy smile vanished as she pinched him hard. 'Patch, why are you so disgusting?'

'Would you notice me if I wasn't?'

She twisted round and threw Patch into the pool. He made a splash like a depth charge. 'Filthy little boy.'

'He's got a point, though,' said Jonah, earning him raised eyebrows from Con and Tye. 'About the swords, I mean,' he added hastily. 'To find out that after all that, Coldhardt's going to give the swords straight back to Kabacra . . .'

'What *is* that about?' Con muttered.

'Guess we'll know what's going down when Coldhardt says, not before,' said Motti.

'Interesting point of view, Mot,' said Patch from the pool. 'But me, I got a better one. *Butt* me – get it?'

Con glanced behind her to find Patch staring up at her ass. She sighed wearily, trod on his head and used it as a springboard for a perfect dive that barely rippled the water.

Motti laughed as Patch bobbed back up, spluttering. 'Hey, can anyone have a go, cyclops?'

Jonah smiled, while Tye shook her head in mockweariness and lay back down on her sunbed. But as the hot sun climbed higher into the sky, the mood seemed a little lighter.

* * *

In the end, the summons to Coldhardt came at six that evening – for Tye and Jonah at least. It turned out they weren't needed for the next stage of Coldhardt's plan – a face-to-face meet with Kabacra. Tye shuddered, happy to leave that little pleasure to Motti, Patch and Con.

An hour later, Tye was back in the plane's cockpit with Jonah bumping along the runway as she took them up. Soon Guatemala's lush landscape was dwindling to a green smear through the windows.

'Looks so peaceful from the air, doesn't it?' said Jonah, looking down over the hills and inlets of Puerto Barrios.

'I guess.' Tye let her mind drift back to her smuggling days there, when *nothing* was peaceful. No big funding and clever friends to fall back on when she was thirteen. Just her and a boy.

A boy who'd promised her the world, then brought it crashing down around her ears.

She glanced across at Jonah as she levelled out the plane. What would *this* boy wind up doing? It felt so weird, there just being the two of them on board. And what was weirder, now she actually had the time and space to talk to him in private, she couldn't think of a thing to say.

'So have you often come up against armed guards trying to fill your back full of bullets?' asked Jonah conversationally.

'Is that, like, a line?' she asked, deadpan. He grinned and so did she, but she caught the anxiety in his eyes. 'Yeah, I have, a couple of times. And yeah, it never stops being scary as hell.'

'But still you do what Coldhardt says.'

'What else am I going to do?' She shot him a look. 'Anyway, you can't be complaining about our latest assignment: Go back to the swanky new base in New Mexico and start mucking about with your precious computers –'

'Hey! I'm sorting out the computer hub, thank you, the heart of Coldhardt's –'

'– *mucking about* with your precious computers in between lounging and doing nothing. Apart from fixing me drinks and food.'

'Oh yeah?'

'Yeah! Coldhardt's not getting a cook in till next month!'

'Well, it's lucky I make a mean Pot Noodle, then.' Jonah smiled. 'OK, I admit it – we didn't pull the shortest straw. I'm in no hurry to meet this Kabacra guy with the others. Saw his picture in the containment vessel, and I'd rather look at Patch's bum anyday.'

'Oh yes?' She arched an eyebrow. 'Something you want to tell me?'

He smiled, then blushed just slightly. 'Lots,' he said.

Tye's mouth went dry for a moment. 'Well,' she said briskly, 'I'm supposed to be teaching you to fly this thing. Not that you really need me. You're getting good.'

Jonah grimaced. 'Can't drive a car to save my life but I'm OK in a plane. My life's turned totally mental.'

She put the plane on to autopilot. 'But you're happier than when you were in prison, right? All alone, no family, no –'

'Of course I am. With you and the guys, it feels like . . .' He trailed off, self-conscious. 'Suppose I'd be even happier without the armed guards, the bullets and all that.'

'Well, I guess we'd all like to make as good a living singing carols in old people's homes and selling cookies door to door,' said Tye. 'But think how quick you'd get bored. Think how ordinary people must have it, doing the same dull stuff day after day.'

'I wouldn't mind taking a holiday to Dullsville now and then.'

'Wise up, Jonah,' she said, not unkindly, as she thought about her time running contraband between the Caribbean islands. 'There's a price on anything worth having.'

'Uh-huh.' He looked out of the cabin window, lost in thought. Then he got out of the co-pilot's seat. 'So I suppose we should get on with the lesson. Can I take over here?'

'Go right ahead,' she told him, rising to take his place. 'You have control.'

He smiled ruefully back at her. 'I wish.'

Coldhardt's newly acquired base was a huge ranch in northern New Mexico set in five hundred acres of wild terrain. Jonah stood on the veranda as the sun slowly set, listening to the gentle rush of the Tierra Amarilla river flowing carelessly through the grounds, just as he had before they'd flown out to Guatemala.

The black speck of a helicopter whirred quietly through the darkening sky, and Jonah wondered where it was going. Growing up, he'd had a thing about planes and their destinations – always wishing he was on board, flying out of his miserable home-life. Now, to his amazement, he was actually glad his feet were on the ground. He'd already made a start on getting the computers up and running. Structurally, everything was in place, so he'd cabled up the patch panels and tonight he'd start on –

'Nice, huh?' Tye had come to join him with a couple of beers.

'Yep, they're the best beers I ever saw.'

It was a lame joke, but he was pleased to see she smiled anyway. 'You can't help but lose yourself in a sunset like that,' she said.

'Er, right.' *That and the joys of network hubs.* 'Cheers.' He took a long swig from one of the bottles. 'So, does Coldhardt's getting this little holiday home mean he'll be losing one of his others?'

'Maybe,' said Tye. 'He had a base in Bucharest he sold off last year when he bought the *castello* in Siena. The main base in Geneva is his only real home, I guess. The others he just buys and sells as and when it's convenient.'

Jonah shook his head, bemused. 'I'll bet that if his car ran out of petrol he'd leave it at the roadside and buy another.'

'Uh-uh. I'm his driver. I carry a petrol can in the back.' She necked her beer. 'There is something about this place though. Found it while I was looking around. Something I haven't seen in any of Coldhardt's other homes.'

'The mysterious act would work better if you didn't have beer froth on your nose,' Jonah teased her.

'Want to see?'

'See what?'

'Follow me.' She took him by the hand and led him back into the spacious living room. The swift clomping of her low-heeled shoes on the hardwood floor was a close match for his heart. He wanted to squeeze her fingers, or grip her hand more firmly, but what if she snatched it away? What if she just stared at him, or laughed in his face – or landed a punch there instead? Tye kickboxed, she was not someone you wanted to mess with . . .

He tried to stay unflustered as she went on towing him through to the dining room, into the hall and down some stairs to the wine cellar, her fingers soft and warm around his sweaty hand. She led him towards the rear of the room, then, to his surprise, squeezed between two large dusty racks of vintage red and drew him up close beside her.

He looked at her in the dim light, confused, excited, silently urging himself to just lean in and kiss her. Surely she would be OK with that if she had led him –

'It's here,' she whispered, then turned away from him to face the wall. Her fingers twitched at a black covering there, pulling at it to reveal a chunky slab of metal. It took Jonah a couple of seconds to process what he was seeing: a door, formidable-looking like it belonged in a bank vault. It gleamed dully in the low light.

Jonah pushed his hands in his pockets, as if trying to stuff his disappointment down there. 'I, er . . . I guess this wasn't something left behind by the last owners. Sneaky old Motti, huh, coming up with this on the quiet.'

'If it *was* Motti.' Tye looked at him. 'You heard the way he was bitching about being overworked trying to secure the grounds before we left. He never once mentioned this.'

'Maybe it's a secret.'

'If he was keeping something back, I'd know.' Tye looked thoughtful. 'Why would Coldhardt send just the two of us back here, Jonah?'

'Duh! Because I'm fixing up the computers here, and as designated pilot you have to take me.'

'But if he's going to meet with Kabacra, does he really need Motti, Patch *and* Con to hold his hand?'

Jonah shrugged. 'He must figure he needs them for something.'

'Or else he doesn't want the locksmith, the security man and the greedy girl to stumble on this while he's away.' Tye's dark eyes were agleam. 'I think it's his private collection. His buried treasure.'

'New Mex marks the spot.' Jonah felt a slow smile spreading over his face. 'I guess he has to keep his stash of goodies somewhere, right?'

She nodded enthusiastically. 'Can you imagine how much his collection must be worth? How much he must have in there?'

'By the look of that door, you'd need a nuclear bomb to get inside.'

Tye grimaced. 'Just ask Kabacra to fetch one.'

Just then they heard a muffled crash from upstairs. Both of them jumped. 'What the hell was that?' breathed Jonah.

'The grounds are secured,' Tye reminded him, rearranging the black curtain. 'Motti designed the systems himself.'

'And like we've just agreed, he's been overworked.'

'Probably just the wind, knocking something over. We left the veranda doors open, remember?' She placed her hand on his chest, gave him a gentle push. 'But we should go check.'

Jonah didn't move. He liked feeling her hand there. She didn't move it. He realised the rhythm of her breathing matched his own. There was a look in her eyes, like she was daring him to make the first move.

He was just edging his face closer to hers when they heard it again.

'Come on,' said Tye, steering him firmly out of her way now, the moment lost. She quickly crossed the cellar and scaled the staircase. Jonah swore under his breath and jogged after her.

But when he emerged into the brighter light of the hallway, there was no sign of her. 'Tye?' he called, and walked through to the dining room.

Too late he saw the dark figure hiding behind the door jump out at him. Jonah twisted round and brought his arms up over his face to deflect the blow he glimpsed coming, but it was like being whacked with an iron bar. He fell backwards, gasping as the heavy mahogany edge of the dining table bit into his spine. As his attacker rushed towards him, masked in black from head to foot, Jonah threw himself back on the table, brought up both legs and kicked out with all his strength. His feet crunched into the face beneath the balaclava; by the grunt of pain that came back at him, his attacker was male.

Swiftly, Jonah performed a backward roll and slithered off the table, keeping it between him and his assailant. The masked man had slumped to the floor, but was he really dazed or just shamming? More importantly, where the hell was Tye?

Leaving the man where he lay, Jonah hurried into the living room – in time to see Tye's prone body being carried out on to the veranda by two burly guys, also in masks. A far shorter man was urging them on.

'Get off her!' Jonah bawled.

'Quickly, Xavier!' the smaller man called back into the house, in a well-educated voice.

Jonah looked around for a likely weapon, settled for a heavy candlestick and started after them. *Please don't be armed*, he thought, feeling sick with fear and adrenaline.

But then sudden ragged footfalls behind him signalled the return of his attacker – Xavier. Jonah turned, swung the candlestick, but it was knocked from his hand by a hard blow to the wrist. Vivid green eyes blazed into his own and suddenly Xavier's other hand was clamped tight round Jonah's throat, forcing him to the floor. Jonah flailed out with both arms but couldn't twist clear of the man's grip, couldn't breathe. The pressure began to build in his head, and the man's masked face blurred in Jonah's vision. He felt something drip on to his cheek. *Blood*, he thought, *I hurt him*. So he reached out, grabbed Xavier's nose through his mask and twisted hard.

With a shout of pain his attacker recoiled, and Jonah tore himself free, gulping down air. *If I'm going to stand a chance I have to end this quickly*, he told himself, and threw himself on top of the masked man. He aimed a punch but Xavier bucked beneath him, and Jonah lost his balance. As he toppled sideways on to the hardwood floor, his fingers snagged on something round the man's neck, something that came away in his frantic grip.

By the time Jonah had rolled over and got up on his knees, Xavier was back on his feet. He kicked Jonah in the chest, sending him sprawling backwards into the fireplace. The metal grate hammered into the back of Jonah's skull, sent bright lights and patterns flashing over his vision. Terrified of what Xavier might do next, gritting his teeth, Jonah forced himself to get back up, raised his fists.

But by the time his vision had cleared, so had the room. He was alone.

'Tye?' Jonah shouted, stumbling over to the veranda. The cold mountain air stung his cheeks, and soon he was shivering. 'Tye!' He put his hand to the back of his head. It came away sticky with a thick slime of blood.

God, that's mine, he thought, and finally passed out.

CHAPTER FOUR

Patch rubbed his good eye blearily, wondering what the hell was going on. He was still shagged out from getting no sleep the night before, and could've done without being on parade in Coldhardt's room at half-two in the morning. Motti and Con stood stiff and silent, one either side of him. They didn't look too happy about it either.

Coldhardt emerged from his bedroom carrying his super-slim laptop, dressed immaculately as ever in his dark suit. He surveyed them each in turn. 'Some hours ago,' he began, 'the New Mexico base was broken into and Tye abducted.'

Patch felt like someone had slung a bucket of water over him. 'What?' he said stupidly, like he hadn't heard, but Con and Motti were just as startled.

'I wasn't finished testing the security,' Motti said. 'I mean, Jeez, we're not even properly moved in there yet.'

'What else did they take?' Con demanded. 'Tye's mobile has all our numbers –'

'Nothing was touched. Apart from Jonah. He's taken a beating, but insists he's fine. He's called Tye's phone. It was still in her room.'

Motti rubbed the back of his neck. 'Why take Tye? Ransom?'

'Then why not take Jonah too?' said Coldhardt. 'More profitable.'

'Kabacra, maybe,' said Con. 'He might have kidnapped Tye to get a hold over you.'

Motti shook his head. 'If he knows we ripped him off, why not grab one of us from this hotel? Hell of a lot easier.'

'It doesn't sound like it was much trouble getting inside the ranch.' Coldhardt fixed him with a glare. 'I shall expect a comprehensive report on the state of those security systems upon your return to the estate.'

'If you'd only let me oversee the guys who installed them like I asked –'

Something pale and dangerous flashed in Coldhardt's eyes. 'Never question my decisions, Motti.'

Motti nodded mutely.

'In any case, Jonah's found us something to go on,' Coldhardt continued. 'One of the intruders left this behind.' He tapped a key to wake up his laptop, and the image of a circular amulet made of jade came up big on the screen. Engraved on the front was some sort of cartoonish birdman, with a big beak, muscular wing-arms and titchy legs like the artist had run out of room.

'The design is antique Mesoamerican,' Coldhardt informed them. 'It is centuries old, and almost certainly worn by a particular sect of Aztec priests.'

'Aztecs,' Patch realised. 'Them people Cortes conquered, right?'

'Lived in Mexico, five or six hundred years ago,' Con agreed. 'Big empire, big on sacrifice –'

'Big whoop,' Motti put in sourly. 'Back to the amulet. Do we think Tye was taken by an art collector?'

Coldhardt shook his head. 'I believe this particular symbol has been adopted by a secret society calling themselves Sixth Sun. Their beliefs are apparently influenced by those of the Mesoamericans.'

'What, they believe in feathered serpents and jaguar men and all that crap?' Motti frowned. 'Gotta be crackpots.'

Con looked less amused. 'If they are responsible for breaching our defences and kidnapping Tye, they could be very dangerous crackpots, no?'

Patch liked the sound of this less and less. 'How'd you know about them, Coldhardt?'

'It was when I heard of Sixth Sun's interest in Cortes's sword some time ago that I became certain the weapon's existence was more than just rumour. Naturally I checked them out, just as I would any business rival.' Coldhardt's face clouded slightly, enough to put the wind up Patch. 'In this case, it seems secret society really does mean secret. I could find out next to nothing about them.'

Con shrugged. 'But if they have links with Kabacra, they must be in the arms trade, no?'

'Whoever they are,' said Patch fiercely, 'we've got to get to these Sixth Sun-of-a-bitches and get Tye back, fast!'

Coldhardt ignored him. 'Motti, a taxi is waiting outside reception to take you to the airstrip at El

Péten. You'll take the six a.m. flight back to New Mexico and go straight to the base to check security. I want to know how these people breached our defences.'

Motti raised his eyebrows. 'Thought I was s'posed to work on getting you into Kabacra's place, once you found it?'

'Plans change. Go.'

Motti nodded. 'Am I gonna have to nursemaid Jonah, too?'

'He is already using his computer skills to scour the Internet for further information on Sixth Sun. Now, get on with it.'

Dismissed, Motti slouched from the room.

'What about the rest of us?' wondered Patch.

'We still have our other business to attend to,' Coldhardt replied, closing up the laptop. 'Namely, this meeting with Kabacra. Thanks to Patch's work at the nuclear complex, we now know the whereabouts of his base of operations.'

Patch frowned. 'What did I do?'

'It seems the number code you cracked with the bit-buster – 15-30-90-15 – was not picked at random. Turns out a similar series of numbers was imprinted on my reconnaissance photos of the nuclear power station – precise latitude and longitude co-ordinates for the location.'

Con raised an eyebrow. 'So Kabacra's code was a set of co-ordinates, yes?'

He nodded. 'Located at 15' 30" north, 90' 15" west in the middle of Guatemala is a large colonial-style mansion. The locals say the owner is a foreigner with a scarred face.' He looked at them both. 'I have invited all three of us round to deliver certain of his missing swords in person.'

'No wonder you don't need Motti.' Con smiled. 'We can walk in through the front door.'

'So you *were* serious about giving them swords back.' Patch sighed. 'Are you gonna 'fess up that we nicked 'em?'

'No. Merely that we have located them, and wish to return them to their rightful owner. I want to put Kabacra in a generous frame of mind. But if he is not prepared to give, then we will take.' He looked at them both, his eyes like cold stones. 'Acquiring Cortes's sword has to be our top priority.'

Along with getting Tye back again, Patch willed him to add.

But Coldhardt's mind was clearly elsewhere. 'Con, book the best car you can find for seven o'clock this morning. Oh, and just so you know – Kabacra has warned me that at the first sign of a double-cross we shall be taken and executed by a firing squad in the grounds.' Coldhardt leaned forwards. 'It goes without saying, we must play this one *very* carefully.'

'Play?' echoed Patch. 'Sounds like this Kabacra don't know the meaning of the word.'

Con looked knowingly at Coldhardt. 'Then we must teach him – yes?'

Jonah stared blankly at his PC, eyes stinging, head still hurting like hell. He'd been online for hours, breaking through firewalls and security protocols, trawling through encrypted postings from all kinds of weird and worrying newsgroups, trying to find some trace of Sixth Sun's existence. But about all he'd dug up after near-enough twelve hours was some background on the amulet design and a possible reason as to how Sixth Sun came by their name. He felt so guilty, just sitting round while Tye was God-knew-where, so useless and frustrated that he couldn't find them another lead –

'Yo, geek!' came a holler from downstairs. 'Your nursemaid's here. Where are you?'

'Mot?' Jonah jumped up from his chair and gasped as the world rocked about him. The back of his head hurt so much he felt sick. He sat down on the bed before he *fell* down.

'Hey.' Motti was standing in the doorway dressed in washed-out black, a distressed *Punisher* logo screaming from his T-shirt, a smudge of stubble infringing on his goatee. He seemed concerned, and Jonah felt pathetically grateful that he should care. 'You look dog rough, man.'

'I know.' It all spilled out of him, everything that had happened last night. The only stuff he skipped was the close-call-clinch with Tye and the mysterious vault in the wine cellar. Motti listened in silence, nodding from time to time, his face grave.

'I let Sixth Sun take her, Mot,' Jonah finished hoarsely. 'I screwed up. Maybe if you or Con had been here –'

'C'mon. You think I didn't spend the whole of the flight over here blaming myself for them getting past security?' Motti sat down in the chair. 'I got scanners, I got motion sensors, I got microwaves . . . I got goddamned Canada geese with spy cams wrapped round their beaks –'

'You do?'

'Well, no, but I thought about it. Look, geek, it ain't no good blaming ourselves.' He snorted. 'So let's blame Coldhardt instead. There's more than five hundred acres to police here, man, including a goddamned river. And does he let me supervise the security installations? No, he's gotta get contractors in . . .'

Jonah thought of the vault hidden down in the wine cellar. *Tye was right*, he thought, *he didn't want you to see*. And for now, Jonah decided to keep quiet about it – he had to be in enough trouble with Coldhardt already.

'Could the contractors have sold the details of security here to Sixth Sun?' he wondered.

'Con wiped their memories with her hypnotism act. They won't remember jack about this place.' Motti shook his head bitterly. 'Nah, Sixth Sun musta had the place under surveillance for some time. We were here, what, four days before Coldhardt sent us off to Guatemala. That ain't long enough to test all the sensors, the alarms, the infra-red . . .'

'So they'd have known the place wasn't totally secure yet,' Jonah realised. 'But how'd they find out Coldhardt was setting up here at all? And why take Tye?' He picked up the amulet from his bedside table and tossed it over. 'They took a piece of me. But at least I got something in return.'

'Saw this on Coldhardt's computer,' said Motti, studying the amulet. 'Looks old. Real antique. Guess Coldhardt attracts a better class of housebreaker.'

'Crazy thing was, one of them seemed more like a professor or something than a burglar. Short little guy.'

Motti looked at the design on the front. 'Birdwatcher maybe?'

'Apparently that's a hummingbird.' Jonah rubbed the back of his neck, felt the muscles all bunched up there. 'It features on a lot of Aztec pottery and jewellery and stuff. Aztec warriors believed that when they died in battle or got sacrificed, they would transform into hummingbirds and flutter off to join the Sun God.'

'Sounds fun,' said Motti. 'What kind of outfit's gonna want that as their emblem?'

'I've been reading up on it – Aztecs were big on blood sacrifice. They killed thousands of people each year, even their best warriors. The priests chopped out their hearts while the victims were still alive.'

'Nice.'

'Creepiest thing is, the victims were cool with it. They believed that by giving their life force to the gods, they would go to heaven and live with them.

Motti snorted. 'Eternity as a hummingbird? You can keep it.' He looked down at the amulet. 'Coldhardt said priests would have worn these. So is that what these guys think they are – priests or something?'

'Priests or warriors,' Jonah agreed. 'Or maybe both . . .'

'Anyways.' Motti chucked the amulet on to the bed. 'You find out anything a little more current that could help us?'

'Not really,' Jonah admitted. 'But get this.' He crossed woozily to the computer and called up a page in Explorer. 'Apparently, the Aztecs had this weird calendar going on. Believed that the history of the world could be divided into cycles of hundreds of years, that they called Suns. And at the end of each Sun, the Earth was pretty much wiped out by a different disaster – flamed up one time, flooded by water another . . . and humanity only just survived.'

Motti fidgeted impatiently. 'Just how bad *was* your knock on the head, geek?'

'Right now, we're meant to be living in the fifth cycle of creation – and the last. The age of the Fifth Sun. The Aztecs reckoned this age would come to an end in the twenty-first century with a load of mega-earthquakes. No get-out for the human race this time. The end.'

'So, what,' said Motti, 'these guys call themselves Sixth Sun 'cause they think they're going to cheat the predictions and see in a new age?'

'Could be. But what kind of new age would it be?' Jonah frowned, staggered back over to his bed. 'Suppose it depends if they're priests or warriors . . .'

'Whatever the hell they think they are,' said Motti, getting up. 'How come they need Tye? As a hostage to use against Coldhardt?'

'Then why not take me along too?' said Jonah. 'Two hostages are better than one. They just beat me up and dumped me.'

'They got taste,' Motti joked. 'Or else not enough room in their transport. Their best chance of getting past the defences was if they took a chopper, and that would mean limited space . . .'

'Oh God,' said Jonah. 'I did see a helicopter a bit before – but it was miles away.'

'Nah. You'd have heard it touch down.'

'But we . . . we were down in the cellar.'

Now Motti's eyes widened. 'You and *Tye* were down in the cellar?'

Jonah blushed. 'We just . . . fancied some wine to drink.'

'Uh-huh.' Motti's voice had hardened, he clearly didn't believe a word of it.

'It wasn't like that, Mot,' said Jonah, getting to his feet – and wincing as the world pitched and tilted.

'Just stay in bed, lover-boy,' said Motti gruffly, getting up too. 'I'll go out and see if I can find any evidence of that Sixth Sun 'copter. And you'd better hope I turn up a better lead than anything *you've* found so far.'

He stalked from the room and shut the door behind him. Jonah curled up on the bed and closed his aching eyes. 'I'm hoping,' he breathed. 'God, am I hoping.'

CHAPTER FIVE

Con sat in the front of the Range Rover, shooting a pained glance at the chauffeur every time he took a bend too fast or drove over one of the many deep ruts in the road. He was a local, stuffed into an ill-fitting uniform and clearly wishing he was a thousand miles away. His presence was a constant unpleasant reminder that Tye had been taken from them.

Poor, serious Tye, always agonising over everything instead of milking the moment for all it was worth. It didn't seem possible to Con that she might never see her again.

She glanced over her shoulder at Patch and Coldhardt but they hadn't shifted; one wearing out his good eye and blasting both ears with his Game Boy, the other apparently asleep. Con sighed. Coldhardt looked so much older when he slept. Frail and vulnerable.

The road was near deserted as they climbed and swooped through the dramatic landscape of Baja Verapaz. They had driven for hours along the Carretera al Atlántico, scrubby bush and cacti slowly giving way to lush pine forest and alpine meadows. Now, as they descended into the heart of the Salamá valley, there was an almost sinister stillness about them. Con's unease grew as the car drew inexorably closer to Kabacra's hidden lair. Hemmed in by parched hillsides, the hard, featureless sky like pale ceramic high overhead, she felt more and more isolated from the real world.

The sat-nav suddenly spoke up, making her jump, warning the chauffeur to turn left at a turning two hundred metres ahead. A chequered flag had appeared on the display, telling them their long journey would soon be over. Quickly Con checked her long, dark wig in the vanity mirror, and put on a pair of chic sunglasses. Being recognised by some random guard as the bogus backpacker from the nuclear power station was something she could live without. Although considering the men had spent more time looking at her legs than her face, she was probably safe so long as she didn't lose her jeans.

The turn was well hidden by straggly, overgrown bushes, but the Range Rover pushed through and on to a track crowded by dense vegetation.

'We there yet?' asked Patch, not looking up from the Game Boy.

'Almost. But keep playing.' He got car sick, and from bitter past experience Con knew that he was prone to throwing up the moment he lost concentration. She allowed herself a weary smile. That would certainly wake Coldhardt up with a jolt.

As they rounded a sharp corner she saw two armed sentries come into view. They both raised their rifles, ready to fire. The chauffeur stamped on the brakes and the car slewed to an awkward halt.

The hum of an electric window broke the tense silence. 'Let us pass,' rapped Coldhardt from the back. Con turned to see he was sat bolt upright, looking alert and confident, a changed man from just a few moments ago. 'Kabacra is expecting us.'

One of the men fished a radio from his pocket and spoke into it. After a brief exchange he nodded to the other guard and they stood aside to allow the car through.

The chauffeur started speaking angrily in Spanish as he pulled away again. Con translated for the others. 'He says he'll wait for us outside for one hour. After that he's driving straight back to Livingston, no matter what we're paying him.'

Coldhardt dabbed at his forehead with a black handkerchief. 'Tell him one hour is all we shall need.'

They were greeted at Kabacra's gate by more armed sentries. Patch buzzed his window open and noisily threw up down the side of the car. The guards stared at him with disgust.

'You'd think they'd be used to people throwing up at the sight of them,' Patch muttered as Con gingerly helped him out.

Once they'd been frisked for anything antisocial, Con, Patch and Coldhardt were ushered inside a large, modern mansion. White and bare with a black carpet, the entrance hall held about as much charm as the stairwells at the nuclear power station. The heavy wooden door creaked like a coffin lid as it was shut behind them.

Coldhardt was carrying the holdall with the swords. One of the guards snatched it from him and disappeared through a doorway without a word. Two more guards remained to watch them.

'They are checking the swords are genuine, yes?' Con said quietly.

'For surveillance devices and signs of damage too, I imagine,' Coldhardt murmured. 'Which is why I brought only those eight that survived the journey to Livingston entirely without harm. Like I say, I want Kabacra in a generous mood.'

'So he might not shoot us the second he sees us,' Patch muttered, still looking green.

A good ten minutes later, the door opened again and Kabacra appeared. Con tried not to grimace, but he was strikingly ugly – thin and bony, with a face like scarred chicken skin stretched over a skull. His sunken eyes were as black and shiny as his lank hair.

'So you're Coldhardt,' Kabacra said in grave, accented English. 'You brought your kids?'

Coldhardt smiled. 'My associates. Con and Patch.'

Kabacra did not acknowledge them. 'I've heard a lot about you.'

'Likewise, Señor Kabacra.'

'Enough to make me want to kill you.'

The guards released the safeties on their weapons, the metallic clatter echoing around the hall. Con held herself absolutely still, and Patch closed his eye.

Coldhardt simply smiled. 'Is that any way to show your gratitude? You have seen for yourself I have recovered certain merchandise that was stolen from you recently.'

'And very swiftly, too.' Kabacra folded his arms. 'Perhaps because you were the one who stole it in the first place?'

'Oh, I hardly think I'm the only suspect. What about Sixth Sun?'

Con wished Tye was here to study Kabacra's reaction to the name – or rather, lack of reaction.

'Sixth Sun?' he inquired.

'News reached me – through my usual secret sources – that they were seeking a particular relic in your possession,' Coldhardt said amiably. 'The sword of Hernando Cortes.'

'Is that so?'

'I had believed it lost for ever. And I imagine the purchase price is very high.' Coldhardt smiled. 'I was concerned that perhaps Sixth Sun's agents might try to steal it and not pay you a damn.'

Kabacra looked no prettier when he smiled. 'And this is why you have tracked me to my private home?'

Coldhardt nodded. 'I am here to make you a better offer.'

'You have come a long way for nothing, Coldhardt.' Kabacra said. 'The deal is struck. You will have to approach the sword's new owners.'

'Really? And how do I set about that?'

'I am afraid I must respect my clients' confidentiality. But thank you for safely returning my swords. For that, I will not use them against you.' His scarred skin puckered further as he bared his teeth in a jackal's grin. 'And I shall allow you to leave here with your arms and legs intact.'

Coldhardt looked unruffled. 'How gracious. But I'm not ready to leave, Kabacra.'

'That is unfortunate.' Kabacra took a threatening

step towards him. 'But consider how much *more* unfortunate if the boy here found his good eye speared on the end of a rapier.'

'Yeah, that'd be well clumsy of me,' Patch squeaked.

'Or if charming Connie here needed stitches in those pretty cheeks of hers.'

'My name is *Con*,' she told him quietly, looking into his blazing eyes. 'Call me Connie again and *you* will be the one needing stitches, yes?'

Kabacra's eyes narrowed, but then Coldhardt calmly stepped between the two of them. 'Since you're so fond of threats, Kabacra, perhaps I should mention that I have also recovered the other swords stolen from your collection – the cavalry sabre, the Civil War cutlass –'

'I want them back, Coldhardt.'

'Should my associates and I suffer so much as a scratch in your company, they will be melted down for scrap and dropped on your head from a great height.'

Kabacra leaned up close to Coldhardt and spoke in a low, dangerous voice. 'You test my patience.'

'I'd sooner test a dry Martini while we talk business,' said Coldhardt. 'I'm willing to pay, and pay well, for information that will get me the sword of Cortes.'

Kabacra held himself still for a few seconds. Then he straightened and gave his grisly smile. 'You know, I deal with so few people who truly live up to their reputation. Just be careful you don't die because of yours.'

'Oh, I'll be careful,' Coldhardt agreed. 'For a start,

I'll fix my own drink.'

'Your associates will remain here, under guard.' Kabacra ushered Coldhardt through the door and into a large living room done out in purples and crimson, like the whole space was bruised and bleeding. One of the guards followed them inside and closed the door behind.

Patch looked nervously at Con. 'Well, that went well, then.'

'Let's just hope Coldhardt keeps him occupied for long enough.'

'Shut up,' said their guard.

'Sorry, was that too loud?' Con smiled, lowered her voice, fixing him with those incredible pale blue eyes of hers. 'How about I speak softly. I don't want to be any trouble to you.'

'*No hablo inglés,*' he said grouchily – Con imagined that 'shut up' was as cosmopolitan as he got.

At once she switched to Spanish. 'You must be tired, no? You are tired. So sleepy . . .' She smiled as he nodded, staring back at her, unblinking. 'And you would like to help me, I think. Yes, of course you would . . .'

Patch looked on as Con did her hypnotism trick. He had no idea what she was saying, but her accent sounded so mindblowingly sexy it actually distracted him from wanting to hurl again for a few minutes. And he felt better still when the guard lowered his gun, a glazed, restful look in his eyes.

'OK, he's under,' Con announced. 'The stupid ones take no time.'

Patch nodded. 'But does he know where Kabacra keeps his client list?'

She asked the guard in Spanish and he answered dreamily, pointing to a flight of stairs. Then, when Con prompted him with another question, he spoke in halting English: 'We tie you up.'

'What's he on about?' said Patch warily.

Con set off for the stairs. 'Up here and second door on the right. The room is locked but not guarded.'

'OK, but what does he mean, "We tie you up"?' Patch bounded lightly after her up the stairs and on to a long landing. 'Is he into bondage or something?'

'He thinks it's the password for Kabacra's computer. Seems the other guard has hacked in before now, looking for scraps of information to sell.'

'Why use an English password if you're Spanish?'

'To make it harder for others to crack?' She shrugged. 'How should I know? Just thought I should ask. I doubt there's a hard-copy of the client list.'

Con stopped outside a hefty wooden door carved with skulls, swords and shields. Two large locks were crafted into the design.

'Bollocks,' said Patch. 'Got us a pair of tubulars.'

'They're hard to pick?'

'God, yeah. The pins are placed all the way round the edge of the cylinder plug.'

'I love our little talks, Patch.'

He lifted up his eyepatch, teased out the glass ball inside and unscrewed it at the middle. Inside nestled a collection of extendible picks and a telescopic tension wrench. He grabbed the wrench, selected a pick and got to work. 'Easy, now . . .' He listened to the soft click of the pins as he probed with the pick, analysing them, trying to predict the way they should rise and fall.

There was a loud click as the first bolt gave way, and Patch beamed at her. 'How's that, then?'

'Not bad.' Con smiled back, put her hands on her hips. 'Crack the second one inside twenty seconds and I'll show you my bra.'

'Deal!' Patch pounced on the next lock, let the tools in his fingers twist and cajole and lightly spring until . . . 'Yes!' he hissed, as with a satisfying clunk the second bolt eased back. Patch opened the door and they both pushed inside a small, drab office. Con raced over to an intricately carved desk and started rifling through the drawers while Patch stood guard.

'Come on, then,' he said, looking back at her over his shoulder. 'That was loads less than twenty seconds. What about the bra!'

She smiled like an angel. 'I'm not wearing a bra today, Patch.'

With a tortured sigh, Patch turned back to the chink in the door and kept his eye on the empty landing while Con started up Kabacra's computer. 'If Scarface comes out of that room and finds we've gone,' he whispered, 'do you realise how dead we are? Why'd you think Coldhardt even wants this sword so much?'

'It must be worth a fortune.'

'I reckon it's more than that. It's like he needs it for something. Something we don't know about.' Her fingers clicked over the computer keyboard – then she swore. 'There's only room for eight characters in the password field. "We tie you up" is ten characters, doesn't fit. The guard must have heard wrong.'

Patch joined her by the computer keyboard. He'd never understood why they didn't put all the letters in alphabetical order. A-B-C made a lot more sense than Q-W-E-R . . .

'Qwertyuiop,' Patch read the top line of keys aloud, and some of the letters leaped out at him. 'Wer Ty. Where Tye?' He sighed. It was a good question, even if the spelling was bad.

Hang on a sec . . .

'Wer Ty U Iop.' Patch stared at Con. 'That's almost the password, innit?'

'What?'

'The guards ain't English, right?' Patch hissed. 'So what if the password's just letters from the top line of keys, and they're saying it as it sounds!'

'Kabacra's being funny, you mean?' Con typed in W-E-T-Y-U-U-P and hit return.

INVALID PASSWORD.

Patch sighed. 'Stick to lock-breaking, shall I?'

'Wait.' Con tried again, but this time changed U-P to O-P. 'That way it's spelled with all different letters but still in sequence along the line of keys, yes?'

'You sound like Jonah.'

'Pity *you* don't look like him.' She smiled sweetly and hit return.

And this time, they were in.

'Yes!' breathed Con, eyes glittering.

'You can snog me to say thanks if you want,' said Patch, before flinching at the look she gave him. 'How're you gonna find the client list?'

'I'm not,' she said, removing two memory sticks from the chunky buckle of her leather belt. 'We have five gigabytes of storage on each of these. I'm going to copy his hard drive across so we can go through it later.'

The minutes crawled by as she copied the files and changed sticks. Patch chewed his lip and checked his watch.

'Done.' Con yanked out the second memory stick, tucked it with the other one back behind her belt buckle and shut down the computer. 'We must leave everything just as we found it. And you must lock the door again.'

'Tell you what, extra incentive. If I do it in less than a minute, you have to show me your pants.'

Con raised one eyebrow coyly.

Patch almost whimpered. 'No pants either?'

'You should get out more, Patch,' Con mused, striding primly to the door. 'No?'

Back in the entrance hall, Con told the guard to forget everything that had happened since he'd been ordered to watch them, and to continue as normal. Like any good guard he did exactly as he was told, and covered them with both his gun and his glare until his boss re-emerged from the living room with Coldhardt, almost thirty minutes later.

Coldhardt looked enquiringly at Con, and she nodded discreetly. 'I'm afraid that Señor Kabacra will still not tell me how we may contact Sixth Sun. Not for any price.' Coldhardt's affable smile belied the ice in his tone. 'Interesting behaviour for a mercenary who values his independence so highly.'

'I think perhaps you may thank me for keeping quiet some day, Coldhardt.' Kabacra gave a bark of cheerless laughter. 'Now, because I have so enjoyed your visit, my men will escort you to your vehicle and you may leave.' But then he grabbed Patch by the back of his scrawny neck, making him yelp. 'That is, of course, once you have told me the location of my other swords.'

Con bit her lip as both guards aimed their weapons at Coldhardt's head.

'You'll find them in the penthouse suite of the Stanley Hotel in Livingston,' he said. 'They are in a holdall beneath the four-poster bed.'

'That is most illuminating. Thank you.' Kabacra grinned through his criss-cross of scars, tightening his grip on Patch's neck. 'But you know, I find myself wondering – why should I not kill you now? If you are telling the truth, I have no further use for you. And if you are lying, you and your young "associates" deserve to die in any case.'

Con cleared her throat. 'You'll let us go free, Kabacra. Because if we do not return to our colleagues this evening, your little hideaway here will be made public.' She fought to keep the tremor from her voice. 'To the FBI, Interpol, the Russian Foreign Intelligence Service –'

'The suite at the Stanley is paid for till the end of the week,' Coldhardt interrupted. 'Why not stay there with my blessing? The tortillas and eggs at breakfast are particularly good.'

Kabacra's scarred top lip curled slowly like paper in

a fire. 'Leave, then,' he hissed. 'But should you be foolish enough to tell others of this place, or to seek audience with me again . . .'

Patch pulled himself free of the man's grip, almost falling over as he raced to reach the front door.

Con set off after him, keeping close to Coldhardt. As Patch threw open the front door and they walked outside, she had never been so glad to feel the sun on her skin.

The chauffeur started the Range Rover, and the guard covering him looked to Kabacra for confirmation they were free to go. He must have received it, since he stepped away from the vehicle and allowed them inside.

'We did it,' Con murmured. 'We actually did it!'

'We ain't out of here yet,' Patch warned her.

Coldhardt said nothing until the pale chauffeur had turned the car around and burned some serious rubber in his haste to get away. 'What do we have?' he demanded.

'Everything on Kabacra's hard drive,' Con told him.

'Excellent,' said Coldhardt, steepling his fingers. 'Well done, both of you.'

Patch remained miserable. 'What are we gonna do now? We can't go back to the hotel, Kabacra will send someone round to do us.'

'We're heading straight for the airstrip and a flight to New Mexico,' said Coldhardt. 'I've had our things sent on. Except for the swords beneath the bed, of course.'

Con frowned. 'You're really giving them to Kabacra?'

'It will keep him off our backs. With the reasons for Tye's abduction still unclear, I don't need any further distractions.'

'Maybe Jonah and Motti have found out where she is by now,' said Patch, forcing a little brightness into the car. 'Yeah, I'll bet they have. Then we can get her out, wherever she is.'

Coldhardt nodded vaguely. Then to Con's secret delight, he leaned forward and placed a hand on her shoulder. 'That was nice improvisation back there.'

She glowed at his words of praise, and did her best to imagine his touch had been warm and paternal on her shoulder; not the careless afterthought of a man already lost in dark, unknowable thoughts.

CHAPTER SIX

'Help me!' Tye croaked. She couldn't move. The heat of the sun was like a solid thing, pinning her down. Her mouth felt claggy and dry, and her head was pounding; every thought was a thistle prickling her mind as she waited for the next inevitable wave of nausea to hit.

Cracking open that second bottle of tequila had been a bad, bad idea.

Unsurprisingly, both the bottle and the idea had belonged to Ramez.

'I said, "Help me!"' she moaned, shifting on the sunlounger and smoothing out her camisole top. 'I can't reach my water. Pass me it.'

'See you ain't learned no manners since you left Haiti,' said Ramez. He was sitting by the pool, waving his feet through the clear blue water.

'Please.' With an enormous effort, Tye propped herself up on one elbow. The view of Santa Fe from the penthouse roof was incredible, but her smile was just for him. 'Pretty please?'

'Better.' He got up stiffly and splashed over the decking to pass her the drink. *Oh, Ramez, Ramez, Ramez.* The boy was looking fine; his olive skin taut and toned, hair razored, smiling back at her. The years in jail had mellowed his pretty-boy looks, but hadn't taken any of his charms away; she guessed he'd never been good at letting things go.

'Thanks,' she said, as another wave of nausea made her shut her eyes. He hadn't looked so hot when they'd parted company four years ago. Weird how she'd only been thinking of him just the day before, high over Guatemala. She'd been thirteen and crazy in love, he'd been sixteen, the big shot wannabe. He'd promised her so much – then tried to grab it all for himself by ripping off Haitian drug-dealers. Tye shuddered at the memory of the beating they'd given him; they'd blown off one of his kneecaps right in front of her, and it was only the arrival of the river police that stopped them putting a bullet in his brain. She remembered hiding in the shadows, rocking with silent tears as his bloodied body was dragged away by police. Remembered the way he'd cried and screamed.

Not for her. For the money he'd hoped to steal.

She opened her eyes again, watched the distant smile playing round Ramez's lips. No more tears and shouting. He clearly had the money now, and lots of it. And now he'd come back for her. Just as she'd used to dream he would.

'Penny for your thoughts, sugar-girl,' he said.

She looked away. 'A penny, with the kind of cash you must have? I don't think so.'

He started caressing the top of her arm. It felt way too nice. She'd been little more than a kid when they'd first got together; surely she should have outgrown those old feelings? But then she'd been smuggling for two years by then. She'd done so much growing up already.

He tried again. 'Hangover not shifting, huh?'

'I'm fine.'

'Never used to have a problem holding your drink.'

She pursed her lips. 'Maybe it's a bad reaction to the chloroform your friends used on me.'

Ramez took his hand away. 'Would you have left there quietly with armed intruders?' The question was so dumb she didn't bother to reply. 'Exactly. Remember, we didn't know if this Coldhardt guy was keeping you prisoner, if he had guards or what. The guys had to get in and get you out nice and quick, no arguments.' Ramez shook his head. 'They're the best. If we'd known there was just that one little kid with you –'

'His name is Jonah.' Tye closed her eyes. 'And you're *sure* those guys didn't hurt him, right?'

'Sure I'm sure. He's fine.' Ramez's cool act seemed to waver for a moment. 'I wasn't busting anything up between you guys?'

'No,' she said, probably just a fraction too quickly. 'It's just the idea of me needing to be rescued from Coldhardt!'

'The guy's got no file, no ID, no official existence, Tye. For all I knew, the guy coulda been using you for all kinds of bad shit.' Ramez shrugged. 'And since I couldn't go in myself with my shot leg, I figured the guys should just take you out of there. That we'd deal with your questions later.'

Tye settled back against the mattress and sipped from her drink. 'You haven't really dealt with any of them. I still don't know how you got off life in jail, or how you can afford to rent a penthouse in Santa Fe just so you could keep tabs on Coldhardt more easily . . .'

'You always had to question stuff,' he said, a trace of disappointment on his face. 'And you're still doing it. Why is that?'

She shrugged. 'I just would like to know –'

'I had to get to you, sugar-girl. 'Sides, I'm only renting this place a while.' He laughed softly, but she caught some sadness in his deep brown eyes. 'I told you, I made friends inside. We fixed a deal, we got an arrangement.'

'What kind of arrangement?'

'You could call it . . . an inheritance.' He shrugged, smiled. 'Now they look out for me. The way I wanna look out for you.'

Tye could tell from his body language that he wasn't lying. Though it had taken some time – and tequila – she was satisfied that whatever else Ramez might be up to, *he* wasn't trying to trick her. But he was clearly holding back one hell of a lot.

She sipped her drink. 'When I went to see you in jail, you sent me away. You said you never wanted to see me again.'

He looked downcast at the memory. 'You'd wasted enough of your life waiting on me.'

Tye looked away. 'So when you were screaming at me that I was a slut and going with any guy who might look at me, that was you driving me away to be kind, right?'

'Maybe. I dunno, I just . . .' He shrugged. 'I couldn't

hang on to dreams of you back then. It was easier to push you away.'

You never did find that so hard, Tye recalled unhappily. *Always pushing me away.* 'So what's changed?'

'Me.'

'Right. Sure.' What were the chances of the first boy she'd ever really cared about, the crush of her life, escaping the pit of a Belize prison, getting rich, and then taking time out from living the high life to chase her to the ends of the Earth?

'No chance at all,' she murmured distantly.

'Huh?'

'Forget it.' This was just way too good to be true. Since she'd got here last night she hadn't wanted for anything – his bodyguards were ready to go out and get whatever he asked for, any time of the day or night. This was apparently the way he'd been living for almost a year now, but how come he'd wound up smelling of roses instead of what roses grew in?

Tye knew that she should press him further, find out exactly what was going down here. But a big part of her simply didn't want to know. Didn't want to spoil the fantasy. Not after last night . . .

'I've spent so long trying to find you, girl,' Ramez said suddenly, taking her hand. 'Wasted so much time. But the time we've got left together, well . . .' His fingers strayed down to stroke above her hip. 'I want it to be special. When I heard you'd got caught up with this big-league criminal guy –'

She brushed his hand away. 'I haven't got "caught up" in anything, Ramez. I'm not thirteen any more. And your sugar-girl has managed to get by without you for four years.' She slumped back on the sun-lounger. 'D'you really think I'd stay anywhere unless I wanted to?'

He gave her that drop-dead gorgeous smile. 'I notice you ain't tried escaping here yet.'

'Maybe I just like your pool.'

'Tye . . .' Ramez looked away almost shyly. 'If it helps you chill, why not speak to Coldhardt? Let him know you're OK?'

'I left a message for him at the hotel in Guatemala already.' She shrugged. 'It's cool.' She sounded so casual; secretly Tye was longing to call Coldhardt and the others properly. But she couldn't take the chance of calling on their private numbers. She was glad her mobile was back at the base. She knew that whatever she wanted to believe, this had all the hallmarks of a king-sized set up; that Ramez's friends might have her down for an easy mark. If she called in on a tapped phone, they could use her to get right to the core of Coldhardt's operation. No, the message she'd left for him and the others at the Stanley – brief and bland, like she suspected nothing – would have to do for now.

'I guess the old bastard's gonna want you back?' Ramez said.

'If he doesn't I'm gonna go kick his ass.'

'You really *want* to go back to that life?'

She stared at him. 'For God's sake, Ramez! What did you think? That you could show up after four years like nothing had ever happened and I would just drop everything?'

'Not for ever,' he told her, his eyes clouding. 'Just for now.'

Tye felt a tingle go up her. The words were simple, but there was something about the way he'd said them . . .

'Ramez,' she said quietly, 'are you going to tell me what the hell is going on here?'

'Nothing to tell. This is the rest of my life – luxury all the way. And I want you to share it with me.' He smiled. 'Now, where d'you wanna go for dinner tonight?'

Just give in to it for now. 'Well . . .' She shrugged. 'I don't know. I'm kind of new in town.'

'I know this great penthouse place,' said Ramez. 'Quiet little table by the pool . . . Real private. Interested?'

'Maybe.' Tye tried to smile. She kept thinking of how assured and grown-up Ramez had become, outwardly so successful; and yet, there in his eyes, a feeling she couldn't fathom.

How much had this 'inheritance' Ramez spoke of cost him?

The distorted scream of an electric guitar woke Jonah as it carried past his doorway. He had fallen asleep on the bed without meaning to. The sun was starting to set. Twenty-four hours had passed since Tye had gone.

It didn't take long to place the angry, discordant music. 'Motti's back,' he realised, and got up cautiously. His head felt a little better – but it wouldn't for much longer if Motti's overdrive pedal had its way.

Jonah walked a little unsteadily towards the hangout – the biggest room in a whole wing of the ranch given over to their recreation. Huge, squashy leather sofas and funky plastic furniture vied for floorspace with snooker tables, arcade games, snack machines and even a fully equipped coffee bar. A gigantic HD TV set dominated one wall, with speakers sited on all sides of the cavernous space. In the room beyond was a full-sized heated pool and, beyond that, a garage full of karts and quad bikes. There were even stables. Coldhardt expected his employees to work hard, but invited them to play hard too – so long as it was on his turf and his terms.

Right now Motti was playing rock god in his private recording studio – built as far from the hangout itself as possible and paid for with his earnings from Coldhardt. Jonah gritted his teeth as an insanely loud and spiky riff burst from the supposedly soundproofed room and threatened to take his ears off. From the noise coming out, Motti wasn't in the best mood.

Jonah pushed open the door to the performance room. Motti broke off and looked at him. 'The neighbours complaining or something?'

'Yeah, in Russia,' Jonah told him, rubbing his ears. 'You were asleep when I got back from checking the grounds, and I figured you needed the rest.' He switched off the amp and sat down on it heavily. 'But, man, I was going crazy brooding on this alone. Needed to blast out some cobwebs.'

'There's now a thousand homeless spiders in Yugoslavia. What did you find?'

'That I was right about the chopper. I checked the motion sensors on the roof of the main building. They recorded strong, consistent movement just within tolerance – the alarms woulda gone off if the 'copter came any lower or touched down, so I'm guessing it hovered just outside the range of the sensors while your pals climbed down on rope-ladders on to the veranda.'

'How'd you know?'

'Faint boot prints in the mud, they go so far and then stop. It was a slick job, Jonah. These Sixth Sunners are clever sons of bitches.' He snorted. 'Maybe that short guy you saw really *is* a professor.'

'I just wish I knew what they wanted Tye for.'

'Let's hope it's not the same thing *you* want her for.'

Jonah glared at him. 'I already told you, nothing happened. It's not like that.'

'Well, that's good,' said Motti. ''Cause we're a team, man. We work together, we chill together, we watch out for each other, but we do not let it get messy. Because if we *do*, and our judgement gets clouded, then everyone else could wind up screwed as a result.' His face softened as he blew out a sigh. 'Anyways, Coldhardt'll soon be on the case. Con called. Her and the others are gonna get back around three tomorrow morning. There'll be a debrief in the hub at eight. We'll get our girl back.'

'Yeah,' said Jonah. 'We'll get her back.'

He only wished he really believed it.

CHAPTER SEVEN

Tye stood at the penthouse balcony, a cool breeze tingling her skin as she stared out over the Santa Fe vista. The lights of the city were like lanterns against the dark, misshapen shadows of the crowding mountains in the moonlight.

Discreetly she poured what was left of her glass of wine over the foliage far below, tired of her head feeling muddy and wishing she'd eaten less of the take-out duck, served to them in silence by one of the ever-present bodyguards.

She heard Ramez come up behind her, and closed her eyes as he slipped his arms around her waist. 'You look amazing,' he said.

'Do I?' Tye looked down at the white silk dress she wore. She guessed it was gorgeous – Con would no doubt be in raptures – but really she'd be much happier in her jeans. Unfortunately Ramez hadn't arranged for her wardrobe to be abducted along with her. She turned in his arms to look up at him. 'How'd you know my size?'

'Lucky guess.'

'Damn lucky. You *sure* you chose it for me?'

'I saw it on local TV,' he insisted. Then he grinned,

a macho shadow of the younger Ramez back in his deep-tanned face. 'I've got three other sizes down in my room. Figured that if that one didn't fit, another one would.'

Reading his body language, she saw he was telling the truth, and finally allowed herself to relax and smile. Why was she trying so hard to ruin things? Didn't she mess up stuff for them before by always probing too deeply, pushing things too far?

'Let's go out,' she said suddenly. 'Out into the city.'

He shrugged. 'I thought maybe we could stay in.'

'We've stayed in all day!'

'OK,' he said. 'I'll go tell the guys, tell them to get the Merc out front for us –'

She put a finger to his lips and silenced him. 'No. Let's go out on our own.'

Ramez gently tightened his grip on her waist. 'We can't.'

'Of course we can.' She pushed him playfully away. 'C'mon, it'll be cool. I'll look after you.' Hitching up the skirt of her dress, she vaulted the balcony rail, landing lithely on the other side. 'We can drop down to the balcony without your bodyguards knowing, follow the parapet round to the neighbouring penthouse. You said it was empty, right?'

'The guys told me it was –'

'And why should they lie, right?' Her eyes challenged him to disagree. 'I can get us inside and we can sneak out together.'

Ramez shook his head. 'Not with my leg.'

'I can help you.' Tye glanced longingly at the city's bright lights. She needed to get out of this place.

81

'Please, Ramez. Your bouncers give me the creeps. You're their boss, right? Tell them to stay home for once.'

'It doesn't work that way,' he protested.

'So how *does* it work?'

Ramez's shoulders tensed. He didn't answer.

'Then we're back to sneaking out,' Tye spoke lightly despite the sudden prickle of sweat on her palms. Setting off along the parapet, she glanced out at the city again. 'Wait here.'

'C'mon, sugar-girl.' Ramez's voice hit an anxious note. 'Come back!'

But Tye ignored him, her heart hammering like the questions she couldn't keep at bay. Just what the hell was it that Ramez had inherited? How did it affect her, and her link to Coldhardt? Trying not to think of the six-storey fall if she slipped, she dropped down for a perfect landing on the lip of the top-floor balcony. She followed it round as far as it would go. The neighbouring balcony stood the other side of a recess maybe a metre-and-a-half wide.

With barely a second thought she hitched her dress up round her waist and leaped recklessly across the divide, landed on the parapet and grabbed hold of the balcony rail to steady herself. Ramez was right, he'd never have been able to get down this way; she should just go back and stop trying to wreck –

Lights were on inside the building. She could hear voices, too. So much for the penthouse being deserted. Why would Ramez's bodyguards lie so blatantly?

Maybe because someone was staying here that they didn't want Ramez to know about. With his bad leg,

Ramez would never be able to climb down to the parapet and see for himself. And since he only went outside with an escort, that would give them plenty of time to switch out the lights, keep up the pretence of emptiness . . .

Tye broke off her train of thought and sighed. The penthouse might be a fair way up, but her paranoia had to be scaling even greater heights.

Even so, she swung herself easily over the balcony rail and padded across to the nearest open window, grateful that the blinds were drawn.

'. . . the pieces are all in place,' a man was saying, his voice a low Midwestern drawl. 'Soon, we'll have everything we need.'

Settling in for a game of chess or something. Tye supposed she'd better scram back before she was caught.

'See for yourself, the latest geological surveys confirm it.' The woman's voice, prim and British, took Tye's attention. 'I am sure that we are on the brink of finding the exact location.'

'And then the prophecy shall finally be fulfilled,' the man said quietly. Tye strained to hear. 'We shall be brought face to face with Coatlicue herself.'

'And the power we seek will be ours.'

So much for chess, Tye decided. Coatlicue was another blast from the past, the Aztec goddess of life, death and rebirth with her skirt of serpents – Tye had known of one smuggling gang who used hollow porcelain statues of Coatlicue to run H between Colombia and Yucatan.

But to be brought face to face with Coatlicue?

What was that supposed to mean?

She listened for another half-minute or so, but heard nothing. The man and the woman must have gone to another room.

She heard a click from the French windows further along the balcony.

Hastily, Tye vaulted the rail again – but the hem of her white dress caught and ripped noisily. Heart quickening, she swiftly leaped the divide, landed neatly on the adjacent parapet, hauled herself over and lay down flat.

Through the stone balustrade she saw a woman with dark, bobbed hair step outside on to the balcony. Her tall, willowy figure was silhouetted against the starry night as she looked all round.

'No, there's nothing out here,' she reported. The moonlight laced her bare neck with silver as she stepped back inside her penthouse to rejoin her companion.

Quickly, Tye scrambled up and scaled the rough and pitted wall. She dragged herself back on to the roof. Ramez was pacing the balcony. He didn't seem amused.

'What the hell d'you think you're doing?' he demanded, grabbing her arm as she climbed over the rail. 'Look at the state of you!'

Tye looked down at her torn and dirty dress. 'Sorry.'

Ramez let go of her, shook his head. 'Why'd you always have to make everything so damned hard?'

'Maybe it's you who always wants to believe everything's so damned easy.' She pointed back the way she had come. 'Your "deserted" penthouse next door is occupied.'

He shrugged. 'So?'

'You were told the place was empty. The guys wouldn't lie, you said.'

'Duh, so maybe someone moved in there in the last coupla weeks. Who cares?'

'There's a man and a woman there talking about power, and pieces being in place, and Coatlicue and –'

'Would you read my lips, sugar-girl?' His voice was low, a sneer on his face, hard and tough and *God*, she loved it when he was like this though it always scared the hell out of her. 'I – don't – goddamned – care.'

'Seems like nothing matters to you now,' she said quietly.

His voice softened. 'Nothing 'cept you, sugar-girl.'

With a weird thrill, Tye saw that he meant it; the words she had always dreamed of hearing from his lips.

'So anyways,' he went on, the familiar swagger returning to his shoulders, 'I told you everything's cool, so why don't you just stop worrying and –?'

'No.' Tye shook her head. 'I used to swallow every word you said because I *wanted* to believe in you. I wanted to think that maybe together we could crawl out of the gutter and –'

'And now we have!' He took hold of her hands. 'OK, so we weren't smart enough to make it by ourselves, had to be *bought* out of it – but that's cool. The important thing was cutting free, right? We both made trades to get everything we really wanted.'

'Everything we really wanted . . .' She frowned.

'And what's that, Ramez?'

'Duh!' He looked baffled that she should even ask. 'Money! Stacks of cash.' He squeezed her hands. 'The high life, babe! Or did I miss something?'

Tye felt a sick feeling in her stomach. 'Yeah, Ramez,' she whispered, pulling away. 'I think maybe you did.'

For a moment they stared at each other, the silence between them thick and heavy.

Tye broke off the look and turned back to the horizon. Now the twinkling skyline seemed to mock her – all those hopeful lights so far away, out of reach. She suddenly found herself wondering where Jonah and the others were right now. What were they doing? She swallowed. Was Jonah thinking about her?

'You know what? Fine,' Ramez said, breaking the silence. 'You wanna go out? We'll go out.' She couldn't bring herself to look at him, but she heard his impatient sigh. 'Just get the dress changed, and I'll tell the guys to take us partying.'

'OK.'

'We can go anywhere. Anywhere you like.'

'Great.'

She heard him leave. A minute or so later, she went to her luxurious bedroom, stripped off the dress, pulled on her old clothes. Wiped her eyes.

Twenty minutes later one of the bodyguards steered her and Ramez out of the building to where the other waited in the limo. Tye glanced up at the neighbouring penthouse. Its windows were dark, the balustrade before them like a big black grin leering out at the night.

CHAPTER EIGHT

Jonah sat impatiently in his swivel chair. Con yawned, and Patch sank a little lower in his seat. Motti was slumped over a steaming mug of coffee. It was like being in another world down here, in an underground bunker beneath the ranch – a climate-controlled could-be-anywhere.

'I thought Coldhardt said debrief was at eight a.m. prompt.' Jonah looked round. 'Anyone seen him?' *Funny how things change*, he thought. Not so long ago, he'd have been terrified, on edge here in the heart of the old man's world, where the plasma screens on the wall looked down like dark, accusing eyes, and the long marble table felt like a headstone to the touch. He'd have been chewing his nails, scared of screwing up or saying something dumb. But he supposed that once you started coming up against maniacs with guns and crossbolts on a fairly regular basis, a high-tech underground conference room lost some of its power to intimidate. 'It's not like Coldhardt to be late.'

'He is going through the stuff we stole from Kabacra,' said Con proudly. 'Looking through the client list.'

Patch sighed. 'Wish he'd start looking for Tye.'

Coldhardt emerged from a back room, dressed all in black save for a tiny white rosebud pinned to his lapel, and sat in a high-backed chair at the head of the table. 'As yet I have had no demands, no threats, nothing from Tye's kidnappers,' he announced. 'But I *have* received a message from Tye, forwarded from the Stanley Hotel in Livingston.'

Jonah's heart lurched. 'When did they get it?'

'Shortly after Con, Patch and I set off for Kabacra's.' Coldhardt produced a small, flat remote, and pressed a button. Suddenly Tye's voice, hollow and speckled with digital noise, boomed out from hidden monitors.

'Coldhardt, it's Tye. I'm safe, I'm being well-treated. The attack wasn't aimed at you; it's me they were after. It's kind of complicated to explain, but you don't need to race to my rescue. I'll get in touch again soon. Be careful, guys. Bye.'

'She's all right,' murmured Patch. He looked totally bewildered.

'That's it?' Motti slammed down his coffee. '"It's kind of complicated to explain"?'

'She must have been forced to give that message,' said Jonah loyally, his insides all bunched up. 'Why else would she phone the hotel instead of our mobiles?'

Con shrugged. 'Perhaps because she didn't really want to talk to us?'

Jonah gave her a look. 'Coldhardt, can we trace where she was calling from?'

'No. The message was already a day old by the time it was forwarded. We have no idea of her location.'

Coldhardt looked at Jonah. 'Did you find anything on Sixth Sun online?'

'Nothing,' Jonah admitted.

'Then I'm glad that Con and Patch at least have not let me down.' He tapped a pile of papers on the desk in front of him and smiled thinly. 'There are some illuminating entries in Kabacra's client list.'

Motti set down his espresso cup with bad grace. 'Like what?'

'For one, a penthouse residence in Santa Fe marked as belonging to Sixth Sun.' Coldhardt looked at each of them in turn, as if to underline the importance of the words that followed: 'According to Kabacra's transaction records, the sword of Cortes was delivered to that address.'

'A drop-off point,' Con speculated.

'Or their base,' Patch offered.

'A top-floor apartment doesn't sound like much of a base,' said Jonah.

'I don't believe it!' Motti was shaking his head. 'We bust our asses getting to Guatemala and ripping off a nuclear power plant, and the whole time it's sitting just about eighty miles down the highway from here?'

'So why kidnap Tye?' asked Jonah. 'They must already have had the sword by then, so it can't be to warn us off. If anything it's going to make us *more* likely to come after them.'

Con shrugged. 'Maybe they're using her as bait, and this is some kind of trap.'

'Then why no messages, no demands, no contact at all?' said Jonah. 'And why do they even want this sword of Cortes so much in the first place?'

'It's the sword of their nemesis,' Coldhardt reminded him, 'the most notorious conquistador of all.'

Jonah looked at Coldhardt straight. 'So why do *you* want it?'

He smiled without warmth. 'Let's confine ourselves to the first question, shall we? Why *would* a secret society dedicated to old Aztec tradition wish to acquire the symbol of that people's absolute defeat?'

'They wish to avenge their defeat by possessing the symbol of his victory,' Con speculated, undeterred. 'Or to destroy it – kind of a symbolic gesture, yes?'

'Pretty pricey gesture,' noted Motti.

'Actually, they paid a good deal less for the sword than I would have expected,' said Coldhardt. 'The payment was recorded in Kabacra's accounts along with a second Sixth Sun address across the border in Colorado, headed "Black House".'

Jonah frowned. The name seemed familiar from somewhere but he couldn't place it.

'Then this Black House must be their base,' Con asserted.

'I'm looking into it,' said Coldhardt curtly. 'In the meantime we must investigate that penthouse. There's a chance the sword has been kept there – perhaps even Tye.'

Motti raised his eyebrows. 'So we're breaking in?'

'You will drive to Santa Fe this afternoon, get the lie of the land,' said Coldhardt. 'You, Patch and Con.'

Patch sighed. 'If it's a radiation-free zone, I'm happy.'

'What about me?' asked Jonah. 'My head's feeling much better this morning. I can go too.'

'I need you here to finish work on the computer set-up.' Coldhardt looked graver than Jonah had ever seen him. 'There are things I need you to do. We can't afford to be exposed now.'

To Patch's eye, being in Santa Fe was like falling through a time warp. Everything was built like it was really old, kind of Spanish-looking and muddy. The car parks were done out in red-brown clay, and even the petrol stations were disguised as ancient Native American monuments.

But the only building that mattered right now was the penthouse.

They drove into the city in Con's powder blue Porsche 911. She couldn't drive, just loved to be seen in it – as did Patch and Motti. But today they sat as quiet as the ride, not getting off for once on all the stares and jealous looks thrown their way as they cruised along the streets.

Normally, it was Tye who did the driving.

Patch looked up from his Game Boy and saw some kids their age hanging outside a bar. One boy eye-balled Motti. 'Hey!' he called. 'D'you steal that car?'

'It's *my* car,' Con informed him. 'And as a matter of fact it's about the only thing I *didn't* steal.'

Motti razzed away the moment the lights changed and left the kids eating Porsche dust. 'Gotta spend your money on something,' he reflected. 'Gotta enjoy it while it lasts. 'Cause you never know when the high life's gonna end.'

'Never know when life's gonna end full stop,' said Patch gloomily, holding his stomach.

'Throw up over my car and it ends right now,' Con promised him.

They stopped near a quiet pizza parlour where Con's charms and talent got them some useful props – including a delivery van. Then the recce began.

Motti dressed up as a pizza delivery guy – possibly the grouchiest pizza delivery guy in the whole world – and took a big box up to the penthouse on the top floor. No one had answered his banging on the door, so he'd pretended to call his boss, all the time taking pictures of the locks and alarms and stuff with his phone-camera.

Patch studied the evidence, worked out which tools he would use, while Motti worked out the best way to bypass the alarms. Con, meanwhile, sat in the back of the van, stuffing her pretty face with decoy pizza all afternoon while she kept watch on the penthouse. The few people who came and went didn't show at any of its windows. She was fairly sure it had stayed empty. No sign of Tye.

Finally, once Motti had returned the van around nine that evening, they were ready to move. Patch felt the familiar drill of nerves building in his stomach as they walked along the street.

'Reckon it's the place next door we gotta worry about,' Motti told Patch as they pulled up in the Porsche a few blocks away, outside one of the ten billion art galleries crammed into the city. The sun was setting, and the mountains on the horizon glowed with fierce red light. 'These two huge guys came out from inside just as I'd finished casing. They did not look happy to see me.'

'They were probably in the mood for a Chinese,' Patch suggested.

'Or perhaps they thought you were lowering the tone of the place, yes?' Con had changed from jeans and T-shirt into a smart, chic business suit with killer heels. She looked like she owned the whole building.

'I'll go in through the front way,' said Con, 'persuade the man on the door that we have every right to be here, yes?'

'Signal when it's safe,' Motti agreed quietly.

There were security cameras in the communal hallways on each floor, monitored from the main reception. So long as Con's mesmerism bit worked, the doorman could spy the Moscow State Circus breaking into the penthouse and not bat an eye. That just left the building's roaming security guard, but Con could take care of him one way or another while Patch and Motti got on with the job in hand.

'You all right, Mot?' Patch asked quietly. 'You been kind of quiet lately.'

He didn't look round. 'I'm fine.'

'Worried about Tye?'

'And about Coldhardt,' Motti admitted. 'He ain't exactly breaking his balls to get her back, is he? This sword's all he cares about. I'm thinking, what if it was one of us? How much do *any* of us count with him?'

Patch frowned. 'He cares about us! 'Course he does!'

'Sure. It's all a nice, cosy game of happy families.'

At that moment, Con re-emerged and stuck her slender thumb up. Nervously, Patch followed Motti into the building to join her. All together they took the lift up to the top floor, where Patch took his lock-pick tools from out of his false eye.

'Do your thing,' said Con as the lift doors opened on to the penthouse approach. 'The guard is on the third floor, he's working his way up. I'll meet him on the fourth and talk him out of going any further.'

'Got it,' said Motti, and breezed off to study the door to the penthouse.

'Take care,' Con told them as the lift doors closed again.

'So what've we got?' Patch asked.

'I'm guessing a sensor in the side of the door. If the door opens, the switch tells the alarm to prime itself. And when that happens we've got, what, fifteen seconds tops to stop the alarms going.' Motti glanced behind him at the door to the penthouse opposite. 'Maybe less if Bozo and Bozo through there stick their broken noses in.'

Patch was already working the lock, teasing the tumblers into turning his way. 'So it's E-bomb time?'

'Risky, but we ain't got no choice.' Motti had taken a small metal drum about the size of his palm from his pocket. It emitted a powerful electro-magnetic pulse; enough high-powered microwaves to completely screw the electrics of anything in the area while leaving everything else intact. Trouble was, you couldn't really aim an E-bomb – they just went off and took out anything electronic within range. The one in Motti's hand was a titch, but it could still easily take out the whole top floor – not to mention their mobiles, the bit-buster, all their gadgets . . .

Patch got to work on the door's lock and was

rewarded just a few seconds later with a quiet click. His hand closed on the door handle. 'Ready?'

'Look out, alarm,' muttered Motti, priming the E-bomb. 'Got ten gigawatts coming up your ass.'

Patch threw open the door, and Motti pushed through into the penthouse, activating the device. The alarm didn't make a sound – but the lights in the hallway clicked off in an instant. Patch checked his digital watch as he followed Motti inside. It was dead.

'Right,' said Motti softly, 'let's hope everyone else in the place thinks it's just a power cut and waits nice and quietly inside for the juice to turn back on.' He pulled out a solar-powered torch and was soon pulling paintings off the living-room wall, looking for a hidden safe.

Patch produced his own torch and started searching the white and minimalist master bedroom. He had a quick poke around in the slatted wardrobes. 'Found the safe!' he hissed. It was large. Easily large enough to hold a sword.

Motti was beside him in a second. 'Can you crack it?'

'Dial combination lock with key-change capability,' Patch muttered. 'In other words, if you wanna change the combination, you need a special key from the manufacturer. You stick it into that hole in the lock case there, see?'

'And you have the special key, right?'

'Nope.' Catching the murderous look in Motti's eyes, Patch moved on swiftly. 'But I do have a fibre-optic scope. I can stick *that* into the lock case and read the correct positioning of the wheels on the combination dial that'll free the bolt.'

'Sounds clever.'

'It's bloody genius, mate.'

'Get on with it.'

Patch got out his scope and set to work.

Jonah rebooted the server in Coldhardt's data centre. 'OK. Firewall should be up and running now.' He glanced over at Coldhardt. 'If you restart, you should be able to access all your shared files.'

The old man did not acknowledge him, staring into space with a gaze as blank as the screen in front of him. Jonah's eyes lingered on the small, unsettling statue upon his desk; it depicted a man in combat with some squat, demonic figure. It was a theme common to many of the artworks Coldhardt put on display, and every variation gave Jonah the same shivers.

'Thank you, Jonah.' Coldhardt snapped suddenly back into life. 'A timely announcement. I need to check some aerial maps of the area.'

'What area?'

'Colorado Springs.' He paused. 'That Black House address I found mentioned in Kabacra's records – it cannot be found on any official maps.'

Jonah frowned as he finished checking the proxy server was up and running – a further protective barrier between Coldhardt's network and any possible attack from over the Internet. 'Could it have been a bogus address? Or maybe encoded in some way?'

'Possibly,' Coldhardt conceded. 'Once you have hacked into a certain satellite scanner in low orbit over the area and secured us a live feed, we can be certain.' He fixed Jonah with those unnerving blue eyes. 'Something's existence may be denied. But that's not to say it doesn't exist.'

For some reason, Jonah found his eyes drawn to the statue of the man and demon again.

He blinked. 'I, uh . . . I know that in the UK some American military bases aren't marked on the maps. Could Black House be something like that?'

'Possibly. There's a good deal hidden in this world from all but the most prying of eyes.'

'Like your treasure vault down in the wine cellar?' asked Jonah lightly.

Coldhardt looked at him stonily.

'If you have to kill me 'cause I know too much,' said Jonah apologetically, 'I figured I should tell you *before* I blow my last hours hacking into that low-orbit satellite.'

'I had hoped you would live long enough to out-grow this flippant streak, Jonah. How do *you* come to know of the vault?'

'Tye found that big hidden door down there. She showed it to me.'

'And you believe I store my treasures behind it?'

'I haven't told any of the others.' Jonah shrugged. 'I just figured you should know that Tye knew about it. Because if Sixth Sun manage to make her talk, well . . . then they'll have found out about it too.' *And if that doesn't get you more fired up about doing something to rescue her,* he thought, *what the hell will?*

But Coldhardt simply got up from his desk and walked calmly away. 'Perhaps, for the time being, you'd restrict your curiosity to the spy satellite's IP address, and the relevant co-ordinates. I want to know more about this Black House.'

Subject closed, Jonah surmised. *For the time being.*

Tye lay on the bed in her dressing gown, still and quiet in the darkness, listening to Ramez breathe beside her. They'd had the lights down low, soft music playing. Then the lights had suddenly flicked off into blackness, the hi-fi went dead. And yet in the darkness Tye had felt suddenly exposed. It came down to just the two of them, their sweat, Ramez's hoarse breathing.

And it was suddenly like it had been four years ago, half-wanting him, but always wary of how far to let his hands wander, of how far to let herself go. '*Give a boy what he wants and he's gone tomorrow,*' she'd heard the older girls say. '*Hold out on him and he'll be back again and again.*' And Tye had never given him what he wanted and look, here was Ramez back again, only it was pure cotton and silk they were lying on, not the bumpy backseat of some crappy car he'd hotwired, and his fingers were way too –

'Hey.' She'd squirmed clear of him, panting softly. 'Who turned out the lights?'

'Power's out, 's'all,' he'd murmured. 'They'll turn back on in a sec.' He started kissing her neck hungrily. 'And so will you.'

She'd held herself dead still. 'Can we slow down?'

Ramez had reluctantly thumped back down on to his back, his breath coming in deep, rapid pushes. Only now, minutes later, was it starting to slow.

Tye could feel his frustration. He'd wanted to jump her from the moment she'd woken up in this place;

that much was obvious. But she'd never let him go all the way before and that wasn't about to change now – no matter what he said about wanting to make the most of every moment they had together, and no matter how much he really seemed to mean it. Because she didn't trust the undercurrents in this situation. They threatened to tow her out with him into some cold, uncharted place. Some place she could wind up lost.

'When d'you think you'll feel ready?' Ramez asked bluntly.

She rolled on to her side. 'You know, I love it when you act so romantic.'

'How much more romantic can I get?' he snapped. 'We went out last night like you wanted. Today I let you lie in, got you breakfast in bed –'

'Made by your bodyguards.'

'– champagne by the bucket load, bracelet of Akoya pearls, watch chick-movies with you, play with your hair . . . and *still* you wanna wait?'

'I'm waiting for you to tell me what this is really all about.' She turned back to face him. 'I've been kidding myself I didn't need to know. That I should just stay in the moment. But that's not me, Ramez. I could have run out on you a dozen times these last two days and I damn nearly did . . .' Tye stared at him searchingly. 'But I still care about you. I care way more than I should, but I guess that's just the way it is.' She swallowed hard. 'So for God's sake, won't you just come out and tell me whatever the hell it is you did or sold to land your dumb ass in the high life?'

There was silence for a while, save for their breathing. Then Ramez pulled his lighter from his jeans pocket and grabbed a tealight from the table. Soon an orange glow flickered into the room, casting spectral, hazy shadows over the wall.

'Guess we've all got to move on sometime,' he said at last.

'Where are you moving on to?'

'Maybe shuffling off's a better way to put it.' He looked at her, his eyes glistening. 'Point is, I want you, Tye. That's all I want now, before I have to go.'

Damn, his eyes could melt chocolate. 'And what happens to me then?' she asked him quietly. 'I'm just dumped, left behind?'

He half-smiled, but a tear fell from his left eye. 'There's no way I can take you with me, sugar-girl.'

'Oh my God,' she murmured, as the realisation hit her like a fist. 'You're ill, aren't you?'

He looked away, his voice soft as the shadows. 'I guess you could say I haven't got long.'

She placed her hand on his bare shoulder, feeling sick. 'What is it? What's wrong with you?'

His smile seemed bitter. 'We all got to make sacrifices in life, right?'

Suddenly a loud click from outside the room made Tye jump. 'What was that?'

'Sounded like the door.' He peered into the gloom, then let his head fall back on the pillow. 'Just one of the guys going out for something.'

'Oh, Ramez, can't we just get out of here together? If you're sick I can get you help, Coldhardt can fix you up with the best doctors –'

'You can't go back to him, Tye,' Ramez told her, pushing himself up on one elbow. 'You mustn't.'

'Why not?' She stared at him, her head hot and spinning. 'Jeez, Ramez, would you try making sense for five seconds?'

He stared back at her, his eyes dark and intense. 'Here's something that makes sense,' he whispered, and pressed his lips against hers.

And though her heart felt like it was splitting, Tye gave herself up to the kiss.

Con took the steps to the top floor, leaving the sprawled body of the security guard at the base of the stairwell. Some people were just too stubborn to be mesmerised. She'd tucked a fifty-dollar bill into his pocket to say sorry for the tap on his head – then pulled it back out and given him thirty. It was possible to get too sentimental about things.

She emerged through the fire door on to the penthouse approach and checked all was quiet. Then she had to duck back out of sight as two large, hulking men emerged and crossed to the window at the end of the landing. They peered out, perhaps looking to see if neighbouring buildings were also out of power.

With a sinking feeling, Con saw the men exchange glances and walk back down the corridor. She quietly re-opened the fire door and peeped round to see where they had gone.

And then she swore.

Patch gave a silent cheer as the last of the dials locked into place and the bolt fully retracted. The safe door swung smoothly open.

'I don't believe it,' snarled Motti. '*Still* no

goddamned sword!'

Patch reached in and pulled out the safe's only contents. 'It's like a book or something!' The cover was thin wood decorated with turquoise discs. Opening that, he found the ancient pages unfolded concertina-style, a bit like a modern map; but they were made from some sort of animal skin, daubed with weird drawings like those on the Aztec medallion. 'What the bleedin' hell is it?'

Motti grabbed the book and tucked it up his shirt-front. 'After all this dicking around, we're taking it with us whatever the hell it is.'

'Uh, Mot?' Patch felt his heart sinking into his shoes. 'I think the Ugly Brothers there might have something to say about that . . .'

A huge man stood framed in the bedroom doorway, an even bigger bruiser just behind him. They advanced into the room, fists raised and clenched.

CHAPTER NINE

'Have you come to fix the lights, then?' Patch asked brightly – as Motti hurled his torch at the first guy's head. The guy ducked, so it smacked into his mate just behind him. The blow did nothing to slow him down; he lumbered on towards Motti while the first guy came running for Patch.

Quickly, Patch flipped up his eyepatch, scooched out his false eye and rolled it into the man's path. Face twisting in revolted surprise, the man slipped on the oversized marble and fell heavily to the floor.

The other man had caught hold of Motti and was crushing him in a bearhug. Patch jumped on to his back, trying to grab him round the neck. Angrily, the guy shrugged him off – but as he did so Motti broke free of his grip, punched the guy twice in the mouth and gave him an almighty shove backwards. With a shout the man overbalanced and landed slap bang on his mate.

'Come on, cyclops,' gasped Motti, 'we're done.'

'Where'd my eye go?' Patch checked quickly about the floor. He liked that eye, it had his best picks inside. But he was too slow, one of the men grabbed hold of his ankle and twisted it round. With a yell of pain,

Patch went down.

As he fell he caught a crazy glimpse of long bare legs, blonde hair and a frying pan fleeting past. A second later there were two ringing clangs and the grip on his ankle relaxed.

Patch pulled himself free to find Con was standing over him, one eyebrow raised, still wielding the pan. Both blokes were out cold, and looked set to stay that way.

''Ere she is,' he said dreamily. 'The domestic goddess.'

She dropped the pan. 'I think I am just practical, yes?'

'That was such a dumb fight,' said Motti grumpily. 'Slipping them up, putting them on their butts, socking 'em with frying pans. That's just embarrassing, man. Coldhardt should ditch us and hire Charlie Chaplin.'

'Charlie Chaplin wouldn't look as good in a skirt,' said Patch, grabbing his eye from the floor. 'He's dead for a start.'

'You two could well have joined him,' Con said pointedly. 'But was it worth it?'

'Oh yeah.' Motti patted the bundle beneath his shirt. 'We got us some Aztec comic book or something. Big whoop.'

'Where's the sword?'

'Ain't here. Unless one of these jokers is hiding it up their ass.' He glared at the fallen men. 'They're the guys I saw next door.'

Con nodded. 'And they had keys to get in here.'

'Then I'm guessing they're more than just caring

neighbours,' said Motti. 'Next door must be a Sixth Sun hangout too.'

Patch caught his breath. 'Then maybe the sword's in there?'

'We go and see, yes?' Con crouched beside the biggest guy and started rummaging in his trouser pockets.

Patch sighed. 'That git's got further than I ever have and he never even bought her a drink.'

Con produced the keys, then led the way back out of the penthouse and across the corridor. A few seconds later she had the door open, and Patch piled in after her and Motti.

The hallway flickered with pale, greasy light from three oil lamps ranged at intervals. In the middle of the room, some slim and swarthy bloke stood angry and incredulous. 'What the hell –?'

Con skipped quickly forwards and high-kicked him in the chest. He gasped and fell backwards against the wall, apparently winded – but as she closed in to send him to dreamland he slugged her with a vicious uppercut to the chin. She tumbled to the floor. Motti leaped over her body and booted the guy in the family jewels, following it up with a punch to the jaw that floored the son-of-a-bitch. But as he knelt to check the guy would be no more trouble, a black girl swept out of the main bedroom in a silky white dressing gown and kicked him in the face, sending him sprawling.

'Tye!' Patch almost screamed. 'Christ on a bike, it's Tye! She's here!'

'Guys . . .?' About a hundred emotions flickered over her features in turn – shock, pleasure, confusion, alarm . . . Patch started forward, ready to grab her and hug her, but hesitated when she crouched protectively over the bloke on the floor, cradling his head. 'He's out cold.' She looked angry and baffled. 'Motti, what the hell were you doing?'

'What was *I* doing?' he gasped, clutching his jaw. 'Jeez, Tye, you nearly knocked my frickin' teeth out!'

'I heard Ramez shout, I thought someone was . . .' She shook her head, like it didn't matter. 'What happened to Con?'

'*He* happened to her,' said Motti, dropping to check she was OK. Con was stirring now, a little dribble of blood oozing from the corner of her mouth.

'Ramez didn't know who she was,' Tye said defensively. 'I mean, come on, this is his place, you guys just burst in here . . .'

'Oh, sorry, I'm sure!' said Patch, hurt and confused.

'Where's Jonah?' Her wide dark eyes looked suddenly fearful. 'Is he here?'

'No, he's back with Coldhardt.'

She looked back down at Ramez, flustered. 'How did you find me?'

'It was Cortes's sword we were sent after.' Motti helped Con to her feet. 'It was bought by Sixth Sun and delivered to their place next door. We just broke in, but it ain't there.'

'Do they keep it here?' Patch added, glancing about nervously.

'Sixth who? *What?*' Tye put her hand to her forehead, looked genuinely lost. 'There must be some mistake.'

'Right,' said Motti. 'And when those two big guys

who were hiding in here came over and tried to kill us –'

'Ramez's bodyguards?'

'– that was a mistake too, huh?' He straightened, his face sour. 'You know, Tye, I'm getting the vibe you ain't exactly overjoyed to see us.'

'It's not that,' Tye protested. 'This is all so sudden, so crazy. I've been dying to get in touch but –'

'Yeah, it musta been tough here,' Motti sneered, 'locked up in just your robe with the topless prettyboy.'

'This is Ramez, we –' Tye broke off. 'We knew each other. Long time ago, back in Haiti.'

'Looks like you been busy getting reacquainted.'

'They are using him against you?' Con dabbed at her split lip. 'You *are* a prisoner here, yes?'

'I . . . I don't know for sure,' said Tye. 'I don't get what's happening.'

'Neither do I!' said Patch, 'but I *do* know we need to get the bleedin' hell out of here. So, Tye, do Sixth Sun have the sword or not?'

'I've never even heard of Sixth Sun!'

'Then here's a refresher,' said Motti. 'Secret society – believes in old Aztec crap. They kidnapped you, nearly killed Jonah, cosied up to that scumball Kabacra in exchange for that dumb sword –'

'And if this place belongs to your "old friend" Ramez, then chances are *he* belongs to Sixth Sun too,' Con told her. 'You're being duped, sweets.'

Patch had wandered back over to the front doorway. They'd left the door open, and through the moonlit gloom he thought he caught sight of movement within. 'Guys, those gorillas are waking up!'

'Hold on,' Tye said, crouching beside pretty-boy who was groggily propping himself up on his elbows. 'Ramez? Come on, we're getting out of here.'

'We are?' he said distantly.

'The bodyguards can't stop us. We're going back to Coldhardt.'

'No.'

'You need help,' she insisted, 'and if you come with me –'

'I told you, I ain't going nowhere,' Ramez said, hanging on to Tye's arms. 'I can't.'

'But *you* can.' Motti looked at her. 'Come on back home.'

'Quick!' Patch begged them.

'Tye?' Motti held out his hand.

'Don't leave me, Tye,' Ramez pleaded, looking up at her, all puppy-dog eyes. 'Sugar-girl, if you ever loved me, don't make me face this alone.'

'I can't run out on Ramez,' she whispered, cradling the boy's head. 'I just can't. Not now.'

'What?' Con stared. 'For God's sake, sweets, he's just a boy!'

'Get out of here,' Tye told them.

Patch felt sick. 'You mean you ain't coming with us?'

'I'm more use to you here. I'll find out more about Sixth Sun, look for the sword. If I find it, I'll get it to you somehow.' She looked at them each in turn in the smoky, flickering light. 'Now *go*.'

'Whatever.' Motti slouched away.

Con tried again. 'This is madness, Tye. You can't just walk out on Coldhardt.'

'I'm *not*,' she protested.

'It doesn't look that way to –'

'Will you just get the hell out?' Tye screwed up her eyes. 'If they know I spoke with you . . .'

Con turned and left without another word, pushing past Patch who lingered in the doorway. There were definite groans and clomping noises coming from next door, and any moment now . . .

'Patch, get going!' she urged him. 'And tell Jonah . . .'

He cocked his head. 'Yeah?'

She looked down at Ramez, her features hidden by shadow. 'Tell him there's nothing like the sunset.'

'Cyclops, leave her to it and shift your ass!' hissed Motti from the end of the hallway.

Feeling like his pounding heart was being tugged two ways, Patch pelted after Motti and tore down the emergency stairs.

'I've hacked into the satellite's programming,' Jonah reported. 'Ready to see what we've got at those co-ordinates?'

Coldhardt was the other side of the hub. He turned as if surprised to find Jonah still there, then crossed to join him at the terminal.

The image on the screen resolved only slowly. 'It'll take a while 'cause I hooked up through five different proxy servers. The images will take longer to load and refresh but at least we stay secure and untraceable.' He paused and stretched noisily. It was later than he'd realised. The minutes seemed to tick away ten times faster when he was busting codes. 'You can say, "Congratulations", any time you like.'

'I expect no more or less from you than complete success,' Coldhardt murmured. 'Ah, now that really *is* interesting.'

'It is?' Jonah stared at the image; it appeared to be a low, wide shed plonked down on a large patch of farmland. 'Doesn't look like much.'

'It wouldn't stay secret for long if it did, would it?' Coldhardt pointed out. 'If that *is* just an innocent farm building, why isn't it marked on any map?'

'I suppose so,' said Jonah.

'And look at that.' He pointed to a large round area where the grass was neatly cut.

Jonah felt a rush of realisation. 'Could be a landing pad for a helicopter. Could be where they took Tye!'

'I'll make some enquiries. We have to know what's happening there.'

Just then a chime sounded from the intercom in the hub doorway. 'Motti and the others are back,' Coldhardt announced, moving a little stiffly over to an intercom device at the hub doorway. 'Come down.'

Jonah felt a tingle of apprehension go through him. A few minutes later, the sound of the concealed lift as it descended the levels from the ranch house above was thrumming through the hub.

At last, Motti stood in the doorway, Patch and Con just behind him. Con looked like she'd lost a fight with a revolving door. There was blood on Motti's face. He passed some kind of decorated book to Coldhardt.

'You ain't gonna like what we've got to say,' he said.

And as Motti started to describe all that had happened, Jonah decided that was the understatement of the decade. 'Tye was actually there in the other penthouse?' He couldn't believe he was hearing about this second hand. 'And you didn't get her out?'

'We couldn't drag her away,' said Con, and from the look of her blackened chin, she had tried.

'Ramez was an active smuggler in Haiti at the same time as Tye,' Coldhardt announced. 'When I was looking for recruits in that sector, he was *not* under consideration. A big talker but no talent to back it up.'

'Tye sure sees something in him,' said Motti, with a knowing glance at Jonah.

'I understand they were involved romantically when he was incarcerated for drug smuggling. I *had* thought he was in prison under sentence of death.' Coldhardt spoke so casually he could have been discussing a game of cricket. He seemed more concerned with the strange book, running his fingers over the pictograms and characters on the ancient pages.

Jonah cleared his throat. 'Bit of a coincidence, isn't it, that this Ramez guy should show out of nowhere and set up with Tye next to a Sixth Sun hideout? Like Con said before, it must be some kind of warning to you, Coldhardt.'

'But why involve Ramez to do that?' said Coldhardt reasonably. 'Purely to keep Tye happy throughout her incarceration?'

'He's doing that all right,' Patch muttered.

Jonah could feel himself flushing. 'We know Tye wouldn't run out on us.'

'And we also know she wouldn't run out *with* us,' said Motti. 'She said she would keep looking for the sword –'

'But it is him she stays for,' Con said.

The words felt like little bruises on Jonah's insides. He remembered the way Tye had looked at him down in the wine cellar, just before the masked men came to the house. Imagined her looking at this Ramez guy in the same way.

Then he tried not to.

'She knew him before she knew any of us,' Patch reflected. 'Old loyalties run deep, I s'pose.'

'Enough speculation.' Coldhardt looked up from the book, a fresh vibrancy in his old, craggy face. 'I'll decide how best to deal with Tye later.'

Jonah frowned. 'Deal with her?'

Coldhardt turned his wintry gaze on Motti, Con and Patch. 'Your expedition may not have been fully satisfactory, my children, but it most certainly was not a wasted effort. I believe you have brought back with you a near-fabled relic of Aztec antiquity.' He picked up the old book reverently. 'The Azteca codex.'

Motti frowned. 'Co-what?'

'A collection of ancient manuscript texts, over nine hundred years old. The conquistadors burned all Aztec books to demonstrate their mastery of the people.' He smiled coldly to himself. 'So little of worth survived.'

'But this is worth much, yes?' Con asked quickly.

'Its value is inestimable . . .'

Jonah looked down at the table. He felt a crushing wave of confusion surge through him. So, that was it for the Tye discussion? Vague threats and then back to the only thing that truly mattered to Coldhardt – the basic value of things, *stolen* things. To Jonah it felt as if Tye had been stolen away; that he'd been standing on the brink of something good, only for the ground to crumble beneath him. And now he was expected to just go on as if nothing was wrong and –

'If I might invite you back to the debriefing, Jonah?' Coldhardt's hardest stare was fixed on him, and Jonah realised he must've looked miles away. 'This codex contains information on temple etiquette. A sort of "what not to do" guide for the high priests, to ensure they did not disrespect the gods. But there were always rumours that other, rather more valuable information was added to it at a later date.' He tapped the final page of the codex. 'And now we have proof . . .'

'What language did they use?' asked Con.

'One called *Nahuatl*.'

'Nah-wattle?' Patch sighed. 'I can't even say it, let alone read it.'

Coldhardt shook his head. 'Before anyone can read it, Patch, it must be decrypted.'

Jonah looked at Coldhardt warily. 'It's a cipher?'

'In part. And that is the part that interests me, that raises its value beyond computation.' The old man's eyes seemed alive with light. 'Do you think you can crack a code that uses both text and pictograms?'

'I've broken a hieroglyph code before,' Jonah admitted, rubbing the back of his neck. 'When I was in the Young Offenders Institution I studied the computational theory of writing systems . . .'

'Someone had already picked up *Playboy* that day,' said Motti wryly.

'Finding the key won't be easy though,' Jonah warned Coldhardt.

'There is a statuette in my collection of Aztec antiquities – a depiction of Coatlicue, Aztec goddess of life, death and rebirth. Certain pictograms are engraved upon its surface. Two of them were thought by experts to be unique, and couldn't be translated.' He placed both palms down flat on the ancient volume. 'But three pictograms have been added to the final page of this codex, along with three lines of encoded Nahuatl. I don't recognise the third, but the first two match those "unique" marks carved into the statuette. Clearly there is a link.'

Despite himself, Jonah felt his interest rising. 'Why's it encrypted anyway? Any ideas what the message is about?'

'I believe it may contain clues to the location of a fabled lost temple dedicated to Coatlicue – the Temple of Life from Death.' Coldhardt paused, steepling his fingers. 'It is said that when Cortes's conquistadors ransacked the Mexican interior, a temple was constructed underground, filled with the Aztecs' greatest treasures, and then concealed to stop the invaders ever getting hold of them. The temple has been searched for over the centuries, but never discovered.'

'So that's what Sixth Sun are after,' Con said quietly.

'Guess Tye must want a piece of it too,' Motti added darkly.

'You don't know that,' Jonah snapped. 'Like we don't know how Cortes's sword figures in all this.' He looked at Coldhardt. 'Right?' The old man nodded slowly, and Jonah wished like hell that Tye was here to know if he was lying or not. 'Now that you guys have told her what's going on with Sixth Sun, that they've got the sword, she'll be planning to find out more. Stuff that can help us.'

'Maybe Jonah's right,' said Patch hopefully.

A long silence followed. Coldhardt broke it. 'Now the computer network is back up and running, we must start a search. I want to know if this third codex pictogram is marked on any other artefacts of the era. If it is, the context may help Jonah deduce a key for the cipher. I will check through my own collection. Your task will be to gather images, schematics, sketches, anything from the late post-classical period. Some will be public domain online, others will exist only in museum records withheld from the public –' he smiled '– but *not* from us.' He stood up from the table. 'You will start work at six a.m. For now, you are dismissed.'

Like any thought of helping Tye, Jonah thought, rising to go, his head spinning. *Like any idea of finding the truth*.

Tye wouldn't have walked out on them, he knew that. And she could never betray them.

Right?

CHAPTER TEN

Why did Tye stay behind? The question went on haunting Jonah as he sat with the others in the hangout.

Not that anyone seemed much in the mood for playing tonight. The raw thud of Motti's grungy homemade music thumped out from the speakers, well-fitted to the spiky, unsettled atmosphere.

'Pretty cool tune, huh,' said Motti, slumped on a couch beside a crate of ice-cold beers. 'This has got hit written all over it.'

'Close,' said Con. 'You missed out an "s".' Draped demurely over a designer chair, she had fixed herself a cocktail almost as dark and vivid as the bruise on her chin, and was staring into space.

'You don't need talent to make it in music. Just cash.' Motti drained another beer. 'And man, life with Coldhardt has got me a lot of cash. Who needs anything else?' He sighed heavily. 'I don't need nothing else.'

Patch belched loudly. Jonah turned to where he lay sprawled in an enormous beanbag surrounded by empty bottles of alcopop. 'Jonah!' he hissed. 'Got something to tell you. Private, like.'

Jonah crouched down beside him. 'What's up?'

'I meant to tell you before. Tye had a message for you, mate . . .'

'She did?' Jonah stared at him, fearing a wind-up.

'She said to tell you there was nothing like the sunset.'

Jonah's mind processed the words with a sting of disappointment. 'That's all she said? What the hell's it meant to mean?'

'Maybe it's enkip – encroute –' He emptied his glass. 'Maybe it's in code.'

'Maybe.' Jonah crossed back to his sofa and slouched back down. He remembered standing with Tye on the veranda that day as the sun slipped down behind the mountains; she had said, *You can't help but lose yourself in a sunset like that.*

Maybe now she was lost in a different way.

The last track on the CD jarred to a stop, and Patch spoke up in the sudden silence, his voice a miserable slur: 'So d'you think Coldhardt will get someone else in to replace Tye, then?' He belched again. 'We're gonna need a new pilot.'

Con looked at Jonah. 'Tye was training you, no?'

'She sure had his head in the clouds,' said Motti.

Jonah ignored him. 'I could probably fly that plane,' he conceded. 'But not cars, not boats, not hovercrafts or . . .'

'And what about the whole human lie detector bit,' Patch interrupted. 'Ain't gonna be easy, finding some-one who can do all that.'

'Whoever Coldhardt chooses, I think we should be allowed to audition him first,' said Con.

'Him?' Motti looked at her sharply. 'Who says it's a him? Coldhardt told you something?'

'Nah, she just *hopes* it's a him,' said Patch. 'She wants some hunky new bloke to fall at her feet.'

Jonah glared over at them. 'Guys, could we give the Tye replacement stuff a rest?'

'Well, I hope he gets another chick in,' said Motti. 'Older woman maybe, late twenties. A real piece of ass . . .'

Con snorted. 'Another boy would be far better.'

'What's up, can't take the competition?'

'*Stop it!*' Jonah shouted, stunning the others into silence. 'Is this all Tye's walking out on us means to you – the chance to get someone hot in to take her place?'

Con looked away. Motti started peeling at the label on his beer bottle. 'Ain't none of us indispensable,' he said quietly. 'Just ask the boss man.'

'OK, but remember when Coldhardt first dragged me into all this? I wanted nothing to do with it. You tried to sell me the set-up by saying you were like family. That after all those years on my own, maybe here was a place I could fit in. Really belong.'

'We *are* like family.' Patch looked at Con. ''Cept we can still fancy each other. It's allowed. It ain't incest or nothing –'

'Yeah, thanks, Patch, shut up a sec.' Jonah looked between Con and Motti. 'I know I'm the newest one to show round here, and maybe I've got no right to say how things should go. But I always figured family pulled together when things got tough.'

Motti grimaced. 'Aw, jeez, geek, save us the moral

hero bit.'

'Suppose Tye has been brainwashed by Sixth Sun,' he argued. 'Or suppose Ramez has some hold over her.'

'Hold *on* her, more like.' Motti mimed groping a pair of breasts. 'Him topless, her in a dressing gown . . .'

Jonah gritted his teeth. 'If we get her back, maybe she could tell us stuff. Important stuff.'

'What, important stuff like –' Motti put on an oochie-coochie voice – '"It's you I love really, Jonah!"'

Jonah turned away angrily. 'Jesus Christ, Motti!'

'She's ditched us, man,' Motti shouted, jumping up from the couch. 'All of us, you included. What you so surprised about? You know in this life you can't trust no one.'

Jonah shut his eyes. He didn't want to hear this. Didn't want to think that Tye could be the same as all those faces in his past, shaking their heads, refusing him, sending him away.

'Tye did say she could help us find out more by staying there,' said Patch weakly.

'Right.' Con looked down at the floor. 'Because she's made *so* much effort to stay in touch since she left.'

Jonah sighed. 'She was *kidnapped*, remember?'

'Was she?' said Motti. 'Seems you put up way more of a fight than she did.'

'What, now you think she went willingly?'

Motti drank some more, shrugged. 'Who knows?'

'It's like you can't wait to turn your back on her!' Jonah threw his arms up in the air. 'But then, maybe you're too scared to do anything else. Too scared to go on believing in Tye because you can't face the hurt if you're wrong.'

'Go to hell, geek.'

Jonah squared up to him. 'Call me geek just one more time –'

'And what, you'll start crying?'

Con shook her head wearily. 'Oh, stop this macho bullshit!'

'Well, if lover-boy don't like "geek", I got a whole bunch of other four-letter words I could –'

'She was the glue!' Patch shouted, silencing them all. He was up on his feet now, swaying about, pissed off his face. 'Tye, I mean. She was quiet and that . . . but she was the glue what held us all together. As a group. What made us a family. Just won't be the same now . . .' He fell back in his beanbag, tears in his eyes, a huge yawn twisting his face. 'It'll never . . . be the same . . .'

His head fell back and he started snoring loudly.

'Dumb mutant.' Motti sighed, the anger suddenly gone from him. 'I'll go take him to his room.' He picked Patch up with surprising tenderness. 'Let him sleep it off.'

'I'll get the doors for you,' said Con quietly.

Jonah watched them go, trembling and unsure. He didn't want to be alone right now but he was too proud to follow them.

And too scared that if he did, and if he listened too long, he might start believing the same as they did.

In the end he slumped back down in his chair and cracked open another beer from the icebox. He contemplated his reflection in the neck of the bottle.

This isn't going to help any, Jonah thought.

But then, what the hell would?

He took a long, deep swig of the beer. Then he hurled the bottle against the wall, where it shattered.

Tye was back with Ramez in the candlelit bedroom, only the atmosphere was a little less cosy.

The bodyguards, bruised and bleeding, had bundled up Ramez from the floor and dumped him on the bed. They'd shoved Tye in there too, ignoring her faked outrage at where the hell those intruders had sprung from and what had happened to the lights. And they'd locked the door as well as the windows.

Patch would have been able to get them out in ten seconds. But she'd told him to leave.

His look of dismay, frozen in the doorway, haunted her now. She'd seen the same look on her own face so many times before, staring into the mirror every time her drunken father had pushed her away.

Only this time *she* was the one who'd done the pushing, choosing to side with her old flame. Motti, Patch and Con must hate her guts now, and what about Jonah? She looked at Ramez, lying listless on the bed, fingers plucking idly at the silk sheets. She'd put her feelings for him ahead of everything she'd achieved since he'd gone.

'Looks like the honeymoon's over,' she said. 'It's time you came clean with me, Ramez.'

'I told you how it is.'

'But I still don't know *why* it is. What hold do Sixth Sun have over you?'

'They don't.'

'You think I'm too dumb to know when you're holding out on me? I know when people lie, Ramez. Especially you.' Tye crouched over him on the bed, put her face closer to his. 'Now. Tell me how much trouble we're in.'

His eyes flicked up and held hers. 'If you were stuck in hell . . . If there were five of you waiting to die in a stinking cell, if the guards beat you and pissed in your food each day . . . If your appeal was kept pending so long that you lost all hope and wanted to die. And then someone showed up out the blue with a deal that could get you out . . .'

'Go on,' she said, dreading what she might hear.

'You know much about the Aztecs?' His gaze was steady and intense. 'You ever hear of the Perfect Sacrifice?'

'Since when was anything perfect about a sacrifice?'

'Each year some guy my age would volunteer to have his heart chopped out and burned in the name of some god or other. For the next twelve months he was treated like a god himself, given anything he wanted – girls, fancy houses, the best food, all of that. The priests gave him a perfect life for a whole year so he was fit to be sacrificed in the name of beauty.'

Tye swallowed, her mouth feeling dry as a desert. 'This is your inheritance?' she croaked. 'Sixth Sun made you the same deal?'

'I figured they were cranks, or crazy. So I had nothing to lose by saying yes. I never thought they could get me out.' He shook his head, broke off the eye contact. 'And I never imagined they could actually make good on the deal. A year. A year of everything and anything I could ever want. Can you imagine that, sugar-girl?'

'But at the end of that year . . .'

'It's been a hell of a ride.'

Tye twisted his face back round. 'How long before it's over?

'Soon.' She saw the raw fear in his eyes. 'Days.'

'You stupid bastard,' she whispered, as a growing coldness swept through her. 'You stupid, stupid bastard.'

He took hold of her wrists. 'Should I have stayed in that cell? A bit more of me rotting each day?'

'I wanted to get you out,' Tye told him miserably. 'I asked Coldhardt about it when he first approached me but he said no, that I couldn't take anything of my old life –'

'I don't blame you, sugar-girl,' Ramez told her fiercely, his thumbs kneading the base of her palms. 'I treated you like shit and I got it in return. That's cool, that's, like, karma. But right from the start, the first thing I asked for was you.'

She caught the flicker in his eyes, gently shook her head.

'Well,' he added, those heart-breaking eyes flashing. 'Almost the first.'

She pressed her lips against his for a few fervent seconds. 'We can escape. Coldhardt and the others will help us.'

'I can't go,' Ramez insisted. 'If I welch on the deal they'll kill my little nephews. They're the only things in my life not been spoiled or screwed up.' He paused.

'And they'll kill you too.'

Suddenly a key turned in the lock and the bedroom door opened. Tye spun round to find a man framed in the doorway. Tall with fair wavy hair, a nice smile and tanned complexion, dressed in a suit and raincoat, he looked like a perfectly regular businessman; the kind of guy who had a pretty wife, a dog and two-point-four kids waiting to greet him home from work.

Which made it all the more freaky that he was pointing a gun at them.

'Ramez is right, Tye,' the man said. 'I *will* kill you if you attempt to escape from here. Him we need. You're just goods requested.'

Tye stared at him. 'You work for Sixth Sun?'

His smile grew wider. 'I *founded* Sixth Sun. As for my work, that's a very different matter.'

Suddenly she recognised his Midwestern drawl. He was the guy she'd overheard talking with the Brit woman at the penthouse next door. 'Just who the hell are you?'

'His name's Traynor,' said Ramez. 'It's all right, Traynor, it's cool. I ain't going to escape nowhere, and neither's she.'

'How true.' The smile slowly congealed on Traynor's face. 'You should have kept your big mouth shut, Ramez. 'Cause guess what? Now we can't ever let her go.'

CHAPTER ELEVEN

With so much heavy stuff preying on his mind, Jonah imagined the time would crawl even if he'd been white water rafting. And since cracking Aztec codes was the cypherpunk equivalent of watching paint dry, time seemed pretty much at a standstill.

Could be worse, he told himself. *You're not trawling every Aztec relic in creation for a special symbol, like Patch and the others.* Then again, perhaps he wouldn't feel so miserable if he could hang with them a bit instead of being sat here at Coldhardt's machine. After the flare-up last night he felt alone and isolated.

It didn't seem real that he might never see Tye again.

He felt a chill at his back, and turned to find Coldhardt hovering behind him. The man had a nasty knack for showing out of nowhere and scaring the hell out of you.

'Any progress, Jonah? Any leads forthcoming?'

'Not yet,' Jonah admitted. *Give me a chance, I've only had eight hours.* 'I'm running the Nahuatl lines through some character substitution ciphers, but it takes time. And it's hard to know what significance the symbols originally had.'

'They stand for words, or places, surely?'

'Maybe. But as you know, the Aztec language isn't exactly straightforward.' Jonah grabbed a biro and doodled an eye on a pad beside him. 'I mean, what's this? Could be a pictogram, meaning an eye. Or it could be representing the idea of sight – an ideogram. Or it could be standing for the *sound* "I" – the start of a sentence, like, "I am drawing a big blank here."'

'A phonogram,' Coldhardt muttered. 'Yes, I see.'

'Their language seems a total jumble of different meanings. And it's not even like you can just read the symbols left to right like words on a page.' Jonah sighed, rubbed his stiff neck. 'The symbols lock into each other to make new symbols. Like, you put together the Aztec sign for mountain and the Aztec sign for a tooth, and what d'you get – mountain-tooth? Nope, you get *Tepetlitan*, the name of one of their cities.'

'So we will need to know the names of all Aztec dwelling places?'

'I'm patched into a database of pretty much everything recorded in their language, that should pick up on all the official stuff. But if it was a nickname, or a place kept out of all proper records so the Spaniards didn't find out about it . . .'

'The objects in that temple were of such importance, there has to be a decipherable clue to its location,' Coldhardt declared.

'Maybe the lines of actual language will give us that,' said Jonah, trying to stay positive. 'But in some of these symbols, all sorts of words and ideas are being shoved together – a real picture puzzle. It would be hard enough to crack the meaning even if it *wasn't* in code.'

'And yet they must hold the key by which the puzzle can be unlocked.' Coldhardt placed a hand on Jonah's shoulder. 'Would it help you if you saw the markings on the statuette for comparison?'

Jonah raised his eyebrows in surprise. 'I suppose it might.'

'Come with me.' Coldhardt led the way from the hub and called the lift. 'It's kept in my vault. The one in the wine cellar you're not supposed to know about.'

Jonah felt a tingle of anticipation as he followed Coldhardt through the ranch house and down to the cellar, trying to push from his mind how it had been when Tye had led him by the hand to this same place.

Without ceremony, Coldhardt pulled the concealing curtain aside to reveal the vault door, then inserted an electronic key in a slot beside it. A red light played over his eye, scanning his retina maybe. Then he spoke aloud: 'I have caught an everlasting cold. I have lost my voice most irrecoverably. Farewell glorious villains.'

A series of clicks and hisses sounded from the heavy vault door.

'Voice recognition?' Jonah wondered.

'The lines are from *The White Devil* by John Webster,' said Coldhardt. 'A revenge tragedy.'

'That's nice. Who says it?'

'Someone who is dying.'

The vault door opened like a cold, dry mouth. Coldhardt motioned for Jonah to step into the darkness beyond the silver gleam. A waft of stale, freezing air prickled his bare arms.

Jonah was uneasy. 'No, after you.'

Coldhardt pulled a small remote from his pocket and strode inside. A moment later the place was blinding bright with the glare of spotlights. Jonah screwed up his eyes, waiting for them to adjust, shivering in the sub-zero temperature.

When he could see, he was disappointed. There were paintings and tapestries lining the walls, wooden swords and clubs lying in display cases, a few weird ornaments littering the floor; judging by the style, they were Aztec. But the vault was definitely not some mega treasure trove. It was dominated by a plain stone altar in the middle, about the length and breadth of a man.

'This search for the lost Temple of Life from Death has become something of an all-consuming passion,' said Coldhardt. 'You could say my future depends on it.'

Jonah looked at him uneasily. 'Could I?'

'Here you see every Aztec treasure I own.' Coldhardt gestured round. 'You know, I was quite prepared to give them all to Kabacra or even to Sixth Sun in exchange for that sword.'

'Why?'

Coldhardt crossed to the far corner. 'Cortes's sword was stolen by an Aztec warrior, and subsequently fell into the possession of the high priests. They saw it as a totem, a powerful symbol of the Spaniards' great strength, and used it in their mystical rituals, hoping to turn that strength against their aggressors.'

Jonah rubbed his arms to try and keep warm. 'I'm

guessing it didn't work, right?'

'Correct. And as a result the priests came to believe that by burying their treasures in anticipation of the conquistadors' victory, they had unwittingly buried the greatest prize of all – the soul and spirit of the Aztec people. They had foreseen only defeat, had failed to believe in themselves – so why should Coatlicue believe in them?' The old man lifted a small grey-green statuette from the floor. 'Abandoning them, she turned to sleep. And they believed she would sleep on until her people regained their glory through victory in war.' He half-smiled. 'Of course, it was a victory that never came. The Aztecs had no resistance to the infectious diseases the conquistadors brought with them from Europe. Smallpox, malaria, measles, whooping cough, yellow fever . . . They died in their millions. And the sword itself was lost for centuries.' He passed the statuette to Jonah. 'Here is Coatlicue, fashioned from green obsidian in the fifteenth century, recovered from the Great Temple excavations in Mexico. And there are our two mysterious pictograms – pride of place on the front.'

Jonah shuddered as he studied it. The figure was beautifully crafted, and yet hideous. The head of the goddess had been severed from her body; two snakes rose up from the neck, each turning in profile to form a face. She wore a necklace of human hands and hearts, and her skirt was formed from writhing ser-pents. In place of fingers she sprouted monstrous claws, while her feet were like talons. And all over, she was tattooed in pictograms, deeply scored with painstaking skill.

'What do the other pictograms mean?' Jonah asked.

'Apparently they celebrate the appetite of Coatlicue. She feasted on human corpses.' Again, Coldhardt's smile stopped far short of his eyes. 'It has been alleged in surviving scraps of Aztec literature that only Cortes's sword, the hateful symbol of the Aztec nation's utter defeat, can rouse her from her slumber.'

'Or in other words, it must play some part in re-opening the buried temple.' Jonah thought hard, tapping his finger against his lips. 'Perhaps it needs to be placed in some hidden mechanism to raise the entrance, or you can use it to defuse booby traps once you're in.'

'Perhaps,' Coldhardt murmured.

'And Sixth Sun have got it.' Jonah turned the statuette slowly in his hands. 'Do you think they've managed to crack the symbols in the codex – that they know where the temple is?'

'I don't know,' Coldhardt admitted. 'Not yet. But while there's a chance the temple's location is within our reach, we must go on working to crack that code.'

'Crack . . .' Jonah blinked, turned the statuette slowly back and forth, frowning. 'Or *cracks*. Hang on a minute . . .'

Coldhardt stood beside him. 'What is it?'

'Where would this thing have stood in the Great Temple or wherever it was?' Jonah demanded. 'A window ledge maybe? Somewhere it would catch the sunlight?'

'Possibly.'

'Then say that spotlight's the sun.' He carefully angled the statuette in front of it. 'The light makes the raised edges of the pictograms cast shadows. And as the sun moves round, the shadows get longer, right? And as they do . . .' He carefully turned the statuette, showing Coldhardt what he'd noticed. There were faint, silvery veins in the obsidian, and as the smudge of the shadows fell on them, they came into sharper relief – and formed distinct, deliberate lines. 'That's why the symbols couldn't be translated – they're meaningless – shaped and styled to bring out the veins of silver when the shadows fall across them!'

Coldhardt snatched the statuette from him. 'So, if viewed from the correct angle and at the proper time, new symbols will be formed,' he murmured. 'After all these centuries, the figurine will give up its secrets.'

'We'll need to simulate proper sunlight on this thing,' Jonah said, 'get the precise shapes of the hidden lines marked up at different times of day, see if we can make anything of them.'

'You have done well.' There was genuine pleasure on Coldhardt's face now as he stared raptly at the symbols. He suddenly looked years younger. 'I gave you a new life, Jonah,' he murmured. 'Now you may well have returned the favour.'

'What?' Jonah frowned.

The smile faded, and a haunted look stole into Coldhardt's piercing eyes. He turned and walked from the vault. 'Come. We still have much to do.'

'I won't say anything to the others,' Jonah assured him, wanting the pleased, paternal Coldhardt to come back. But abruptly the lights flicked off, leaving him in freezing darkness. He hurried back out into the cellar, just as the vault door began to close. Coldhardt was already climbing the stairs stiffly, slipping the remote back in his pocket, his face lost in shadow. Jonah followed him back up to the house, still gripping the statuette in one icy hand. There was something about that haunted look . . .

Jonah couldn't imagine feeling warm again for some time.

Tye had spent a tense day by the pool with Ramez, their every move watched by the two bruised bouncers. They'd been given food and beers and even champagne when Ramez requested it – but weren't allowed to leave the penthouse.

She and Ramez had hardly spoken since Traynor's arrival. The spell was broken and, as the hours passed, Tye had felt as flat as her untouched Cristal.

Now, as night began to swell like a dark bruise over the Santa Fe skyline, Traynor had returned to interrogate her.

On the surface, the questioning was a civilised affair – no harsh light shining into her eyes since the power was still out, only cosy candlelight. Ramez had insisted that no harm was allowed to come to her, and as Perfect Sacrifice his voice still seemed to count for something round here. Even so, the possibilities of sudden violence – the bruised bouncers on the door, the gun in Traynor's shoulder holster, the intimidating way in which he wound and unwound a length of wire around his fingers – were not lost on her.

'You've made no attempt to contact Coldhardt since you arrived here,' Traynor noted.

She shrugged. 'I called him at his hotel in

Guatemala.'

'I mean proper contact. You're one of his operatives, you must have set instructions about calling in.'

'You make it sound like the FBI or something – and it really isn't.' Tye smiled coolly. 'I'm freelance. I just happen to be under contract to Coldhardt at this time. Doesn't mean I owe him anything.'

'Not even an explanation as to your disappearance?'

'I was having a good time.'

Traynor toyed with the wire. 'Why didn't you leave with your friends when they turned up here?'

'They're not my friends,' she insisted. 'They're just colleagues.' She affected disinterest. 'I don't owe *them* anything either. I just wanted to get things straight with Ramez. I mean . . . it's been a long time since I saw him, you know?'

'Indeed it has.' He smiled. 'You do realise that Ramez owes his current predicament to you, my dear?'

A sick feeling went through her. 'To me?'

'Coldhardt's interest in Cortes's sword and the Temple of Life from Death came to our attention some time ago. Word has it he's obsessed with chasing after any relic connected with immortality or new life – however tenuous. What's frightening him? Simply old age? Or something more?'

'I wouldn't know,' said Tye breezily, though inside she was rattled. She was well used to Coldhardt reeling off the ambitions of other high-movers, but to hear it being done to him felt all wrong. 'He keeps his aims to himself.'

'I know. I've been hacking into his secure files for some time. That's how we knew where to find you at his new base.' He smiled. 'Coldhardt's never posed any serious threat to our operation, but the possibility always remained that he might some day. So when choosing our Perfect Sacrifice, who better than young Ramez? A boy so desperate he'd do anything for freedom, and with an emotional attachment to one of Coldhardt's field agents to boot.'

'Then this all comes down to Coldhardt, not me?'

'You are our insurance, now events are nearing their conclusion.' Traynor yanked the length of wire taut. 'Coldhardt's been blundering about in the dark, but now the race is almost won he's starting to get close. That's why we had you picked up. If he gets any closer, knowing your life hangs in the balance may deter him from pressing on.'

Tye looked away. 'Don't count on it.'

'And hey, it's given Ramez such a boost in his last days. His only unfulfilled dream come true – reunited with his old flame, right at the end.' He grinned, shook his head as if puzzled. 'You know, Tye, given the circumstances of your final meeting, I honestly thought you wouldn't give him the time of day. But my colleague assured me you would.'

'A woman's intuition?'

'Apparently so.' Traynor's smile faded, as he realised he'd given something away. 'How did you know my colleague was female?'

'Lucky guess?' she suggested. 'Here's another. You're hoping to be brought face to face with Coatlicue herself, aren't you? That'll give you power, right?'

He stood up, his face darkening. 'How did you come by this information?'

She cast her mind back to what was said that night on the balcony. 'Have you discovered the precise location yet?'

Traynor flexed the wire between his hands. 'I asked you a question.'

'Thing is – wherever you choose to rendezvous, it's going to be kind of tricky, hooking up with an Aztec goddess. Which makes me think that Coatlicue's got to be a codename for someone . . .' Tye watched his eyes closely; even the smallest reaction would give her a clue as to whether she was right. But all she caught was scorn as he advanced, apparently ready to garrotte her.

'Use that on me and Ramez will never willingly go through with what you want him to do,' she said quickly. 'Don't you think your Aztec goddess will be kind of offended when you have to drag her Perfect Sacrifice kicking and screaming to the knife?'

Again, she was testing him. He should be saying, *What are you, crazy? You think I really believe in that Coatlicue crap?* But instead he was just sitting back down, his anger smouldering away like a smoking match near gunpowder. Still dangerous.

'I asked how you knew these things,' he said at last.

'I'll trade the information,' Tye told him with a coolness she wished she felt. 'But only if you'll let Ramez go. Find another sacrifice.'

Traynor smiled indulgently, like she'd tried to be funny. 'I'll get the answers I want,' he assured her. 'Remember – we choose how Ramez dies. How slowly we make the incision in his chest. How long we stretch out his death agonies.' His eyes held a hard, fanatical gleam that chilled Tye as much as his words. 'Yeah, I think you'll tell me what I want to know.'

There was a knock at the front door. The bruisers slipped out of the room to answer it, and Tye found she felt more intimidated now she was alone with this weirdo sadist.

Distantly, she caught a harsh, accented voice from behind the front door. 'It's Kabacra, open up.' Her heart lurched and she looked down at her hands, fighting to keep her reaction muted, like the name meant nothing to her.

Traynor rose quickly and turned for the door. 'We'll pick up where we left off shortly, Tye.'

She heard the key turn in the lock behind him, and an exchange of cordial greetings followed as they went next door into the living room. What the hell was Kabacra doing here, so far from home turf? Motti had said the arms dealer had already sold Sixth Sun the sword – what had brought him here in person? Tye pressed her ear up to the wall and strained to listen in.

'The consignment will be ready for collection the day after tomorrow,' Kabacra was saying. 'A dark red freight truck, marked Pomarico Eucalyptus, will be heading east on Interstate 40. Cargo's untraceable, with no serious security. The truck will pass exit 85 around 23.30 hours.'

'Excellent,' drawled Traynor.

She frowned. The I-40 ran through north-western New Mexico. But what was this cargo?

'So is everything set for the demonstration?' Tye

could hear the eagerness in Kabacra's voice. He sounded like a little boy who couldn't wait to pull the wings off a fly.

'The agent at the Black House is almost ready for the final tests,' Traynor replied. 'We'll leave for Colorado midday tomorrow.'

'Excellent.' A pause. 'What happened to the lights around here?'

'Just a fault in the power supply.'

'Right,' Tye whispered to herself. Clearly Traynor didn't want Kabacra knowing there had been trouble here. But who was this agent they were talking about – a secret operative of some kind? If so, maybe Coatlicue *was* a codename. And yet Traynor hadn't given away a flicker of confirmation when she'd suggested that – quite the reverse, in fact. He'd acted as if he really believed in a pagan goddess with dominion over life, death and rebirth . . .

As her head crowded with thoughts of cargoes and demonstrations, of gods and secret agents, Tye knew one thing for certain – she had to get out of here, get help for Ramez before his time was up. He would be safe for now – Traynor couldn't kill him twice.

She had to go and get Coldhardt.

Tye slipped into the en suite bathroom and locked the door behind her. The window was split into two – a solid pane of frosted glass beneath a smaller one that opened on a hinge, too small for her to get through. Smashing the larger pane was her only option, but the sound of the glass breaking would surely bring Traynor or the bodyguards running.

Quickly she grabbed a bottle of shower gel and

slathered the scented goo all over the glass. Then she grabbed yesterday's *Santa Fe Tribune* from beside the toilet, doused it in water in the sink and squelched it into place against the pane. She flushed the toilet, and while it gurgled noisily she grabbed the chrome toilet brush holder and swung it against the window with all her strength.

There was a dull crack as the glass broke – but at least the newspaper held it in place, stopping it from shattering everywhere. Wrapping each of her hands in a thick layer of toilet roll, Tye managed to pull the newspaper away complete with the broken glass, then set about removing the largest, most lethal shards still lining the frame. If she could clear a good space before the thirsty, hissing cistern stopped filling –

She jumped to hear a bang at the door. 'What's going on in there?'

It was one of the bodyguards; of course, Traynor wouldn't come himself – why alarm Kabacra if he could help it? 'Nothing,' she shouted back.

'What was the noise?'

'I knocked a stack of shampoo and stuff into the shower screen,' she called, still pulling at the glass. 'Now could you let me use the toilet in peace?'

She listened for the sound of footsteps moving away. Nothing. He was waiting for her right outside.

Tye flushed the toilet again, ran the taps as fast as they'd go, and punched out the remaining glass. Wrapping a towel around her midriff for protection she swung herself through the broken window feet first. She gasped as jagged edges cut into her ribs even through the thick fluffy fabric, and arched her back.

The evening was gusty; it prickled her bare legs as they dangled down, as she tried to get a foothold.

Twisting lithely round, she balanced on the narrow ledge beneath the window. The wind whipped at the towel. She pulled it away, felt a rush of nausea at the thick crimson stripe left on the white cotton, and stuffed it back through the window. She was afraid to look and see just how much she was bleeding. Below to her right was the balcony outside the living room – if she dropped down, Traynor and Kabacra would surely see her. And yet what else could she do?

The decision was made for her when she heard a crash from the bathroom. The bodyguard knew something was up and he was trying to kick the door down. Tye jumped and landed lightly, pressed herself flat against the balcony floor and scuttled along commando-style to the far side, praying she wouldn't be seen.

But the only person up there listening was Ramez on the roof – and he'd sure seen her.

'Tye!' he shouted. 'No way. Don't you dare leave me!'

She climbed up on to the balcony rail. She wanted to yell at him, 'I'm not leaving! I'll be back for you!' But if she advertised the fact to Traynor and co . . .

'She's on the balcony!' Ramez yelled. 'Someone stop her!'

Swearing, Tye leaped across the divide and hit the ground running. He must honestly believe she was running out on him – that the only way he could keep her was by force. The gash in her ribs was still pouring blood; her pale green top and the waistband of her shorts were sodden. But no time to think about that. It wouldn't take Traynor long to work out she'd jumped across to the penthouse next door.

Especially once she'd kicked in the French windows.

Gritting her teeth she swung her hips round in a circular motion, snapped her knee upwards so her kicking leg was parallel to the ground, pivoted on her supporting foot and struck the glass with all her strength. The ball of her foot jarred with the impact, but the crash of the pane exploding was like applause in her ears. She recoiled and recovered, then gasped as her ribs flared white hot with pain. *Get going.* Clutching her sticky side she ran through into the dark penthouse and threw open the front door.

Just as the biggest bodyguard burst out on to the landing.

He threw a punch at her but she feinted back, swung herself round and used her other leg this time to snap-kick him where it hurt – where it *really* hurt, judging by the way he squeaked and fell with a thundering crash to the floor. Tye was already sprinting for the stairwell. She threw open the door, and by the time it had crashed against the wall she was halfway down the first stack of steps, taking them three at a time. A knifeblade of pain jabbed between her ribs with every footfall – but adrenalin was sweeping her on as she swung herself round flight after flight, faster and faster, pounding down the steps.

And then suddenly she was out in the lobby, tearing across the marble, exploding out through the revolving doors. She looked all round, clutched the stitch in her side and gasped as her fingers closed on the sticky wound there. Her head was tingling, pins and needles were creeping into her arms and legs. She forced herself to breathe more deeply but it was so hard when she was running again, across the street, trying to get out of sight.

The other bodyguard would soon be after her, no question. But she knew Traynor wouldn't stop there. Who knew what resources he could put on her tail with a single call?

One thing was sure – she couldn't have long to get the hell out of here and back to Coldhardt's base. Either Traynor would get her back, or she would black out from blood loss.

Feeling sick and scared and close to tears, Tye forced herself onwards. She risked just one look back over her shoulder at the penthouse that had been both her palace and prison for days now. She could see no sign of Ramez up there. But still his last frantic shouts echoed on in her ears.

Echoes hard enough to bruise.

CHAPTER TWELVE

'Screen break.' Jonah looked up at the hub's dark ceiling and moved his head all around to ease his stiff neck. 'My eyes are killing me.' The rush of euphoria that maybe he and the others were about to solve the statuette's enigma had long since passed. The ugly thing was clinging on to its secrets with all the strength in its obsidian claws.

'No delays,' Motti complained, turning the anglepoise lamp he held so it shone into Jonah's face. 'Let's just get this crap over and done with.'

'I wish!' said Jonah. 'Don't forget I'll still be here long after you've packed up and gone to bed.'

'Aww.' Motti put the lamp back in its carefully marked position on the table. 'I think the world's smallest tear just rolled down my cheek.'

Truth was, Jonah could cry with frustration himself. The night was not going well.

His discovery of the shadow-symbols had got Coldhardt fired up, and everyone else had welcomed the apparent breakthrough too. It helped clear the air of awkwardness that still lingered from the night before – though sadly for Patch, his hangover was a lot harder to shift.

Con had located a plan of the Great Temple where the little idol had been discovered, and recreated the layout on top of the meeting table. Coldhardt had calculated the position of the sun as seen through the various temple windows, and it soon became clear there were only two likely places in which the statuette could have caught direct sunlight. Now Motti was training an anglepoise desk lamp on the statuette a careful distance away, while Patch feebly manned the camera phone mounted on the table. He was capturing images of the silvery veins that rose in the shadows of the special symbols.

In turn, these were Bluetoothed in batches over to Jonah at Coldhardt's PC. He was tracing the patterns in Photoshop each time and rearranging them to see if they formed any recognisable shapes or symbols. But of course the shadows – and so the shape of the veins – varied depending on the time of day. Motti had started by simulating sunrise through the eastern window of the temple (a spice rack balanced on an encyclopaedia), and now he was shining his light through a square AM aerial balanced on a box of tissues, doing sunset. Jonah half-smiled. *And doing his nut too by the sound of it.*

'This has gotta be the dullest day of my life,' Motti complained. 'Most of the day searching through papers and pictures looking for symbols that don't mean nothing, and the rest doing my impression of a frickin' sunbeam.'

'Stop shouting,' Patch mumbled, fumbling with the phone keys to catch another image. 'Why's everyone gotta shout?'

'We aren't,' said Con breezily, not bothering to look up from her catalogue of Aztec symbols. 'Your hangover only makes you think we are.'

'You know, Con, I once heard an old wives' tale that the sight of a pair of boobs heals a hangover just like that.'

'So ask some old wives to flash their boobs at you,' Con recommended.

'Just keep taking the snaps, cyclops,' Motti growled. 'You wanna look at a nice rack, check out the east window of this dumb imaginary temple.'

Suddenly the computer chimed, and Jonah's attention was riveted back to the screen.

Con was by his side in a moment. 'You have rearranged the silver lines into the new symbol, yes?'

'No,' he admitted. 'But I think we've got a result on the Nahuatl code. I patched the decryption program into this ancient languages database they use at Yale, right, and –'

'Geek,' Motti burst in, 'just tell us what it says, huh?'

Jonah shrugged and clicked on the dialogue box that had sprung up from the desktop. Con leaned in beside him and read aloud: 'When the earth shakes the sun from the sky. When the bloodied sword is wiped clean. When Perfect Sacrifice is made. When her attendants reach into their hearts, Coatlicue will arise from her temple and feast on the poison in men.'

Silence hung a while in the air, till Motti broke it. 'Well, that's nice to know.'

'The bloodied sword,' Jonah muttered. 'Cortes's sword?'

'Yeah, but what's that stuff about the sun falling from the sky and reaching into hearts meant to mean?' Motti snorted. 'Mystical crap.'

Jonah nodded. 'And nothing about the temple's location.'

'I wish I could say I was having more luck finding a match for the third pictogram on the codex,' Con added, straightening and stretching. 'But there's nothing. I mean, it looks like a heart dripping blood into a box, but there's nothing like it anywhere else.'

'And we should know,' said Motti with feeling. 'Since we musta studied just about every Aztec relic in the world.'

'There are still many more documents to check,' Con reminded him.

Patch clutched his head in both hands. 'I just wish everyone would stop shouting.'

At that moment, an alarm went off – high pitched and piercing. Motti swore and jumped up from the table. 'Intruders!' he shouted, and ran over to some controls beside the lift. 'They've breached the perimeter defences.'

'Not again!' Jonah looked anxiously at Con, and they both stood up. Patch on the other hand, did his best to curl up into a ball.

Motti switched off the alarm. 'Need to hear myself think,' he muttered.

Then Jonah realised he could hear the sound of the lift descending. 'Jesus, they're coming down here!'

Con stared at Motti in horror. 'How could they get past every sensor in –'

'I dunno!' he hissed, rushing to Coldhardt's desk

and elbowing Jonah aside so he could get the security controls on-screen. The twelve monitors on the wall of the hub switched on, showing views around the ranch and grounds. Nothing untoward showed on any of them. 'How many of them are there? Where're they hiding?'

Jonah looked around for anything he could use as a weapon. 'That lift will be here any minute.'

Patch was still holding his head. 'I knew I should never have got up today.'

'They can't open those lift doors unless they've got the proper passcode,' said Motti, calling up a different menu.

'Tye could have given it to Sixth Sun,' said Con.

'She wouldn't,' said Jonah automatically.

'C'mon, we've got to get out the back way,' said Motti.

Patch frowned. 'Back way?'

'After the Siena base got busted that time, Coldhardt insisted on having a hidden exit built into every hub. It's in his data centre through there.'

The lift doors glided open – to reveal Tye standing inside. Everyone stared, speechless, as she took an uncertain step forwards and collapsed face-first on the floor.

'She's hurt!' Jonah shouted. 'Come on!'

Motti grabbed hold of his arm. 'Don't touch her, man.'

'Are you crazy?' Jonah pulled himself free. 'You can see she's –'

'It's a trick,' Motti insisted, looking round at Con and Patch, who were also hanging back. 'She's brought her Sixth Sun buddies straight to us.'

'Right, and I suppose that's just ketchup all over her top?' Jonah hurried over and crouched beside her. 'Tye? Can you hear me?' She was sweating hard and breathing shallow, and his stomach turned as he clocked the messy wound in her side. 'We need bandages or something. Who knows first aid?' Jonah stared up at the others, still staying put the other side of the hub. 'For God's sake, we've got to do something!'

'Indeed we have.' Coldhardt stood framed in the doorway to the data centre, his face unreadable. 'The question is – what does she deserve?'

The night passed for Tye in a delirious blur. She remembered Jonah and Patch carrying her to a bland, spacious room with white walls and ceiling and dark floorboards. She realised it was *her* room, though there was nothing but her coat and her suitcase to say so. She'd spent more nights in Ramez's penthouse than she'd ever spent here.

They'd laid her on the bed. A doctor, some old guy Coldhardt produced out of nowhere, had come up and warned her that the needle would hurt. But by then she felt like she was floating, could hardly feel a thing. There had been some talk of how much blood she'd lost, and Tye thought back to the way it had stained the seat of the car she'd stolen to get here. She felt a twinge of guilt for the owner – then she realised that Coldhardt would have already arranged for the car to be destroyed. The ranch was the only property anywhere near to where she'd stolen it, and an international criminal would hardly welcome the police making inquiries about a missing Buick.

Strange dreams licked around the edges of her unsettled sleep. She pictured Ramez laid out across the bonnet of the car, Traynor with a knife held over his head. But then Ramez was Jonah, yelling her name, disgust in his eyes. She was begging him not to hate her, but now he was Ramez again and he was telling her he loved her, how they would go away some place and be together, but Motti and Con were barring the way, their faces livid with rage and bruises, and Patch was like a puppy yapping round her ankles, and Coldhardt was driving the Buick straight for her, forcing her to run towards a misshapen figure, a huge, terrifying figure who stank of the dead, who wore hands and hearts and skulls around her severed neck, whose claws were swiping down to tear her flesh and –

'No!' Tye shouted, sat bolt upright – and almost passed out with pain. She felt the skin just below her bra, brushed her fingers over the stitches, the surgical stubble sprouting from the puckered wound. Wincing, she closed her eyes and sank carefully back into her pillow.

The door to her room opened a little. 'Tye?' Jonah stuck his head through the gap. 'Are you OK? Can I come in?'

Tye nodded, pulling the covers up over her chest, too glad to see him to worry about how much of a mess she must look. She opened her mouth but found she couldn't think of a thing to say to him.

He didn't seem to mind, just looked down at her, his blond hair all mussed up, his smile crooked with concern. 'We've been worried to death. Is the pain bad?'

'Well, it's not good.' She forced a smile. 'But it is good to see you.'

'Course it is!' He grinned back at her, and held up a thermos. 'Tea? Hot and sweet.'

'Sounds good.'

'And that's just the waiter.' He grinned and poured her a cup. 'You pushed yourself too hard getting here. You lost a lot of blood.'

'I had an argument with a broken window. I had to leave quick before –'

Jonah shushed her, dragged a chair over and sat beside her. 'You can tell us all about it later. The important thing is that you made it back to us. Right now, you need to rest.'

She sipped the hot tea and looked to the window, where pink streaks were flaming across the dark grey sky. 'Oh God, how long have I been out? Is that sunrise or sunset?'

'Sunrise.' His smile faltered a little. 'Though I hear there's nothing like the sunset.'

'You got my message, then.' Tye gulped the tea too quickly, burning her mouth. *Can't handle emotions right now.* 'Where's Coldhardt? I've got to speak to him.'

'He wants to speak to you too. In the hub. Soon as you're feeling well enough.' He shrugged. 'So just tell me when you're ready, and I'll tell him.'

Tye checked the clock on the wall. It was only six something. 'Have you been up all night?'

'Had stuff to do,' Jonah explained. 'Trying to make

a picture out of little lines and squiggles. There was this Aztec statuette, see, with weird carvings on it, and . . .' He must have caught the frown on her face. 'Long story, and an even longer process. But I think I've cracked it now.'

'What picture did you get?'

'Looks like four trees and a giant egg.'

Tye blinked. 'And what the hell does that mean?'

'I think it's a code. Either that or I've got it completely wrong.' He was drifting off into his own thoughts, burbling aloud – he was always like this when he was trying to crack something. 'But it must be right – the shadows cast at the start of sunset pick out the lighter veins, and if you trace them and slot them all together, that's what you get – an egg surrounded by four trees. So what the hell does it mean?'

'Jonah, I have no idea what you're on about.' Tye squeezed his wrist. 'But that's good. That's *normal*. It's good to be back.'

'But *are* you back? To stay, I mean?' His eyes looked wide and hopeful. 'What happened to Ramez?'

'Something bad is going to happen to him. We've got to stop it.'

'We?' Jonah's eyes hardened. 'Right. Got it. *That's* why you've come back.'

She sighed and put down the tea. 'Do the guys hate me? Think I'm a fink?'

'I stuck up for you. I didn't want to believe it.'

'Believe what?'

'That you would pick Ramez over us.' He slumped back in his chair. 'Was I wrong?'

Tye felt a spark of anger. 'You have no idea what

I've been through.'

'Yeah? So come on and tell me. Tell me how hard you've had it, lying in your bathrobe with your old flame!'

'What happened to, "Tell us about it later, you need to rest", Jonah?' She closed her eyes, suddenly so, so tired. 'I guess this is what I'm going to get from *all* of you, isn't it?'

'Must have been *sooo* good, being back with your true love. I can guess how the two of you passed the time.'

'Can you?' She narrowed her eyes at him. 'He's going to die, Jonah. It's some crazy ritual, he's going to be sacrificed to an Aztec goddess or something –'

'Sacrificed?' The anger suddenly drained from Jonah's face; he looked puzzled like a kid in class. '*Perfect* sacrifice?'

'How would you know that?' asked Tye slowly. 'What do you know about it? What's been going on?'

'I guess we've all got some catching up to do.'

The silence that grew between them was thick enough to smother.

Jonah looked down at the floorboards. 'You need some sleep. I should go.'

Like I could ever sleep now. She nodded. 'Tell Coldhardt I'll come to the hub at eight-thirty.'

'I will. See you then.' He crossed to the door, hesitated there. 'I really missed you, Tye.'

I missed you too, she wanted to say. *So much.* But the words wouldn't leave her lips, and after a few seconds he went through the door and closed it quietly behind him.

It was only minutes later, when she was certain he wasn't coming back, that Tye allowed the first tears to fall.

CHAPTER THIRTEEN

Somehow, it didn't seem real to Jonah that Tye was back.

There she was, dressed all in black like a widow in mourning; even the wide headband that held her braided hair from out of her eyes was black. She'd sat isolated at one end of the hub's meeting table as Coldhardt had brought her up to speed on all they had been through.

Now it was her turn to talk. Coldhardt sat directly opposite her, Jonah and Con to his right and Motti and Patch to his left. Patch looked to be listening closely, while Con sat stony-faced. Motti was a study in surliness, but then he was never exactly sparkly before nine.

Coldhardt himself remained as impassive as ever. He inclined his head now and then to show he was listening, but gave little else away.

As for Jonah, he felt the same about Tye's homecoming as he had when he'd finally put together the hidden pictogram – elation giving way to the realisation that he'd simply swapped one puzzle for another. The question in his mind was no longer, 'Why did Tye stay behind?' It was, 'Why did Tye really come back?', and it was no easier to answer. Ramez had meant a lot to her once, and now the guy was in big trouble – facing death, for God's sake. How could he expect her not to want to save him? She wasn't like Con, always ready to cut her losses and run; she *cared* about people.

But did she have to care in a luxury bedroom, wearing just her dressing gown? The thought of Tye and Ramez together was clawing at Jonah's insides. He willed himself to focus on the story she was telling instead of the one he was imagining in his head.

'. . . and then guess who turns up?' Tye stared at each of them in turn. 'Kabacra. Like he and this Traynor guy are old friends. I mean, I know Kabacra sold Cortes's sword to Sixth Sun, but there's a whole lot more going on with these two than that.'

'What do you mean, Tye?' Coldhardt murmured.

'I heard them talk about an agent who's nearly ready for testing. I don't know who, or where from. But Traynor said he was going to Colorado for some demonstration and Kabacra's going along too.'

'Colorado.' Jonah looked at Coldhardt. 'The place with a helipad that's not marked on any map?'

'Which means the agent in question is likely to be a biological agent.' The old man steepled his fingers. 'No wonder Kabacra sold Sixth Sun the sword at such a heavy discount. Traynor must be giving him a biological agent as part payment. To coin an overused phrase – a weapon of mass destruction.'

Tye stared at him. 'What?'

'I've been digging around in some unpleasant places,' said Coldhardt, with the wintriest of smiles.

'This man Traynor can only be *Michael* Traynor, a known collector of Mesoamerican antiquities. In the nineties he owned a private sector plant that made chemicals and production equipment for the biological weapons programme of foreign powers. But he sold up some years ago and disappeared.'

'Around the time he started Sixth Sun?' Motti asked.

Coldhardt nodded. 'I believe that soon afterwards he was recruited to head up a top-secret, government-sponsored biological weapons research centre.'

'His Black House,' Jonah murmured. 'And he's opened it up to a maniac like Kabacra.'

'Incidentally, after further research I should point out that Black House is not just a codename,' Coldhardt went on. 'It was the term given to the place of retreat and meditation used by Motecuhzoma, the last of the Aztec rulers. A philosopher king – tricked, captured and finally executed by the invading Spanish.'

'I knew I'd heard that name before,' said Jonah. 'Must've been when I was trawling online.'

'So this Traynor thinks of himself as a new philosopher king of the Aztecs,' Con ventured, 'and yet he's planning to rob their temple of its treasures?'

'If he thinks he's king, he probably reckons the treasure is his by rights,' Jonah suggested.

'Or maybe it's not only the treasure he's after,' said Coldhardt.

'I know *something* they're after,' Tye offered. 'Kabacra talked about an untraceable cargo being ready for collection from a freight truck on Interstate

40 tomorrow night.'

'What kind of cargo?' yawned Motti.

'I don't know. I only know a dark red freight truck with no real security, meant to be carrying eucalyptus, will pass exit 85 on I-40 around half-eleven – and Traynor's going to be picking up whatever it's carrying.'

'That sounds like plenty of detail,' Con observed. 'You say you overheard this information?'

'I was in the next room.'

Motti nodded. 'And were you dressed yet?'

'That's enough, Motti,' Coldhardt warned him. 'You heard no other details, Tye?'

'That's when I made a break for it. I figured the info could be useful to you.' She paused. 'And I didn't want to stick around to face Traynor again.'

'The information is intriguing.' Coldhardt tapped his lips with a finger. 'What cargo, I wonder? Another significant antique weapon from his strongroom?'

'Or more modern weapons,' said Motti. 'Guns and stuff.'

'Whatever the cargo, it must be relevant to their plans . . .' Coldhardt looked round at them. 'So we shall steal it ahead of them.'

'Suppose it could be another clue as to where to find the temple,' Jonah suggested.

'Maybe,' said Tye doubtfully. 'But Traynor and some woman were talking about being close to finding an exact location a few days back.'

Con arched an eyebrow. 'More information you just happened to overhear?'

Tye glared at her. 'Yes.'

Coldhardt looked grave. 'Well, if nothing else, stealing something that Sixth Sun needs should set back their plans – buy us the time we need to locate the temple ourselves.'

'I don't trust this,' said Con. 'It feels like a set-up.'

Tye stared, and Jonah winced to see so much hurt in her eyes. 'You really think that?'

''Course we don't,' Patch piped up, frowning in Con's direction. 'Do we?'

'Tye cares about Ramez, and Sixth Sun have threatened to kill him,' Con retorted coolly. 'She could be betraying us in order to save him.'

Coldhardt looked at Tye, his expression unreadable. 'Tye, you must know that Sixth Sun will kill Ramez whatever you do. If he is their Perfect Sacrifice then he is vital to their plans. They will have invested far too much time, money and effort to let him go now.'

'I know,' Tye snapped, 'that's why we've got to go back to Santa Fe and get him away.'

Coldhardt shook his head. 'Out of the question.'

'But we *have* to! And we have to get hold of his nephews too, Sixth Sun will kill them if he . . .' Tye leaned forwards in her seat. 'Coldhardt, *please*. Ramez is going to be hacked open for a goddess no one's worshipped for hundreds of years!'

'It must be something to do with the codex prophecy,' Coldhardt remarked. 'When the earth shakes the sun from the sky, the bloodied sword is wiped clean and Perfect Sacrifice is made, and when her attendants reach into their hearts, then Coatlicue will arise from her temple and feast on the poison in men.'

'Oh God. I get it.' Tye was watching him closely. 'You *want* him to die, don't you? You want to know what will happen when he's sacrificed – you think Coatlicue really *will* rise up, like Traynor.'

'The prophecy's stuffed full of figures of speech,' Jonah said quickly. 'That bit must mean that a way into the buried temple will appear if –'

Tye wasn't listening. 'You do, don't you?' She bunched her fists, stalked closer to Coldhardt and shouted, '*Don't you!*'

Jonah held his breath, waiting for the inevitable reaction.

But Coldhardt seemed unfazed. 'If you want me to consider helping Ramez, Tye,' he said calmly, 'first you must prove yourself to me once more.'

She turned and sat back down in her chair. 'What do I have to do?' she said dully.

'That's better,' he whispered, leaning back in his chair, the faintest smile on his face. 'For a start, why not drive your colleagues along Interstate 40 tomorrow night and help them to hijack a freight lorry?'

Jonah decided to stay out of Tye's way for the rest of the day. He was dying to talk with her again, but didn't trust himself not to mess up like before. Besides, she needed to rest, while he needed to make sense of those sodding pictograms – both the one he'd put together with the help of the statuette, and the one in the codex.

After another few frustrating hours he went to see Con, to see how her own researches were going. He found her in her room, sprawled on her stomach on the bed, crunching crisps and flicking through a big pile of printouts.

'Good afternoon, Jonah.' She smiled at him and pulled off her glasses. 'Delight me. Tell me you have had a breakthrough.'

'A breakdown's more likely,' he sighed. 'My latest theory on those symbols is that they both mean, "anyone trying to translate these will go mental".'

She smiled. 'I have a theory too. The heart in this pictogram – it could be a cacao pod.'

'A what?'

She grabbed a piece of paper and leaned up to pass it to him, affording him a view down her pale blue blouse that Patch would have killed for. Jonah took the printout and tried to focus on the line drawing. It showed a man striking another man with a knife, and the blood falling against a tree covered in strange fruits.

'It's a cacao tree. The pods are its fruit – and from the seeds are made cocoa and chocolate, yes?'

'The Aztecs were big on Dairy Milk, were they?'

'They were very big on *real* chocolate,' she told him. 'Not sugary stuff – strong, bitter and spicy. They made drinks from it. People drank it at marriage ceremonies and baptisms, priests made special chocolate pastes and daubed them over temple walls.'

Jonah was left none the wiser by the picture and handed it back. 'Is the guy in the picture being sacrificed?'

'No. He is simply a nobleman, spilling some of his blood to honour the gods.' She knelt up and patted the bed, indicating Jonah should sit beside her. 'Chocolate was felt to be the blood of the earth, and there was a sacred association with human blood. Chocolate held deep symbolic meaning.'

He perched himself beside her. 'Guess the Aztecs liked their deep, symbolic meanings, huh?'

'Yes.' She smiled at him, her pale eyes holding his. 'In Nahuatl, Aztec poets and thinkers would often pair two words together to create a metaphor for something totally different.'

Jonah frowned. 'How d'you mean?'

'For instance, the words for "mat" and "seat", when paired, were taken to mean "rulership", yes? Because the rulers sat in judgement over the people, I suppose.' Her eyes glittered. 'And according to the experts online, "heart" and "blood", when paired, were taken to mean "cacao".'

'So, you think the pictogram could be showing a cacao tree pod and not a human heart?'

'It is possible.'

'But not very helpful,' Jonah pointed out. 'We go from a heart dripping blood into a box, to a cacao pod dripping chocolate into a box.'

'Or boxes. Look at that outside edge. I am thinking there might be one behind the other.'

'Well, then, dripping chocolate into boxes. What kind of a clue is that?'

'I don't know . . .' Con deliberately leaned against him as she reached for something under the covers. 'But it seems a tasty proposition, yes?'

She produced a small box of posh chocolates, opened it and waved it under his nose so he caught the enticing scent. Then she smiled up at him. 'Help yourself.'

Jonah regarded her warily. Con knew he was Tye's biggest supporter – was she making a play for him in the hope of weakening Tye's position further?

'They look great. But I don't fancy one right now.'

'Oh.' She popped one of the chocolates in her mouth and put her specs back on. Was that just the faintest trace of red in her cheeks? 'You are saving yourself for supper, yes?'

'Mm. Patch says he's making pizza – God help us.'

Con didn't reply. Already she seemed a million miles away, poring over her papers like he'd never been there. How could she just turn it off and on like that? Just how strongly did she ever feel anything?

Shaking his head, Jonah walked away from her cool enigma and back to the puzzles on his PC.

Around seven o'clock, Jonah was brooding in his room when his mobile went. He hoped it would be Tye. It was Patch.

'Dinner's served in the hangout in about ten minutes,' he announced. 'Can you call for Tye and bring her over?'

He blinked. 'Why me?'

'Just thought you might want to.'

And because you knew Motti and Con would tell you where to go. 'OK, fine.' Jonah held the phone between his cheek and shoulder as he pulled on his trainers – no point in wasting time. 'Pizzas doing OK?'

'I'm not sure about the *foie gras* one. It smells gross.' Patch paused. 'But then it's posh, so it's probably meant to.'

'Uh-huh.' Jonah took a vague stab at styling his

hair one-handed in front of the mirror. 'I think I'll stick to ham and pineapple.'

'Closest I could get was ham and blueberry.'

'Then I think I'll stick to toast!'

'Just make sure you get her here, right? I gotta surprise for her.'

'As if the blueberries weren't surprise enough,' Jonah muttered as Patch rang off. He checked his reflection again – he'd do – and set off down the corridor towards Tye's room in the east wing, his heart slowly crawling up his throat.

He knocked, but there was no reply. 'Hey. It's me. You in there?'

'Somewhere,' came the muffled reply.

Jonah licked his dry lips. 'Patch wants us to get down to the hangout. He's got something special cooking.'

There was a pause, and the sound of unenthusiastic movement. A few seconds later the door opened and Tye looked out at him. She looked like she hadn't slept for days. 'I'm not hungry.'

'Probably a good thing.' Jonah offered an awkward smile. 'I could try to tempt you by saying everyone's going to be there, but I guess that's not much incentive right now.'

'You guess right.' She sighed. 'Still, I suppose I've got to start "proving my loyalty" sometime.'

'Not to me,' he murmured.

She opened her mouth to say something, but then seemed to think better of it. She closed her bedroom door and they set off together along the corridor. 'I just don't want a big fuss, you know?'

'It'll be fine,' he assured her, hoping for the best. 'It's just pizza. No one's going to make a song and dance out of it.'

No one except Patch, it appeared.

A homemade banner was draped above the entrance to the hangout – WELCOME BACK HOME. From the writing and messy felt-tip scribbles, it was fairly obvious their most junior member was responsible.

'Oh, great,' murmured Tye.

'Here she is!' Patch cheered. 'Let a banging evening commence!' He shook up a bottle of champagne, which exploded with a loud pop and a rush of white foam.

'You wanna watch out, man,' said Motti, slumped in one of the leather armchairs. 'You could have your eye out with that.' He let off a party popper with an ironic expression. 'Hey, Tye, Jonah. Come on in. Hope you ate already.'

'And no one's allowed to be lippy,' Patch warned him. 'Or they get a *fat* lippy.'

'Can they *wear* lippy?' Con was still doing her make-up as she breezed into the hangout without a glance at Tye and Jonah. 'I mean, this is a special occasion, yes? And so of course I wish to look my best.'

Tye threw a daggered look at Jonah like he had led her into a den of lions. He shrugged helplessly.

'Nice banner, Patch.' Con sat down opposite Motti. 'You even spelled everything right.'

'I looked up the words. I may not have been to school much but God can I ever rustle up some grub!'

Patch gestured to the coffee bar counter, which was piled high with sloppy slices, and hit a button on a remote control. Music started blasting out of the speakers, naff cheesy disco stuff, as he came over to join them and let off another popper. 'Help yourself, peeps! Sooner they're finished, sooner we can let off the fireworks. I bought up two grands' worth – my own cash, mind. The bloke thought it was a wind-up . . .' When no one moved he looked crestfallen. 'Aw, come on, then. I worked my bum off making this lot.'

'Jonah does not have much appetite at the moment,' said Con, carefully applying her eyeshadow. 'But I expect he will manage something, won't you, Jonah?'

Tye looked between Jonah and Con, then turned quickly to Patch. 'Well, I'm going to stuff myself.' She gave him a hug, and he responded with enthusiasm. 'Thanks for going to all this trouble, Patch.'

'But no, she still won't lay you,' added Motti.

'Oh, Patch?' Con batted her heavily mascaraed eyelashes in his direction. 'Would you fetch me a slice of each?'

'I'm the chef, not the waiter!' he protested.

'So fetch yourself some, too.' She wriggled in her seat. 'We can sit and eat them together, yes?'

'On my way!' Patch cried as he scooted off.

'Like a dog thrown a bone,' murmured Jonah.

'Nuh-uh. That's a dog with a *boner*.' Motti mooched over to Tye. 'Hey. Want me to get you something?'

Tye smiled. 'Sure. Except I don't know what there is.'

'It smells like crap and looks like roadkill.' He paused, as if suddenly awkward. 'Wanna check it out?'

She nodded. 'We can talk about the plan for tomorrow while we eat.'

'Uh-huh. Eat, drink and be merry, for tomorrow we rip off a lorry for its unknown cargo ahead of a secret brotherhood into human sacrifice.'

Jonah watched them walk off together, feeling a bit of a spare part.

Patch was smiling to himself as he headed back from the bar with two loaded plates. Jonah intercepted him, lowering his voice. 'You do know Con's going to try and use you to get at Tye, right?'

'Oh yeah,' Patch said cheerily. 'It ain't gonna work, but I can't wait to see how far she's willing to go!'

Jonah watched him sit eagerly beside Con, then headed off to examine what was left of the buffet. *Tonight the roadkill's on some dodgy pizza*, he reflected. *Tomorrow it could be a lot more personal.*

CHAPTER FOURTEEN

Tye was feeling the usual tangle of nerves in her stomach that came before a job, and she was quite glad to have the drive along the Interstate to focus on.

She stared out at the scenery. It was real Lone Ranger stuff around here. Not just because you could imagine cowboys riding the vivid red plains or Native Americans charging down the steep sides of the mesas, but because 'lone' seemed to sum up the whole experience. There was no traffic behind or in front of them, just the landscape.

Majestic. Sweeping.

And kind of lonely.

They'd hired a large, white van and set off mid-afternoon to get ready to intercept the truck. The boys were sat in the back of the van – Patch absorbed in his Game Boy, Motti staring out the window, and Jonah with his eyes closed. The hours awake these last few nights must finally have caught up with him, and if Tye was being honest, it was a relief. Since their disastrous talk the other night it felt like he was always hovering, trying to say something he couldn't quite put into words. And meantime, she was trying to deal with her fears about Ramez. How long did he have left now? How was he coping, knowing the end would soon be here?

A bump as they hit a pothole made her realise she'd been accelerating without even knowing it. The wound in her side felt tight and sore. She just wanted to get this job over and done with, to get back in Coldhardt's good books.

Only he could help Ramez now. If he chose to.

'Become a top-class thief for a shadowy millionaire master criminal,' Con said suddenly, shifting in the passenger seat, 'and you too can enjoy the glamour of driving a van along the Interstate.'

Tye glanced at her in surprise. Con never travelled in the back of a car – not since the crash that killed her parents – so Tye knew she hadn't sat up front for the company. They had barely spoken since she'd come back.

'Wishing you were somewhere else, sweets?' Con asked lightly.

'Wishing you could believe me when I say I'm glad to be back.'

The van fell silent for a while, until Con spoke again. 'When you accused Coldhardt of wanting to see Ramez sacrificed, of believing in this goddess . . . were you just angry? Or were you reading him?'

'A bit of both, maybe.' Tye considered. 'He definitely knows more than he's letting on. Like that freak Traynor, he didn't bat an eye at the idea of some ancient Aztec goddess rising up from the underworld.'

Motti snorted. 'That's crazy.'

'He told me he'd invested a lot in looking for this lost Temple of Life from Death,' Jonah murmured.

'Said his future depended on it.'

Tye checked him in the rear-view. His eyes were still closed. 'What the hell is that supposed to mean?'

'I don't know.' He opened his eyes, met hers. 'But those were his words.'

'Traynor said Coldhardt's been chasing round after relics that are linked to stretching out your life, or cheating death, for ages.'

'So he doesn't want to die,' said Con defensively. 'Can you blame him?'

But is that all there is to it? Tye wondered.

'Guess he is cracking on a bit,' said Jonah.

'Shut up,' said Patch, still staring at his Game Boy. 'Nothing's gonna happen to him.' He paused. 'Or else what happens to the rest of us?'

There was a gloomy pause in the conversation. Jonah lightened the moment. 'Motti'll be OK. He's going to be a rock star.'

'Uh-huh,' Motti deadpanned. 'Maybe I'll let you all be in the video for my first single. Song's about freaks. You'll be perfect.'

They journeyed on in silence for a few miles.

'How long till we reach the right bit of road?' Patch asked.

'Not long,' Motti informed them. 'Checked out the view from that low-level satellite you hacked into, geek.'

'I'm getting quite good at breaking those,' Jonah declared.

'There's a gas station under construction coming,' Motti went on. 'It's a gift for us – should give us some cover and it's on a dead straight. We'll see a dark red truck coming a mile off.'

'Won't the workers notice us there?' Patch asked.

'We won't get there till they've knocked off, numb-nuts. We shouldn't be disturbed.'

'It's miles ahead of exit 85, too,' Tye added. 'So we should intercept the truck way ahead of Sixth Sun.'

'It is a shame you don't remember its registration number,' Con said.

'Kabacra didn't give it.'

'Funny, he gave all the other details.'

'I only overheard them talking.' Tye's fingers had tightened round the wheel. 'He probably had the registration written down somewhere.'

No one spoke again until the construction site came into view, white and chrome against the dusty desert red.

'Slow down to sixty,' Motti told her. 'Big truck shouldn't be doing more than that. Let's time how long we'll have to get our asses in gear once we've spotted the sucker.'

Jonah counted the seconds aloud from his watch. He'd reached twenty just as she sailed past the entrance.

Tye decided to take advantage of there being no one behind her and no one coming the other way. 'Hang on!' she shouted. Putting the gearstick into neutral, she turned the wheel sharp left and yanked up on the handbrake, wincing as her stitches pulled. The rear wheels locked and with a protesting screech the van began to spin through 180 degrees. Three-quarters of the way through the turn Tye shifted into first gear, released the handbrake and stamped on the accelerator. The stink of burning rubber filled the van as the tyres chewed on the asphalt. Then they were moving forwards again. Tye steered them bumpily into the site before coming to a sharp stop behind a stack of construction supplies.

Jonah was looking a bit shaken. 'Take it you don't like reversing?'

'Figured it was best we got in quick,' Tye told him. 'Never know who's watching.'

'That was cool!' Patch enthused, though he looked clammy and pale. 'But now I think I'm gonna –'

Jonah frantically slid open the passenger door beside him while Motti grabbed Patch by the back of the neck. He almost hurled him out of the van – before Patch could hurl all over the front seats.

'Good handling,' Con remarked.

'Me, or Motti?' asked Tye, and was rewarded with the smallest of smiles.

'Definitely Motti,' Jonah joked, as the sounds of retching carried from outside.

By eleven o'clock, Jonah was sure his heart must be pounding hard enough to rock the whole van. But it almost stopped altogether when a loud banging started up on the side door.

That was Motti's signal.

The five of them had been wearing hardhats and fluorescent jackets all night, hoping to pass themselves off as a late shift of construction workers – clanking around with wooden pallets and shoring poles, rigging a ready-to-go instant roadblock. Now Motti, their advance lookout, must have spied the truck coming.

'I can see its headlights,' Tye confirmed. 'We're on.'

'There's another car just behind,' said Con. 'I'll take care of whoever's inside.'

Patch wielded the big knife beside him. 'Once I've taken care of our trucker mate.'

'Get hacking, Patch,' Jonah encouraged him.

Patch started sawing away at the length of rope Jonah had tied, which was securing a large, teetering pile of pallets and shoring poles to the side of the van. When the rope was cut, they fell loose and tumbled out into the highway with a terrible din, blocking the carriageway. A loud hiss of pneumatic brakes carried through the night to Jonah, and a screech of tyres as the truck swerved to avoid the debris – and failed.

With a loud smack and a crash, the truck tore into part of the barricade. As if cued, Jonah and the others sprang into action.

'It's marked "Eucalyptus!"' Motti shouted. 'The job's on!'

Holding a fresh length of rope, Jonah joined Patch as he sprinted over to the driver in the cab, while Tye took the passenger side.

Patch yanked the driver's door open. 'Get out the truck!' he hollered. 'Move!' But the driver – middle-aged, plump and baffled – simply sat there. 'Bugger. He don't talk English.'

'*Eu sou Portugese*,' the driver offered.

'He's from Portugal.' Con was jogging over to the family saloon that had stopped further up the highway. 'Try, *Saia do caminhão*!'

'Do what? Oh, sod it.' Patch pulled a large pistol from his jacket pocket and aimed it at the man's face.

'How about, *Hasta la vista*, baby!'

Jonah stared at him in horror. 'Patch, have you gone crazy?'

'Stay out of this, Jonah.' Patch jabbed the gun at the driver and then gestured to the side of the road.

Raising his hands, the driver made to obey – until suddenly he stopped, his face darkening. 'Is water pistol!' he cried.

'Sod it,' said Patch.

The driver lunged for him, and he opened fire – squirting jet after jet in the man's eyes and mouth. Then Motti came along and hauled the spluttering driver bodily out of the cab, holding his arms behind his back while Jonah got to work binding the man's wrists.

Patch smiled and blew at the barrel of his water pistol. 'The name's Bond. Patch Bond.'

'Patch "Ass", more like,' Motti retorted. 'Dumb cyclops. Get clearing this barricade.' He smiled grimly. 'Wouldn't wanna cause an accident or something.'

'Did you check inside the lorry, then, see what we've got?' Jonah asked, pulling the last knot tight.

'Couldn't get in. But from the locks on the rear doors there, I'd say we got a hell of a lot more than eucalyptus oil loaded up inside.' Motti frisked the driver, then scowled. 'Where are the keys to the rear doors?'

The driver shrugged miserably. 'No have.'

'He means it,' said Tye. 'He's just the delivery man. A stooge.'

Motti shoved the driver away from them. 'OK, pal. Start running. Don't stop, you get me? *No pare el funcionar!*'

With a last, wholly baffled look at his attackers, the man turned and stumbled off, away from the highway, heading cross-country. And while Tye adjusted the truck driver's seat, Jonah and Motti joined Patch in clearing the road of poles and pallets.

Con rejoined them. 'That was Spanish, Mot.'

'Close enough.' Motti nodded after the dwindling figure of the driver. 'Anyway, he got the idea.'

'He probably just thinks we're a bunch of escaped psychos and can't wait to get the hell away,' Jonah decided, dragging a wooden pallet over to the layby. 'Con, did you deal with the driver of that car behind?' But even as he spoke, he saw it was carefully manoeuvring past the lorry, the man at the wheel casually continuing his journey. 'Guess you did.'

'He will remember nothing of this incident. In five minutes he will pull over and call the police, alerting them to a major incident a few miles from exit 85.' She smiled wickedly. 'Many police cars might make our Sixth Sun friends feel uncomfortable, no?'

Motti grinned. 'Nice work.' He looked up at Tye in the cab. 'The front fender's screwed but no other damage. Can you drive her?'

'Get inside and see,' she suggested, as the engine roared back into life.

Traffic was starting to gather behind them now, and a few drivers were hitting their horns. Con smiled and held up her hands to them in apology while the others piled inside the cab. Then she jumped aboard herself, squeezing on to the seat beside Jonah. 'We did it!' she shouted.

'Piece of cake,' Motti agreed.

Patch cheerfully squirted Jonah with his water pistol. 'Like shooting fish in a barrel.'

Tye swung the big wheel round and suddenly the rig was off. They did a U-turn and were soon speeding back the way they had come, heading for home.

Jonah wiped the water from his face. 'You don't think it was *too* easy, do you?'

'Here we go,' sighed Motti. 'The king of doom.'

'I mean, that driver was a pushover, he barely put up a struggle,' Jonah argued. 'Would you put a guy like that in charge of a valuable cargo without any backup?'

'Not unless I was stupid. But maybe his bosses *are* stupid. Must be why Kabacra targeted them.'

'It isn't far to Gallup,' said Tye. 'A few miles. Then we can see what we've stolen and let Coldhardt know.'

Jonah nodded, still feeling apprehensive. The plan now was to dump this truck just outside the small town and – if Coldhardt approved of the cargo – to transfer it across to another rig Motti had hired from a haulage depot.

After what felt like ages, Motti motioned Tye to take an unmarked exit. 'The depot should be off here.'

Soon, the truck was rumbling into a sprawling, apparently deserted industrial estate. They parked outside the depot, and Con went out to convince the night watchman into letting them switch transports without paperwork or awkward questions.

Patch was looking a bit green after the journey, and Motti shoved him out of the cab quick. 'Get busy with the locks, cyclops. Sooner we're away and done, the better.'

Feeling he could use a bit of fresh air himself, Jonah went outside with him. The night was cloudy and moonless, the only light coming from a couple of dim streetlamps further down the road.

There was a heavy padlock and chain securing the lorry's back doors. Patch hoiked out his glass eye from beneath his scrap of leather and extracted his tools.

'Should be a piece of cake, shouldn't it?' Jonah observed.

He shook his head. 'That padlock's a tricky sod. Multiple combination type – twenty-five possible ways to turn the tumblers, but only one unlocks it. Get the wrong one, the inner workings collapse and you ain't getting in without serious cutting gear.' He approached the padlock. 'G'is a bunk up, then.'

Jonah made a stirrup with his hands and took the boy's weight. Patch pressed his ear up against the lock and gently fed in his pick and torque wrench. A few seconds later, the padlock sprang open and he jumped down.

'Wa-hey!' Jonah clapped his hands together, both applauding Patch and wiping them clean. 'Thought you said it was tricky?'

Patch grinned and popped his eye back into place. 'To anyone who's not a complete genius, yeah.'

Together they pulled the chains away from the doors. Tye came round the back to join them, followed by Motti. 'What have we got, then?' she asked.

Jonah turned the stiff handles and opened up the doors. A pale white light flicked on, illuminating the spacious hold. Not that there was very much to see.

'Oh God,' Tye breathed. 'Don't tell me it's empty.'

Motti climbed up and went inside. 'No. There's something here right at the back. A couple of metal boxes.'

Intrigued, Jonah scrambled up to see for himself. But he found Motti standing some way back from the two boxes, pointing, apparently speechless for once. 'Geek, do those signs mean what I think they mean?'

He peered at the cases. Each was marked with lurid yellow stickers, a black circle flanked by three black triangles. Hazard warnings.

'They're well shielded,' Jonah muttered. 'This stuff must be radioactive or something.'

Motti nodded. 'What the hell are we on to here? What would Sixth Sun want with crap like that?'

Tye had come up behind them. 'Maybe it's a trick, meant to put us off opening them.'

'It's working,' Jonah assured her.

'She could be right.' Motti took a step closer to the boxes. 'Kabacra's goodies are locked up in a shut-down nuclear plant, he's bound to have some old crates lying around.'

'Yeah, but we also know he's dealt in plutonium and stuff.' Jonah wiped his sweaty palms through his hair. 'This whole set-up is dodgy!'

Motti knelt in front of the cases to examine them more closely. 'I'll bet it's a trick. Why the hell would anyone wanna go transporting nuclear rods in a eucalyptus truck?'

'Uh, guys?' Patch was peering in worriedly. 'We might have company. Chopper out here. With lights.'

Everyone fell quiet, and heard the approaching

drone. Jonah went to see, legs trembling, heart thumping.

'Must be the cops,' said Motti, stomping back across the truck's hold to see. 'I bet they picked up the driver.'

Tye's braids bounced about as she shook her head, peering up at the helicopter, which was dropping steadily from the sky. 'Looks unmarked.'

'Wait a sec.' Jonah swore. 'Of course! Kabacra didn't give Sixth Sun the registration number of this truck because there was no point. They wouldn't have been able to see it – not from the air! That's why he gave them the colour and the brand name and stuff.'

Patch pointed at the helicopter, his one eye wide. 'You think it's *them*?'

'We know they got a chopper,' said Motti.

'And we thought a big truck would mean a big cargo. But Traynor can snatch it and be away in minutes with that thing.' Tye slammed her fist against the side of the lorry. 'The truck didn't pass the exit when it was meant to, so they've come looking.'

The helicopter's approach made a grinding, raucous din, shattering the quiet of the darkness as it came in to hover over the roof of the three-storey depot. A blinding white light shone down from its underside, bleaching the street. Motti, Jonah and Tye scrambled down from the back of the lorry and ran round to the far side where they were shielded from view.

'Tye, get back in the cab and start her up,' Motti hissed. 'Whatever's in these cases, we ain't letting those bastards get it.'

She made to go but Jonah caught hold of her arm.

'I hate to point it out, but Sixth Sun must be prepared to hijack a moving lorry. They'll be ready for us!'

'Then we'll have to get some place populated, where they won't dare try anything.' Tye pulled away from him, ran round and opened the cab door. 'And fast.'

'Go with her, cyclops,' Motti told Patch. 'The two of you take off. Now.'

'And what do the rest of us do, Mot?' Jonah demanded as Patch ran off. 'Throw sticks and stones at the 'copter?'

'Con's gotta be ready with the other truck by now. We leave in that, fast – and hope they think we've had time to switch the cargo. They won't know which of us to follow – and we can give them the slip.'

'You ever driven a lorry before?'

'Looks like there's gonna be a first time.'

The red truck's engine roared into life and Tye pulled away. Jonah and Motti were exposed again, swamped in blinding brightness as they sprinted towards the depot car park. The lorry they'd hired now stood in its centre. Con was cowering in its thick black shadow as the chopper swooped down over-head.

And suddenly the harsh rattle of gunfire added to the deafening din. The ground seemed to explode around Jonah's feet as bullets strafed the concrete, kicking up clouds of dust and shrapnel. Terrified, he ran still faster, pushing himself to the limit. He and Motti practically bounced off the side of the lorry as they reached Con and its cover at last.

'What the hell are they playing at?' Jonah shouted.

'We have to get out of here!' Con shouted, her

usual cool composure cracked wide open.

'Working on it.' Motti was just reaching for the door of the cab when the whole lorry shuddered under the impact of a barrage of bullets. Two of its tyres blew out and the windscreen shattered.

'We're not going anywhere in this thing,' shouted Jonah.

Then the chopper circled round to attack them again.

'Get under!' Motti shouted, and the three of them ducked and rolled underneath the truck. More bullets raked the ground around them. Another tyre burst, and the underside of the lorry lurched down, grazing the back of Jonah's head. For a terrifying moment he thought they were going to be crushed beneath tons of metal.

Then the firing stopped, and the roaring drone of the helicopter picked up in pitch. The light began to lose some of its neon brightness as it shifted away.

'They are leaving,' Con breathed. In the fading light, Jonah could see the tears streaking her face. He reached for her hand and she clutched hold of it tight. 'I felt sure we were dead.'

Motti cautiously dragged himself from beneath the ruined truck. 'Here's why we're not.'

Jonah wriggled out too and saw that the lorry's rear doors had swung open during the onslaught to reveal the bare interior. Shakily he helped Con stand up. 'All they're after is the cargo.'

'And now they've gone after Tye and Patch to get it.' Motti whumped his palm against the side of the lorry. 'While we're stuck here.'

'I told you this was a set-up,' Con shouted. 'Tye must have told them –'

'No.' Motti shook his head. 'She couldn't have. Coldhardt was monitoring all signals in and out of the base. Anyway, Tye didn't come up with the hijack plan, *I* did. I never told her where this place was, and she never asked.'

'When the lorry didn't show, they must have traced the route it took in reverse. Spotted us miles away!' Jonah pulled his mobile from his pocket, speed-dialled Tye's number. 'We've got to warn them to get the hell out of that truck, fast!'

Tye was speeding around the industrial park, gritting her teeth against the pain in her side. Her first thought had been to try and reach Gallup along the Interstate before Sixth Sun could put whatever plan they had into operation – but it was a good six miles away and she didn't like their chances. Instead, she was looking out for some place they could park the truck, get it under cover and out of sight, throwing Sixth Sun off the scent. If they could only find a garage or something, and if Patch could get them inside and safe . . .

Her phone trilled into life, made her jump. Patch grabbed it and stabbed the OK button. 'Jonah? Is everything – you *what*? Bleedin' Nora!'

'What's happening?' Tye demanded.

'Chopper's coming after us,' Patch reported, pale-faced. 'Sounds like they'll shoot us full of holes the second they see us!' He spoke into the phone again. 'All right, we'll clear out. Cheers, Jonah.' Patch hung up. 'Tye, we gotta jump.'

'No way.' She stepped on the accelerator and aimed the truck at the perimeter gates of some metalwork company.

'But they're gonna kill us! If you don't kill us first –'

The truck slammed straight through the gates, the impact rocking the cab, almost jarring Tye's hands from the wheel. The cut burned red hot in her side. Wincing, she checked the rearview – just as the chopper swooped into sight from behind a building. She swore as its lights flooded on, dazzling her.

'We gotta get out of here!' Patch pulled at her arm. 'Please, Tye!'

Tye bit her lip, swinging the truck round a corner. She knew it was no good hiding the truck now they'd been spotted. But if they could only hide the cargo, make out it had been unloaded back in the depot somewhere . . .

Spinning the wheel round sharply, she sent the truck careening through a flowerbed, bringing it to a sudden halt. But as the growl of the engine died, the noise of the chopper soon rose to replace it. Tye threw open the door. 'We've got to hide the cases.'

'We've got to hide full stop!' Patch hissed back. 'Come on, I'll do the locks on this warehouse, we can sneak inside –'

'Get on with it!' Tye ran to the back of the truck and opened the doors. She could hear the thrum of the helicopter's rotors building, like angry bees swarming ever closer. She clambered inside the back, grabbed hold of one of the cases and started dragging it to the doors.

Too late. She saw the bright white light flooding down outside, the flowers and undergrowth whipping about in the wind from the screaming rotors. The judder of automatic gunfire tore through the night, the noise reverberating through her head.

'Patch!' she shrieked.

But a second later he scrambled into the truck to join her, one eye clutched in his hand, the other wide and terrified. 'I couldn't crack the door in time,' he shouted. He reached out and pulled the doors shut, then ran across and hugged her tight. She clung on to him. What else could she do? They both knew there was nowhere to hide. Not now.

The thrum of the rotors pitched down in intensity. The chopper had landed. Tye heard footfalls outside as people surrounded the truck, and the clatter and clicks of safeties disengaged.

'This is it,' Patch whispered in Tye's ear. 'We're dead meat.'

CHAPTER FIFTEEN

Jonah stared out at the New Mexico sunset, cold and alone. Over the mountains, the deepening red was the same colour as the stolen lorry.

He remembered when he, Con and Motti had found it, abandoned, all doors flung wide open as if in despair, bulletholes in the nearby walls. The image had haunted him on the long flight back – his first trip flying solo.

He could've wished for happier circumstances.

At least you know Tye and Patch aren't dead, he told himself. The monitoring satellite had shown that much – the helicopter with its mysterious cargo had flown straight to the Black House in Colorado, and his friends along with it. There had been cars and trucks coming and going all day, and it was impossible to know if Tye and Patch were still there or if they'd been removed to another location.

Jonah imagined Tye would have been reunited with Ramez by now. And he'd want to keep Tye happy, so surely he'd insist on nothing happening to Patch. But the thought of them, surrounded by so many enemies, being marched off to face God knew what . . .

And what did Coldhardt have to say on the

subject? Not much below one hundred and twenty decibels. Jonah had never seen him lose it so noisily. He seemed more disappointed that his 'children' had let him down than he was upset to hear of Tye and Patch, and had insisted that Jonah redouble his efforts to crack the meaning of the stubborn symbols.

Then he'd gone off by himself.

Jonah reckoned he knew where.

With a sudden, steely resolution, he made his way to the wine cellar and marched down the steps. The curtain was pulled away from the vault door, which stood wide open. It was bright inside. Coldhardt stood before the altar like some dark, silver-haired angel.

'Is there news, Jonah?' he murmured, without turning round.

'No. Only questions. And I want real answers.'

'The truth can be disturbing.'

He glowered at the old man's back. 'Just why is finding this temple so important to you?'

Coldhardt was silent, his fingers caressing the stone altar. Then, after a slow, weary sigh, softly he began to speak. 'If we can only locate it ahead of Sixth Sun, I might stand a chance.'

'A chance of trading the info for Patch and Tye's lives?' No answer. 'Nah, I didn't think that was on your mind. So what *is*? And what's with the altar? It's not Aztec like everything else, doesn't even look like it's worth much.'

'What are any of us worth?' Coldhardt whispered. 'When I was a younger man I thought of nothing but money. I was prepared to sell everything I possessed, thinking I could acquire so much more.' He leaned against the altar. 'A policy that in my later years, as the sands of time run out . . . I have come to regret.'

'Oh, Jesus. I get it now.' Jonah sucked in an icy breath. 'This isn't a treasure vault at all, is it? It's a tomb. It's going to be *your* tomb, isn't it?'

'We're all dying, Jonah, all of us decaying a little more each day. And what waits for us on the other side?'

'I don't know,' said Jonah. 'But I think you have a pretty good idea of what's waiting for you. And you don't like it.' He remembered the little statue on Coldhardt's desk, the man struggling with the demon, and shuddered.

'As a young man, the thought of what would happen to me after death never bothered me.' Coldhardt turned and gave his wintry smile. 'I was more than willing to sell my soul.'

Jonah felt a shiver down his spine. 'Is that a metaphor . . . or for real?'

Coldhardt remained impassive.

'Who d'you sell yours to?'

A tight smile. 'The highest bidder.'

Figures, thought Jonah. 'And now you're trying to get out of it?'

Again, silence.

'So that's why you've been so busy looking for the secret of eternal life. And why you're banking everything on finding this temple, the Temple of Life from Death. It's not the treasure you want – it's that promise.'

Coldhardt was staring into space. 'Eternal life doesn't seem to be an option. And although deep and

185

deathlike trances can extend the body's lifespan dramatically, it isn't much of an existence.'

Jonah stared wonderingly at Coldhardt. 'So unless this temple can offer you another way out, you'll end up hiding your body away in this deep freeze, hoping it'll keep out whatever comes digging for you –'

Coldhardt leaned forward suddenly – 'Shut up,' he hissed, and for a split-second Jonah caught a glimmer of something ancient and inhuman in the old man's hard blue eyes. Then the moment passed, and Coldhardt leaned back heavily against the altar, wiping a hand across his brow. 'You have no conception of the fate that awaits me.'

'I know what's waiting for Patch and Tye,' said Jonah shakily. 'Tye said Ramez will be sacrificed soon – which means Sixth Sun are almost ready to move. If they *do* know the location of that temple, and now they've got whatever that lorry was transporting –'

Coldhardt pushed himself up from the altar. 'We *must* find out the temple's location for ourselves.'

'But how? We're still no closer to deciphering those symbols!'

'So work harder,' he snapped. 'If we reach the temple ahead of Traynor we can deal with him, bargain for the safe return of Tye and Patch.'

'What if he's already had them killed?'

'I will not be questioned, Jonah,' Coldhardt thundered. 'This is our path of action. I have made my decision.'

Jonah turned and walked away. *In that case*, he thought, *so have I.*

* * *

Tye had been waiting in the room for what felt like for ever. The majestic view from the huge windows was no kind of comfort, showing as it did – with sick irony – the other side of the *Sangre de Cristos* mountains she'd stared out over from Santa Fe. She wondered vaguely if, given that Sixth Sun were a pagan outfit, there was some kind of symbolic reason for their choosing locations overlooking a mountain range named for Christ's blood.

She had no idea where Patch or Ramez were; all she knew was that she was somewhere in Colorado Springs. She guessed that she was being held to convince Ramez to play along, while Patch was being held to ensure that Tye didn't try to escape again. Otherwise, Traynor's thugs could have killed them both in the back of that lorry. Instead they'd had their phones snatched, been bundled off into the helicopter along with the cargo, and flown straight to some big industrial plant in Colorado – the Black House. She and Patch had been separated, and driven thirty minutes into the hills . . . a striking old mansion set all alone in rugged countryside, shaped like a black arrowhead pointing up to the stars.

Presumably Traynor and Kabacra were nearby – and maybe the woman from the penthouse too, that 'colleague' Traynor had been so edgy about.

Suddenly the door opened and a tall, stocky middle-aged man entered. He was dressed in black and wore a jade amulet around his neck. A band of dull yellow make-up was daubed across his face from ear to ear, framing his mouth.

Tye glared at him. 'Nice look. Can I help you?'

'The Council of Thirteen Heavens has summoned you,' the man said, quietly. He sounded more like a librarian than hired muscle. 'Come with me. No funny business.'

'I'm not feeling very funny,' Tye assured him. With nerves flickering grimly through her stomach, she followed the strange-looking man out of the room. Any thoughts of trying to take him were abandoned when she saw a second man waiting outside the room, younger and fitter-looking than the first. He was wearing make-up too, though the stripe across his face was a livid red. As if to press home his advantage in the flamboyance stakes, he wore big, gold ceremonial earrings and a kind of headband festooned with turquoise sequins.

'You guys could have told me the party was fancy dress.' It may have been a lame joke, but it was still defiance, and to Tye that was the important thing. She tried to put some of Motti's swagger into her step. She was going along with these bastards because she had no choice, but she wasn't about to act all cowed and helpless. Not now, not ever.

They led her downstairs and through the hallway to a set of double doors. Here they paused. The doors were dark, made of some kind of smoked glass that absorbed all light.

'O great black mirror, we seek to enter the highest heavens,' yellow-mouth announced. 'We seek to enter the homes of storms and winds, of colours and remote gods.'

Then the other man started spouting off. 'We are only paintings in your book of pictures,' he intoned.

'Destroyer of eagles and jaguars, we ask that you let us enter.'

The doors swung open. Yellow-mouth grabbed Tye by the back of the neck and marched her through the double doors.

Tye almost gasped as she was thrust suddenly into a large, cold, circular space. If the weapons plant was Traynor's Black House, his space to think and plan, then this place must be where he went for all-out worship of his own cult. It was done out like some strange, two-storey temple – and since there were no windows she guessed it must form the centre of the house. Weird effigies lined the sandstone walls high above their heads, fantastical creatures that resembled crocodiles or birds of prey or big cats, dramatically lit with spotlights above and below. Images of the sun and six smaller circles that might have been planets were carved above and below them. A muted light-show was playing on the upper reaches of this bizarre space; the ceiling slipped between light and shadow, colours bled, then clotted, then dissolved and turned black or white in turn. It was soothing and unsettling all at once.

At ground level, a table shaped like a giant horse-shoe dominated the space. On the wall above it, in pride of place behind the table, an elegant but dangerous-looking rapier had been mounted. The hilt was swathed with coils of swept steel to protect the owner's hand, and the blade was pitted from frequent use.

'Guess you've got to be Cortes's sword,' she murmured. 'Finally found you. Way, way too late.'

All but four of the thirteen chairs ranged around the table were taken – the two at both ends of the horseshoe sat empty. Tye's escorts drifted away to stand either side of the doors; she supposed they must usually occupy two of the seats, but where were the others?

Whatever, it didn't take Einstein to work out that they must make up the Council of Thirteen Heavens.

The members present varied in age from maybe mid-thirties through to sixty. They were all done up the same, in headdresses and make-up, and all except one was wearing the distinctive amulet – a blond-haired guy with staring green eyes and a swollen nose. Perhaps he wasn't the necklace-wearing kind.

Then, with a shock, Tye recognised Traynor at the centre of the table, in a kind of crude crown. She noted that the only woman was sat to his right – the woman she'd glimpsed on the balcony back in Santa Fe. She was tall and thin, her black bob emphasising her sallow skin, her dark eyes made up black, and a streak of gold make-up accentuating her narrow lips.

'Nice 'ere, innit.'

The familiar voice echoed all around the temple. Tye turned to find Patch stumbling forwards from out of the shadows. He looked pale, the rigid way he was holding himself betraying his fear. 'Patch, are you all right?' she whispered.

'I've been better.'

Tye took both his hands in hers and whispered, 'Can't you break us out of here?'

'Got no tools, have I?' he reminded her. 'Lost 'em when they snatched us.'

'Quiet,' Traynor snapped. 'You defile Omeyocan with your ignorant speech.'

'Defile who?' Tye frowned.

'Omeyocan. Highest of all heavens.'

'You really do take this Aztec stuff seriously, don't you?'

'Sixth Sun was founded to celebrate the achievements, the culture and beliefs of the Aztec people, last and greatest of the Mesoamerican races.' Traynor spoke quite casually, as if talking to someone over tea. 'They picked up the baton of progress from other chosen peoples, of course. The Izapan civilisation, the Maya, the Olmecs . . .'

'Let us not waste time, Michael,' said the woman. 'We should receive Coldhardt's emissary.'

Tye glanced at Patch but he seemed none the wiser. 'What are you talking about?'

'A man called on your cell phone,' said Traynor, who seemed vaguely amused. 'Says he wants to make a deal in exchange for your lives. Of course, at the first sign of treachery, you and the boy will be killed.'

Tye caught movement behind her, and now she realised that the last two members of the council stood in the shadows around the perimeter of the circular chamber. They must have brought Patch here. The shifting light in the ceiling gleamed on their guns.

'Does Ramez know you're treating us like this?' Tye demanded.

'Poor Ramez doesn't even know that we have caught you again,' the woman informed her with a smile. 'Now, kneel down. Try anything and we'll kill you – along with your mystery knight in shining armour.'

Patch dropped to his knees like he was ready to scrub the floor. Tye crouched down more slowly, nerves buzzing inside her.

Traynor raised his voice. 'The priests shall now receive the unbeliever.'

The doors were opened and Ramez's bodyguards from Santa Fe appeared in the doorway with a slim, suave figure in a dark, well-fitted suit. The doors closed behind him as he breezed into the temple with a slim, titanium flightcase, apparently unfazed by the strange surroundings.

Tye stared. '*Jonah?*'

Jonah looked over and smiled in friendly greeting, like this was no big deal. 'Hey, Tye, Patch. Good to see you're still in one piece.' Then he noticed someone sat at the table, the man without an amulet. Jonah fished into his pocket and produced one. 'Xavier, right? Your friend called out your name that night you tried to kill me. I'm sorry I took your hummingbird.' He tossed it over to the man for an easy catch. 'Peace offering, yeah?'

The woman reached out with bony fingers and snatched the medallion from Xavier's hand. She scrutinised it while Jonah waited, before passing it back, apparently satisfied.

'It's the real deal. Even gave it a polish.' Jonah smiled round the table. 'My case has been searched too, by the way.'

'Who are you?' Traynor inquired.

Good question, thought Tye. It looked to be Jonah,

but he was talking the talk and even walking the walk in a way she'd never imagined he could. He was playing everything so cool – only the wet, matted hair at the back of his neck pointed to the nerves he must surely be feeling. The eyes of this Council of Thirteen were on him, cold, wary and mistrustful.

'His name is Jonah Wish,' the woman announced unexpectedly. 'Coldhardt's encryption and decryption specialist, from England.'

Traynor looked at her. 'How do you know of him?'

She shrugged. 'The boy is unusually talented, aroused a lot of interest in high places. Coldhardt got to him first. Broke him out of a Young Offenders Institution.'

Tye could tell from the way Jonah self-consciously straightened his shoulders that his confident front had been shaken a little. She knew it freaked him out, the idea that so many powerful, shadowy people had been interested in his talents while he was away inside, how they'd been waiting to make their approaches . . .

'Yeah, well,' said Jonah, forcing the flippancy back into his voice. 'Now I've broken *myself* out of Coldhardt's care. And I'm available for hire – at very unreasonable rates, of course.'

'What's he on about?' Patch hissed, but Tye shushed him.

'I want to get with the winning side.' Jonah glanced over at Patch and Tye, then stabbed a finger at Traynor. 'You're Michael Traynor – you head up the big secret biological weapons research labs around the corner, right? Nice to meet you, great place you have here.'

'I am the king,' said Traynor evenly. He gestured round the table. 'These are my priests. You will show us respect.'

'Er, do your shady government bosses know about the Sixth Sun stuff, Mike? About what you've been up to behind their backs – kidnap, dealing with international arms dealers, wearing funny make-up . . .'

Traynor said nothing, watching him intently.

'And what about *you*, lady?' Jonah shrugged his shoulders. 'Sat at the big guy's right hand, you've got to be important. You might know me, but who the hell are you?'

'My name is Honor Albrecht,' she replied, icy amusement on her face. 'I am the High Priestess of Sixth Sun.'

'Got to be high on something to take this old Aztec crap seriously.'

Now Traynor got up slowly from his seat and walked round the table. His council of minions didn't turn to look at him. They seemed frozen in their seats as he approached Jonah, who stood his ground. Tye felt a sick feeling start to build.

'Pretty impressive entrance, kid,' said Traynor softly. Then he lashed out with his fist, striking Jonah in the breastbone. Caught off-guard, Jonah staggered back, but Traynor lunged forwards and grabbed a handful of his hair. Twisting it savagely, the man forced Jonah to his knees.

'Leave him alone!' Tye shouted – then flinched as Traynor kicked Jonah in the face, knocking him flat on his back.

'How impressive is *that*, huh?' Traynor shouted,

clenching his fists as he screamed down at Jonah's prone body. 'You impressed now, you piece of shit? Huh?'

'That's enough.'

Tye started as Honor rose from her seat. Traynor slowly turned to face her.

'Coldhardt's teen puppet thinks he can just stroll in here and make fools of us,' he said, spit catching at the corners of his mouth. 'Thinks he can mock –'

'I want to know what he has to say,' Honor insisted calmly. 'Jonah. Get up.'

Jonah dragged himself to his feet. Tye winced at the size of the welt on his cheek. He dabbed at it, gingerly.

'Just don't take me for a fool, Wish.' Traynor's cold, quiet voice made Tye shiver. 'Remember, you're here on sufferance. We can end your life, or the life of your friends here, any time we choose, without hesitation. So, from now on, you're going to treat me, and my organisation and my beliefs, with respect. You got that?'

Jonah looked at him for a long time, rubbing his chest. Then, slowly, he nodded.

Traynor returned to his seat at the table and smiled evenly. 'Now. Tell us what Coldhardt is planning or we'll kill your friends right now.'

'He's hoping to find the temple ahead of you,' said Jonah, meeker now. 'He's got the codex, and the symbols marked upon it match those on a certain statuette of Coatlicue.' Tye stared in amazement as Jonah placed his flightcase on the edge of the council's table and produced a jade statuette from inside it. 'This one.'

Traynor motioned to another man sat a few places away, who was small and fat and wearing thick glasses. 'Douglas?'

Douglas got up and peered at the ugly object. 'Looks to be from the Eagle House of the Great Temple. Taken from the excavations.'

'That's right.' Jonah carefully passed it to him. 'There's a hidden symbol picked out in veins in the stone, it only shows up if the light falls on it in just the right way . . . And that symbol holds the key to the location of Coatlicue's temple. If you can crack it, that is.'

'This is genuine,' Douglas confirmed, reverently.

'But are *you* genuine, Wish?' Honor remarked. 'Do you really want to get with the winning side? What of your loyalties to Coldhardt?'

Jonah turned and gestured to Tye and Patch; he looked terrible, half his face had turned purple-black. 'I have loyalties to my friends,' he said. 'Coldhardt wasn't prepared to save them. He's set on getting to the temple above all else.'

Honor smiled. 'And so you came here to try and rescue them yourself.'

'I'll trade my loyalty, my skills, all I know.'

'Quite a risk you've taken,' said Traynor. 'What makes you think we need you? We are all of us experts in Mesoamerican peoples, culture and rituals.'

Jonah shrugged. 'How would it be if I guaranteed to get Coldhardt out of your hair for good?'

Traynor smiled through his thick ochre make-up. 'He's hardly been much of a threat to us so far.'

'How about you showing *me* a little respect?' said

Jonah, his voice hardening. 'Why else would you have brought me here, to the heart of your little organisation, if not because you wanted to know what Coldhardt was planning? He's a thorn in your flesh. Made you change your plans for hijacking the lorry, stole your codex, found not one but *two* of your secret hideaways.'

'How *did* he find them?' Honor enquired.

Jonah leaned heavily against the horseshoe table, he sounded short of breath. 'Blame Kabacra. We stole the info from his client list.'

Traynor's eyes narrowed. 'What?'

'So it's for all those reasons that you agreed to see me, Mr Traynor. You couldn't get me here fast enough. You want to keep Coldhardt out of your way and you couldn't be sure killing Tye and Patch would achieve that.' Jonah looked straight at Traynor. 'And I've got news for you – it wouldn't.'

'Coldhardt is irritatingly persistent,' Honor admitted. 'But what can *you* do for us?'

'I can hand him to you on a plate.' Jonah promised. 'But first of all, I'd like some answers. I'd like to know what it is you're actually up to.'

Traynor just went on looking at Jonah, staring him out. Then finally he cleared his throat, like he was ready to give a lecture, and started to speak.

Tye watched him as he talked.

And with a thrill of horror, she realised he meant every crazy word he said.

CHAPTER SIXTEEN

Jonah stared at Traynor, working hard to keep his composure, starkly aware of how much danger he was in. Even with Tye and Patch beside him, he had never felt quite so helpless. His chest still ached from Traynor's blow. And while this mysterious Honor might be smiling, her teeth looked sharp enough to shred bone; maybe she would pick up where Traynor had left off. His cheek felt burning hot, and Jonah found he couldn't stop pressing his tongue against his aching teeth, checking they weren't loose. If any fell out now, he imagined one of these creepy Council types would scoop them up and thread them on to a bracelet.

'Millennia ago now,' said Traynor, beginning his story, 'Mayan records spoke of men who communed with the gods themselves. Men they termed "knowers of occult things – possessors of the traditions". This was a time when science and superstition came together as never before or since.'

'To achieve what?' Jonah asked quietly.

'A classic age. The birth of a true and extraordinary civilisation.' Traynor rose again from the table, and Jonah tried hard not to flinch. 'How do you think the

Mesoamerican peoples came to enjoy unsurpassed cultural and scientific achievements? Did you know they counted in base twenty, or that they accurately calculated the duration of a lunar month to five decimal places? They measured the movements of Venus as accurately as we are able to today. Their medicines and use of herbs were far more advanced than those of the Europeans at that time. The list goes on and on.'

Jonah nodded nervously as Traynor moved slowly, menacingly round the table towards him. 'You were right, Wish. I did found Sixth Sun as a kind of hobby. To start with, anyway.' He walked closer, a happy smile on his face. 'The group was conceived as a meeting of experts, of like minds – those who respected and revered the achievements, the customs and the art of the Mesoamerican peoples. Of course, we dreamed of finding great, lost temples and fantastic archaeological finds. And so I took to arranging weekend expeditions into Mexico. I'd scout out prospective sites myself.'

Jonah swallowed hard. 'And did you find anything?'

Traynor came in close, too close for Jonah's liking – as if he were about to lean in for a kiss. Jonah could smell his breath, see every red-thread vein in the whites of his staring eyes. The man looked rapt as if at some secret, special memory. 'I never found a temple. But in the tropical lowlands I discovered an Olmec tomb dating back to 400 BC, made from basalt pillars and covered in earth. I fell through an opening, a drop of seven metres or more. I lay there, broken, like the jade offerings given up to the priest who lay buried there, my blood seeping into the cracked stone floor. And then . . .'

Jonah watched nervously as a tear squeezed its way out of Traynor's eye and down his cheek, while the other members of the council lowered their heads as if in reverence.

'. . . then *She* communed with me.'

'She?'

Traynor seemed to become aware of the tear and wiped at it briskly. When he spoke again there was a still stronger note of passion in his voice. 'I have come to believe – we *all* have – that the founding fathers of Mexican civilisation made connection with some higher force. A *presence* native to the region. A presence that somehow gave them knowledge so advanced they could just barely assimilate the basics.'

'What kind of a presence?' Jonah was careful to keep the sneer from his voice – this guy had to be a grade-A nutjob. 'You mean, like, aliens? Or a kind of ghost or something?'

'Modern day jargon is not helpful,' Traynor said curtly, looking away.

Honor spoke up. 'We own documents that show how, at the start of the Fifth Sun, the shaman priests reawakened the presence through ceremony, abstinence and human sacrifice. By the time of the Spanish invasion the presence was revered as the goddess Coatlicue.'

'And that is how we shall address her when we raise up her resting place from beneath the Mexican rainforest,' said Traynor fervently. 'The Temple of Life from Death.'

Jonah stared at him. 'You really do believe this . . . *presence* exists.'

Traynor nodded. 'She tasted my blood and it revived her. She communed with me.'

'What did she say?'

'How could a piece of trash like you possibly understand a moment that spiritual? It was . . . It felt to me as if . . .' He trailed off and took hold of Jonah's shoulders. 'I know what I felt. Just as I knew that the place I had stumbled upon was not the true dwelling place of this presence. Here there were only the after-echoes, still bound to the bones of the long-dead priest in his tomb.' His fingertips dug into Jonah's skin. 'Imagine how often that priest must have communed with the presence in the Temple of Life from Death.'

Jonah licked his lips. 'You said you fell seven metres; you hurt yourself bad. This "presence" could just be some bad dream or a hallucination.'

The rest of the council didn't seem to take kindly to that idea. A round of scandalised mutters and whispers started up. He looked round at them all – little men for the most part, who clearly dreamed of bigger things.

'You have no faith,' said Douglas, the fat expert with the glasses. '*We* do.'

An old professor-type nodded proudly. 'Faith is what binds the council in fellowship. It sustains us.'

'Seems the kid thinks I'm a liar.' The council chamber fell silent again as Traynor pushed Jonah down to his knees, then hissed in his face. 'I know what I felt that day, Wish. And I knew from that moment, it was my destiny to commune with Her again. Only next time, I would be prepared. Next time I would *summon* her – and from a position of strength.'

Jonah closed his eyes. Good old destiny. It would have to be the rich, influential head of a secret weapons research facility this kind of freaky crap happened to, not some student backpacker who'd put it down to a bump on the head and laugh about it with a bunch of Aussies back at his hostel.

Suddenly Traynor slackened his grip and let go. Jonah decided it was wisest to stay on his knees – he didn't trust his legs to support him any longer. He risked a glance at Tye and Patch. They both looked as scared as he felt.

'We have read the sacred accounts,' Traynor went on more calmly, 'experimented with the scraps of knowledge the priests wrote down – depictions of the temple, the ways to summon Coatlicue, the great prophecy . . .' He looked into the distance and smiled. 'Soon I will prove to the presence that I'm worthy of all Her secrets and mysteries. If She will share them with me and my priests, then I will work to welcome in a new age – a Sixth Sun – where She shall be worshipped again. Her influence and power shall grow . . .'

'With you as her right-hand hummingbird,' Jonah murmured.

Traynor reacted as the little jibe hit home, and Jonah flinched as he swung round to face him. But then the new Aztec king seemed to recover himself, almost starting to backtrack as he crossed back to his ceremonial seat. 'I cannot lose. Should my attempts to commune with Her fail, I will still have raised up the fabled lost Temple of Life from Death from Mictlan, the underworld. All the Aztecs' greatest treasures shall be ours to share, riches beyond imagining . . .'

Jonah didn't buy this rational act for a moment. 'You mentioned the great prophecy. How does it go again? "When the earth shakes the sun from the sky, when the bloodied sword is wiped clean, when Perfect Sacrifice is made and her attendants reach into their hearts . . . then Coatlicue will arise from her temple and feast on the poison in men."'

Honor smiled, and even Traynor seemed grudgingly impressed. 'You've translated it very quickly.'

'Oh, I'm good,' said Jonah coolly, getting up from his knees. 'Just ask Miss Albrecht here. I'm guessing the bloodied sword is Cortes's?' He nodded to the rapier mounted on the wall. 'Suppose that's it there, right? Courtesy of Kabacra.'

'We shall destroy it in the heart of the temple,' hissed Traynor.

'First, you've got to *find* the temple,' Jonah reminded him.

Honor just laughed. 'I have known of its location for some years, now.'

'Years?' he heard Tye echo behind him.

Jonah turned to her and mouthed, '*Is she telling the truth?*' Tye nodded, clearly uneasy.

'So where is it, then, Miss Albrecht?' he demanded.

'Really, Wish.' Honor shook her head, disapprovingly. 'You don't seriously expect me to tell you?'

'But if you know where the temple is, then why wait?' Jonah checked himself. 'Sorry, stupid question.

There's only one possible reason. You've had to hold fire till you had all the other elements of this so-called prophecy sorted.'

Traynor inclined his head, as if conceding a point. 'We must convince Coatlicue that we are worthy to understand her mysteries. I intend to make sure that the moment of our meeting is perfectly orchestrated.'

Jonah nodded, looked at Honor. 'You're putting a hell of a lot into this, aren't you?'

'We are merely doing what is necessary,' she said.

'Like selling the very latest biological weapons to the likes of Kabacra?'

'He's not getting what he *thinks* he's getting,' said Traynor smugly.

'Or like giving Ramez one last, perfect year as you fatten him up for sacrifice?'

Traynor shrugged. 'The Aztecs knew that the gods gave things to human beings only if they were nourished by human beings in turn.'

'You're sick, all of you!' Tye shouted suddenly. 'Nothing's gonna happen if you kill Ramez! How's his blood supposed to bring anything back to life?'

'That's enough, take her out of here,' snapped Honor, and two heavy types moved from the doors to obey. 'The one-eyed boy, too. I think we have passed beyond the need to make threats against them . . .' She looked up at Jonah, and he caught a hunger in her black eyes that made him want to shudder. 'Perhaps it is time we started talking business?'

'Jonah, we've got to stop them doing this!' Tye shouted, struggling as the two men tried to bundle her out of the room after the unresisting Patch. 'Traynor believes everything he's told you – but *she* doesn't!'

He turned to her anxiously. 'What?'

'She doesn't believe like he does!' Tye insisted. Then she was gone, the dark, mirrored glass of the door swung back into place, and Jonah was left looking at the distorted reflection of himself, his face livid with bruising, half lost in shadow.

Honor smiled at Jonah. She seemed entirely unruffled. 'I'm glad not all Coldhardt's operatives are so . . . hysterical.'

Give me time, he thought darkly, alone now before the Council of Thirteen Heavens – which was fast becoming his private hell.

Feeling wretched and hollow inside, Tye let herself be led out into the comparative normality of Traynor's opulent house. But the atmosphere of oppressive gloom lingered.

'It'll be all right, Tye,' Patch assured her, as he was dragged off to some downstairs room while she was marched upstairs. 'We're better off out of there. Jonah will sort things. You'll see!'

'I know,' Tye called back loyally. 'Don't worry, I'll see you soon.' But inside she felt a lot less certain, both of seeing Patch and of Jonah's chances of saving any of them.

She just didn't know what to make of this Sixth Sun set-up. Traynor was clearly some kind of psychopath – as clever as he was violent. So how come he had lost the plot so badly? She had heard endless people claim that they had communed with spirits – back in Haiti where she'd grown up, the voodoo priests reckoned they did so all the time. How much was down to imagination and how much came from genuine spiritual union had never been clear to her, but Traynor was a true believer all right; Tye had seen that mad glint in his eyes.

Honor Albrecht, on the other hand . . . Tye's instincts told her that the woman's beliefs were entirely different, that when she'd chipped into Traynor's story she'd only been going through the motions. There was no passion when she spoke, no sense of conviction. And for the high priestess of a secret society like this, even allowing for her sense of English cool, that seemed kind of odd.

Marched up to the landing, Tye waited wearily in red-mouth's grip while yellow-mouth unlocked the same room she'd been held in before. But then her heart jumped as she heard movement inside.

'Keep back from the door,' yellow-mouth called through the heavy wood, 'and you'll get a nice surprise.'

Tye heard feet retreating, meekly. Yellow-mouth opened the door and she was shoved roughly inside, fell forwards on to the wooden floor, gasped with pain as the wound in her side burned hot – and felt a shadow fall over her. She recoiled and rolled over, started to scramble up –

'Tye?'

She stared up in disbelief. It was Ramez. He crouched down beside her, and she could see how red his eyes were. Then he grabbed her and held her close.

Tye could feel him trembling. 'Are you OK? Where'd you come from?'

'My bodyguard drove me here. But they never

said . . .' He pressed his face up against her neck. 'I thought they'd killed you.'

'I got away. I tried to get help for you.' She stroked the back of his neck. 'But Sixth Sun found me again, took me back.'

'You can't escape them,' he murmured. 'You just gotta accept that.'

She pulled away from his grip and looked into his glistening eyes. 'The way you have?'

'I used to hope against hope . . .' His fingers were digging into her arms now, but she barely felt it. 'Used to think that maybe there was a way out.' He pressed his lips against hers in a clumsy kiss. 'There's nothing. Tonight they're bringing me my last supper, and that's it.'

'Last supper?' she echoed, numbly.

'Tomorrow. Tomorrow I'm gonna die, sugar-girl.' He kissed her again, rough, hard. His saliva was thick, his mouth tasted sour. She stayed rigid in his arms. 'I'm gonna have my heart cut out with a rock. They're gonna kill me. Sweet Jesus Christ, they're gonna kill me.' His teeth scraped into her lip, she tasted the blood and felt sick. 'Tye, will you hold me?' His voice was all choked up, he wiped his nose on her cheek. 'C'mon, just hold me.'

'We're going to get out,' she whispered, trying to pull away from his kisses. 'Jonah's here, and Patch, and we're – we're not giving up, Ramez.'

'We.' Suddenly he pushed her away, sneering. 'You and your crummy little band of super-crooks, huh?'

She stared at him, hurt balling in her chest. 'Me and my friends.'

'You ran out on me before to get back to them. And what good were they, huh?' He pushed her again, and she fell back awkwardly on her ass. 'What could they do? Jack. Nothing.'

Tye wiped the blood from her lip. 'It's not over yet.'

'*Everything's* over!' Ramez grabbed hold of her shoulders.

'Get off me,' Tye warned him.

'You just don't see it, do you? We're dead – both of us.'

'Don't say that.'

''S'true!' he spat in her face. 'You just get to watch me go first.'

For a moment, Tye was thirteen again, hiding in the shadows as the dealers closed on Ramez.

One of them took out a gun, pointed it so casually, fired. She saw the blood spatter the floor, so much blood, heard Ramez scream, loud and high, a baby wail. Heard sirens, footsteps running. Opened her eyes, saw cops with their arms round Ramez, medics with a stretcher. Ramez never stopped screaming for the money he'd lost, begging someone to bring it back. He couldn't know what had happened to Tye, didn't seem to give a damn. She was shut out, left behind, forgotten in the dark.

'And what do you care, huh?' He started to shake her by the shoulders. 'I said, what do you *care?*'

She brought up both arms to break his grip. Then she twisted his left wrist round behind his back, ready to break that too. He gasped with pain.

'You want to know what I care?' she hissed. 'You need to even *ask* that question?' She threw him forwards. He fell heavily against the leather sofa, twisted round on his knees, and looked up at her. He was clutching his wrist, panting for breath. Then his mouth twisted. 'Help me.' He held out his arms to her, eyes imploring. 'I'm so scared. Oh God, I'm so, so scared, sugar-girl.'

Tye watched him there on his knees, snivelling, reaching out to her.

'So am I,' she said. Slowly, stiffly, she joined him on her knees, held him to her, shushed him gently as he shook and sobbed like a little kid in her arms. 'God knows, so am I.'

'So what's with the earth shaking the sun from the sky stuff?' Jonah asked Traynor, still trying to play it casual but keen to get as much info as he could. 'How d'you read that part of the prophecy?'

'Simple. The Aztec architects who sealed the temple and secreted it underground built in an extraordinary mechanism.' Traynor paused impressively, though Honor seemed less enthralled. 'The age of the Fifth Sun was supposed to end with an earthquake, and the priest-architects planned that the temple would rise up from the deadlands at that time. Therefore the mechanism is designed to respond only to powerful tremors in the area.' He laughed. 'Isn't that beautiful? Only an earthquake can make the temple rise!'

'Beautiful,' agreed Jonah. 'But how do you *know*?'

'The temple was rediscovered by accident,' Honor explained impatiently. 'Nuclear waste is often sealed and buried deep in the ground, all over the world – the Mexican mountains included. A surveyor stumbled upon the foundations of the temple, marked with Aztec runes –'

'And the surveyor sold you the information,' Jonah surmised.

Honor's eyes glinted. 'Of course, he had to be persuaded to keep very quiet about his discovery.'

'Yeah, I'll bet.' Jonah nodded grimly. 'So what are you going to do – come up with your own earthquake?'

'That is *exactly* what we are going to do,' Traynor agreed. 'The eucalyptus truck contained industrial nuclear waste products ready for illegal dumping. Enough plutonium has been extracted from the waste to construct a small nuclear device secretly in my weapons labs. Soon we shall detonate it deep underground in the vicinity of the temple.'

Horrified, Jonah stared at him. 'You've made a nuclear bomb?'

'A simple enough procedure,' said Honor. 'And now we've found the perfect place to set it off.'

Jonah recalled the snatches of conversation Tye said she'd overheard on the penthouse balcony. 'When you said you were close to finding the exact location with those geological surveys, you weren't talking about the temple, were you? You were talking about where best to explode a bomb.'

'It has taken some time to find the precise site among the many fissures and tunnels beneath the mountains,' said Douglas gravely. 'Too deep underground, and the tremors will not be sufficient to set off the temple mechanism. Too close to the surface, and we risk irradiating the area.'

The old professor type piped up. 'There is also the local water supply to consider, which, of course, cannot be polluted –'

Honor got up from her chair. 'Enough of this.'

'Hang on,' said Jonah quickly, turning to Traynor. 'We haven't got on to Coatlicue feeding on the poison in men, yet. What's all that –'

'It is time we discussed how you will rid us of Coldhardt,' said Honor. 'We may have beaten him to the prize on this occasion, but no doubt he will go on attempting to involve himself in our affairs at any opportunity.'

Jonah shrugged. 'I can tell you how to bypass his defences.'

Traynor looked smug and condescending. 'Aren't you forgetting we already got inside his New Mexico base when we abducted your friend?'

'And dealt with you,' added Xavier, his green eyes hard and unblinking.

'No, I hadn't forgotten,' said Jonah evenly. 'It's one thing breaching an unfinished security system in one of his outposts. But I can tell you how to get inside his main base – the heart of the Coldhardt empire. I can tell you how to decrypt all his passwords and get at his secrets.'

'I'll deal with this matter personally, Michael.' Honor gave Jonah her hungriest smile yet. 'We clearly have much to discuss, Wish. You shall join me tonight.'

'Sounds good.' Jonah found his smile was genuine, just at the thought of getting out of that place alive.

Traynor didn't look a hundred per cent about the

idea. 'Do you need assistance?'

Her hair flapped round as she turned to him. 'I believe I can manage, Michael,' she said smoothly. 'Thanks all the same.'

'He's not the pushover he looks,' Xavier warned her.

Traynor smiled. 'Really?'

Honor looked at Jonah. 'I don't think Wish will cause me any trouble.' She took hold of his forearm and pressed her thumb against the flesh. At once he gasped, as a blinding pain tore through his shoulder up to his neck – she must have hit a nerve or a pressure point or something.

'Point proved,' he gasped, and she let go of him. His arm was bristling with pins and needles, but he refused to show any more pain in front of her.

'Xavier will go with you,' Traynor insisted. 'I'm not about to allow one of Coldhardt's operatives to meet with my high priestess unguarded, the night before our plans come to fruition.'

Jonah stared at him. 'This all kicks off *tomorrow*?'

Traynor nodded slowly, picking up Coldhardt's statuette. 'Now, if there are no more matters arising, I declare this extraordinary meeting of the Council to be concluded. We shall meet again at eleven, to rehearse tomorrow's ritual and to purify ourselves for the coming rebirth.'

The excitement in the air was almost tangible. Jonah didn't want to know what purifying entailed. He remembered the drawings Con had shown him of the Aztec lords spilling their own blood on to the land to please the gods, and shuddered.

While the council members turned to each other, chattering excitedly in low voices, Honor was already up and heading for the door. She paused and looked back at Jonah, like he was a wayward dog she was calling to heel. Jonah threw a quick glance at Xavier, pleased to see him wearing the amulet round his neck again. 'No hard feelings, I hope?'

Xavier's expression didn't change. *They might get a lot harder if you ever work out there's a radio transmitter hidden in your amulet.* If Motti's bug was working correctly, then he and Con should have picked up every word back at their motel in Florissant, just a few miles away.

What they could do about all this information with so little time left till kick-off was another matter.

Xavier gave him a shove in the small of his back. Jonah meekly followed Honor from the council chamber, rubbing his numb arm and wondering what the hell he was going to do next.

CHAPTER SEVENTEEN

'Gotta hand it to the geek,' said Motti, pulling off his headphones and turning to Con. 'He's got balls of steel. He did good in there.'

'For what it was worth.' Con was sprawled in an armchair with a Coke, staring at bits of paper scattered on the floor. He guessed she was still trying to work out hidden meanings in the pictograms. She hadn't stopped for hours; languages were kind of her thing, Motti supposed, and she didn't like being beaten on a problem. Shit, none of them did.

But this time, winning through was looking less and less likely.

'Can't believe they're ready to move out tomorrow.' Motti shook his head. 'We're royally screwed.'

'They have all the cards,' Con agreed, not looking up from her work. 'The sword, the location of the temple and the means to open it. And now they have Jonah as well as Patch and Tye.'

'Looks like it's just you and me, baby,' Motti agreed. He gave a heavy sigh, checked the MP3 recorder was still getting down everything that Xavier's amulet was receiving. Considering the radio mike was the size of a pinhead pressed into a crack in the jade, the sound quality was incredible. 'Well, at least we can tell Coldhardt how things are. Maybe now he knows it's no good, he'll give up on this temple and concentrate on getting Patch, Tye and Jonah back safe.'

Con snorted softly, turned a page. 'That's about as likely as an old Aztec goddess speaking in Traynor's ear.'

'C'mon, Jonah, speak into mine,' Motti muttered, pressing one headphone pad back against his ear. He heard a dull, steady drone – a car engine. Jonah, this Honor chick and medallion man were in a car, on their way to her place. Motti listened on, but no one was speaking. He had an uneasy feeling building in his belly. Probably because he knew that it was partly down to him that the geek was now in this mess.

Jonah had come to him and Con, begging them to help him persuade Coldhardt to let him go to Colorado. It had been Motti's idea to wire up the amulet – and this had finally sold Coldhardt on the big gamble. The boss man knew time was tight, and since Jonah was willing, he had decided to risk the geek's life smuggling the hidden mike into the heart of Sixth Sun's sanctum, in the hope they'd hear something that could help them get ahead – maybe even the location to the temple. But it looked like Traynor and co were keeping that info to themselves, and meantime Jonah had been beaten up and Tye and Patch dragged off to God knew where . . .

'So – radio mike. Great idea,' murmured Motti. 'All we know now is how much we still *don't* know. Aside from the fact that Traynor is crazy and Jonah's in big, big trouble.'

Con shrugged. 'It was a gamble. We may not have won but we've found out why Sixth Sun are doing this – and how.'

Motti looked over at her. 'Y'know, if Jonah gives us the address they're going to, maybe we can spring him, or get the chick and force her to take us to the temple . . . Even trade her for Tye and Patch.'

'Can we follow the signal from the radio mike?' Con wondered. 'Use it to track them to the temple?'

'We don't got the range,' Motti told her. 'Why'd you think we came way out here to listen in on 'em? In any case, by the time we've followed them to wherever the temple is, they'll have emptied the whole goddamned place – well, so long as the sleeping goddess don't wake up and have something to say about that.' There was no reaction from Con, and Motti glowered at her. 'Tell me if I'm boring you, OK?'

'Wait. I think I might have something . . .' Con held up the same old pictogram, the one that showed the heart thing hanging over the two boxes. 'Coffers!'

Motti pushed his glasses up his nose and squinted at the picture. 'Huh?'

'Maybe the boxes aren't just boxes. Maybe this longer one is meant to be a coffer, yes?'

'So what?'

Con started rifling through her papers. 'By combining words, the Aztecs changed their meaning, remember? If you take "heart" and "blood" and put them together, you get cacao, their bitter chocolate drink.' She stabbed her finger at a point on the page and shoved it under his nose. 'And according to this old lecture on their language, if you put the phrases "in a box" and "in a coffer" together, you create a new meaning – the word "*secretly*".'

Motti frowned at her. 'So, taking the picture altogether we're left with, "secretly cacao". What the hell does that mean? Sounds like a perfume or something.'

'I don't know,' Con admitted. 'But this other pictogram, the one that was hidden on the statuette . . .'

'The one that looked like a big egg in the middle of four trees? Even the geek couldn't make no sense of that.'

Con looked at him, her blue eyes brilliant. 'Maybe they're cacao trees. Maybe the egg represents the temple – a kind of rebirth thing, yes? Maybe it's buried beneath four trees.'

'But the pictogram's a code,' Motti argued. 'Isn't it? I mean, how the hell would we find four cacao trees in the whole of Mexico? There must be millions of 'em out there.'

Con slumped back on the bed. 'I suppose you're right.'

'Wish I wasn't.' Motti turned back to the head-phones and placed one pad to his ear.

It was dead.

Swearing, he twiddled with the receiver. There was just static.

'What is it?' Con asked.

'Damn mike must have gone out of range.' Motti stopped the MP3 recorder and started skipping back through the contents. 'We only got us a twenty-mile operations zone, enough to take in the weapons centre and Traynor's place. Wherever Jonah is now, we can't get to him – and we can't listen in, neither.'

Con swung herself off the bed. 'Let's look at the map. If they're out of range already, we can work out which direction they've taken from the positioning of Traynor's place, no?'

'And then drive round, see if we can pick up their signal again. We might hear something that gives us a clue where they've gone.' Motti nodded in agreement. 'OK. Let's do it.'

'And hope we pass a McDonalds somewhere on the way,' Con added, giving him the tiniest of smiles. 'I'm starving.'

Jonah stared at the bloody steak Honor placed in front of him, fresh from the fridge. 'I'm, uh, not hungry,' he said.

'It's for your cheek,' she informed him. Without the freaky make-up, she was a striking woman, stick-bony and ashen-skinned, but with a steely strength about her. It showed in those dark eyes that seemed somehow just too big for her face. 'It will help with the swelling and constrict the blood vessels to stop further discolouring of the skin.'

Jonah gingerly picked up the meat and placed it against his sticky cheek. 'You a doctor or something?'

She turned that white, voracious smile on him again. 'I know a very great deal about the way the body works, Jonah.'

He nodded vaguely, looked away. The steak did actually feel soothing, but the smell of the raw meat threatened to turn his stomach. Or maybe that was down to his situation. He was trapped in a fancy rented top-floor apartment in downtown Colorado Springs. A man who had nearly killed him a few days back was guarding the door outside, while he was left alone with a woman at least five times as tough as she looked, the high priestess of a murdering cult of loopers.

He hoped that Motti and Con were still listening in, that they had some idea where he was. That they were coming to get him. Otherwise he was in big trouble.

'So where did you meet Traynor?' he asked conversationally.

'I heard of his reputation in certain areas that interest me, and sought him out.' She smiled. 'It's been well worth it.'

Jonah sucked in a breath as he pressed on the steak. 'Does he often beat up his visitors?'

'He has something of a temper.' Honor shrugged, and smiled. 'But then, so do I. If you're thinking of trying to escape from here, I should warn you that what I did to your arm I can do to just about any part of you.'

Jonah didn't like the way she was looking him up and down. 'I wouldn't want to upset a potential employer, would I?' he said, hoping she actually bought his story about running out on Coldhardt.

'So,' she said, moving closer, her eyes fixed on him. 'You would like to please me?'

'If you're happy, I'm happy.'

'You're, what – seventeen? Eighteen?'

'Eighteen, last December.'

'And yet so highly-skilled, and pleasing to the eye. Yes, I may have need of someone like you, Jonah.' Standing right in front of him, a predatory look in her eyes, she wiped a finger over the plate that had held the steak and licked it – just as there was a bang at the door. 'How very tedious.' Her black bob swung glossily as she turned to the door. 'Xavier? Who is it?'

'Kabacra,' he reported.

'I want to talk,' came a hoarse voice.

Jonah had never imagined feeling overjoyed to have a crazed gun-runner drop in unexpectedly, but right now he felt like punching the air. 'Damn,' he said, acting rueful. 'Just as things were getting interesting.'

'They'll get interesting again, I assure you.' Honor steered him towards the hallway. 'Now, there's a guest bedroom along here. You will stay there, safely out of the way.'

'Couldn't I stay with you, listen in?' he asked casually, lowering the steak from his face. 'I mean, if I'm going to be a part of all this –'

'Trust is earned, Jonah,' she told him, 'not given.'

'Worried I'm going to tell him what Traynor said – that he's not getting what he thinks he is?'

'Actually, no.' She smiled knowingly and opened a door on to a small, plainly furnished room that was just about empty save for a bed, a dresser and a flash stereo. An inner door led to a small en suite bathroom.

Honor switched the stereo on to a local radio station, turning up the volume loud. 'I appreciate how tempting it must be for you to listen in on my business meetings, but that's not going to happen. Not until I'm truly satisfied . . .' She widened her dark eyes, all but licking her lips. 'Satisfied, that is, as to where your loyalties truly lie. Now, make yourself comfortable and enjoy the music. And don't try to turn it down, Jonah –'

'Or you will turn *me* down, right?'

She shut the door behind her and locked it, leaving him with only a soft rock guitar solo for company. He heard the door open faintly, but could catch only a murmur of conversation.

His mouth felt horribly dry, so he went into the en suite. No surprises – just a sink, shower and toilet, all done out in white and chrome. A waterproof radio hung from the shower's housing. Great, he could listen to cheesy old rock songs in here too . . . He ran the basin tap, swilled water around his mouth. *Come on guys, get me out of here!*

Then an idea gripped him. There was a radio mike in Xavier's amulet, right? That had to mean it broadcast on radio waves. Could a regular radio pick up those wavelengths? He grabbed the one in the shower, a flash digital job. Surely there was a chance?

He closed the door to quieten the music. Then he dumped the steak in the sink and pressed the shower radio to his ear, scrolling through the stations. The auto-tune didn't pick up anything, but maybe if he tried it manually . . .

Soon, with a thrill, he caught faint voices. It was Kabacra and Honor. He grinned in disbelief – their voices were carrying from the living room through the front door to where the mike in Xavier's amulet was picking them up and broadcasting them to the little radio!

Jonah kissed the speaker, then pressed it up against his ear. The quality of the sound was terrible, peppered with weird digital whoops and harmonics. But he could just make out what was being said, and thanked God it wasn't in Spanish.

'. . . the demonstration was very convincing.' Kabacra was speaking, and Jonah shuddered to recall that scarred, scary face on the computer screen in Guatemala. 'Now I know how deadly this stuff is, I can think of a dozen groups who would take it – we could name our price. But if Traynor truly imagines he can part-pay me for Cortes's sword with a substitute formula a thousand times weaker . . .'

'Bloody hell,' Jonah breathed. *So that's what he's getting. And he already knows about the stitch-up.*

'Try to see it from Traynor's point of view,' said Honor. 'He sees himself as the instrument of Coatlicue's vengeance – and the power of life and death on such a scale certainly makes him godlike. He's not going to hand it over to just anyone – particularly someone like you.'

'That's why you must get me a sample yourself,' said Kabacra menacingly. 'That weak junk Traynor's trying to foist on me is no better than most other products on the market. We'll get a fraction of the cash we could get for the real thing.'

'Bloody, *bloody* hell.' Jonah felt sick. The latest in biological weapons, to be used on God knew how many people, and all so Traynor could stage the last part of the prophecy – *Then Coatlicue will arise from her temple and feast on the poison in men.*

'I can't simply ask him to hand over samples of cutting edge bio-weapons, can I!' Honor protested. 'What use would I have for them? I'm supposed to be Traynor's priestess, supposed to accept all that trippy garbage he spouts!'

Tye was right, Jonah realised, remembering her last words to him. *She doesn't believe like he does.*

'He honestly thinks he's going to find the spirit of Coatlicue in that temple,' she went on. 'Once he thinks Coatlicue has blessed the phials of the biological agent, he will give them to his priests to disperse. I will give you their intended destinations, and you can send someone out to the closest location and intercept the delivery. *Then* you will have your sample.'

'I had better . . .' A pause. 'You know, I really don't understand you, Honor. You stand to make a phenomenal amount of money from the treasures in that temple. Why seek to make a deal with me on top of that?'

'Because I have invested three years of my life getting this close to Traynor and Sixth Sun,' she said curtly. 'I do believe the temple will contain priceless treasures as they all maintain, but if something goes wrong – if we can't raise it, if it's been ransacked or whatever else – I am *not* coming out of this affair a loser.' Another pause. 'I will take a cut of your profits from the sale of the full-strength bio-weapons as willingly as I'll take Traynor's treasure.'

Through the digital static, Jonah heard the sneer in Kabacra's voice. 'You're a greedy bitch.'

'Oh, yes. But one who takes sensible precautions.'

'So what happens to Traynor?'

'When the temple is exposed and the treasures transported to a place of safety, I shall have no further use for him. He'll probably be quite insane by then in any case, once he realises his deluded dreams have come to nothing . . . that not even the deaths of millions of Europeans can wake up this ludicrous "presence" of his. I'll make sure he meets with an accident before the authorities can track him down, along with his pathetic followers. And those riches in the temple will be mine.'

'Yours alone?' Kabraca said quietly. 'Or perhaps you would consider sharing?'

The conversation stopped. Jonah jammed the radio harder against his ear.

Kabacra spoke again, his voice hardening. 'Don't look at me like that. Without me, Traynor's plans would have come to nothing – and nor would your dreams of wealth. *I* sold Cortes's sword to Traynor so he could play at talking to gods. *I* located and acquired the plutonium needed to make that bomb.'

'So you could get your hands on the agent,' she retorted. 'Traynor could have got the fissile material from anywhere.'

'What if I was to tell Traynor the true reason you involved yourself in his affairs? That you are a tawdry con-woman?'

'Ah. So the gun-runner thinks he can blackmail me.'

He seemed to think exactly that. 'When I tell Traynor your plans, show him how many broke and broken men you have left in your wake . . . what will he think of his high priestess then? And how might he reward me for protecting him?'

Jonah was wide-eyed, but Honor sounded unruffled. 'You'd have to move quickly.'

'I could confront him tonight. You and I have been working together for some time. Long enough for me to compile plenty of evidence.'

'Are you sure it's still in your possession? Coldhardt's operatives got hold of your client list – presumably when they came to call on you in Guatemala.'

'Impossible,' Kabacra hissed.

'I know it for a fact,' she went on, cool as ever. 'Three of Coldhardt's agents are our prisoners.'

'Then I will kill them.'

'*I* shall sell them back to Coldhardt – or to the highest bidder.' She paused. 'After all, I'll need the extra funds, won't I – if I'm to share Coatlicue's treasures with you?'

Jonah imagined he could hear Kabacra's creepy smile spreading through the static. 'A wise decision, high priestess. Very wise.'

'Let's drink to it, shall we?'

Jonah heard the chink of glasses and lowered the radio from his ear, his head crowded with thoughts and fears. He'd come here to try to get his friends back from a dangerous bunch of fanatics in fancy dress. Now he found himself caught up in some mad world where homemade nuclear bombs would awaken ancient Mexican deities, where biological weapons were primed to poison the water supplies of who-knew-how many cities . . .

His head began to spin, panic rose up inside him. Millions of people could die, and he was the only one who knew. What the hell was he going to do about it? He was in way over his head. This couldn't be happening, *no way* could this be happening –

Suddenly Jonah felt his guts turn, and saliva flood his mouth. He dropped the radio, lifted the lid of the toilet and threw up. His throat burned, his cheek felt like it might burst with the pressure.

Then the stereo in the room outside shut off and the door pushed open. With a spasm of fear, he saw Honor standing in the doorway.

'What's wrong with you?' she demanded.

'Don't know.' Jonah flushed the toilet, wiped his mouth on a towel. He didn't even want to look at her. 'Something I ate maybe.'

'Well, pull yourself together,' she snapped. 'It's time you earned a little trust. Prove yourself now and I'll allow you to join us on our expedition tomorrow.'

'Has Kabacra gone?' Jonah asked.

'Come through to the living room,' she said.

Jonah followed her a little unsteadily, breathing deeply. He soon saw Kabacra was still here.

On the floor. Dead.

The arms dealer's swollen tongue lolled out of his frothing mouth. His eyes were staring, wide and sightless. Thin yellow bile seeped along the scars that scored his face from lips to ears. A glass, empty and cracked, was clutched in one hand.

'Take a good, long look, Jonah,' said Honor softly. 'And don't ever dream you can betray me.'

Jonah looked between the tall, bony woman and

the corpse of the man she had poisoned. Then he pelted back to the bathroom to be sick again, half wishing it was him lying on the floor, out of the game for good.

CHAPTER EIGHTEEN

Patch was feeling the strain in his makeshift cell, jumping every time a sound carried down the corridor to the little storeroom he was locked in. How long did he have? While Tye was needed to keep Ramez happy, and while Jonah was convincing Sixth Sun that they couldn't get by without him, Patch guessed that Traynor thought of him as just a little kid whose only use now was as a corpse to send to Coldhardt if the big man got too close.

Naturally, Patch had decided not to tell these spooky sods about his talents – they'd either leave a dozen guards outside his door, or else kill him right now before he could cause any bother. So here he was, jammed into the narrow space of the storeroom.

There wasn't much to do in here. Facing him was a row of filing cabinets and a long shelf packed with dusty old books about Aztec history. He'd checked for any dirty mags salted away between volumes – you never knew, after all – but no, there was nothing of interest anywhere.

Finding another use for his hands, at least he'd managed to convert two paper clips into a set of makeshift picks. But there was no chance of him using them on the main door – the key had been left in the lock on the other side, and anyway the tumblers were too big to be budged by something so flimsy.

So he was picking the locks on each of the filing cabinets in turn to see if there was anything he might use there instead.

The first one was stuffed full of old newspaper clippings about archaeologists in Mexico exploring the highlands, the lowlands – probably the in-between lands while they were at it. The second cabinet was stuffed with hanging files. Patch took one out and sorted through it. Just photos of jungle and stuff. He ditched it, picked up another, marked TEMPLE. That looked more promising. But there were only a few photocopied drawings inside, in a weird, old-fashioned style. One showed a step-pyramid surrounded by skulls. Another showed a big snake-headed figure, like Coldhardt's statuette, standing in-between two pillars. Thirteen circles hovered around the figure's clawed feet, evenly spaced. God knew what they were supposed to represent.

With a shrug he folded all the papers together and stuffed them in his back pocket. Then he sorted through a few more folders full of archaeological reports and more newspaper clippings, until he found a file marked SURROUNDING AREA. Sounded a winner. Patch opened the flap and started to flick listlessly through the black and white photographs inside. Jungle. Mountainsides.

Then, a few pictures in, he stopped dead. 'Bleedin' hell!' he breathed, pulling it out and studying it closely.

That clinched it. Now he *had* to get out of here.

Frantically he rooted through the rest of the cabinet's contents. There had to be something he could use to poke the key out and pick the lock. Then he realised that about a dozen candidates were staring him in the face – the hanging files themselves. Each card wallet was edged with thin metal strips.

Quickly Patch tore one away. Either end of the strip was hooked so it hung snugly from the chrome runners. It would make a pretty good pick and would be strong enough to poke out the key so he could –

'Dummy,' he muttered. Why make life hard for himself? He crossed to the door, listened hard to check no one was waiting outside, then folded the vandalised card wallet flat and slid it partway under the door. With the metal strip, he poked about until the key was indeed nudged clear; it fell from the lock and landed on the card. Then he slid the card back under the door towards him, and the key came with it.

Patch smiled and squeezed the key tight in his hand. As tricks went it was olden but golden.

The key turned smoothly, and the door opened without a sound. Patch slid the photo up his top, closed the door and locked it behind him. Hopefully no one would call in to offer him a bog-break or whatever. At least, not till he was miles from here.

He paused in the roomy corridor. There was a window at the far end, he could maybe open it and slip outside. But what about Tye and Jonah? He couldn't leave them behind. If all three of them escaped they could call Coldhardt, tell him all they'd discovered, hide out some place until they were picked up . . .

Tye had been taken upstairs. Patch decided he'd try to find her first.

Cautiously, his heart banging away, he crept through the house. There was no one about. Maybe everyone was still sat inside that creepy room. Maybe they were all dancing about naked and painting each other funny colours, or practising their sacrifice moves.

Patch ran up the stairs, one hand pressing against the photo through his top, grateful that the deep pile carpet muffled his footfalls. After a minute or two spent checking various doors, he found a locked room. The key was in the lock. He turned it quietly and peered inside.

Bang on. There was Tye, lying asleep on a leather couch. That Ramez bloke was here too, crashed out on the floor beside a table loaded with grub – roast chicken, burgers, crisps and champagne. Patch eyed it hungrily, realised he was starving. But first things first.

'Tye?' he whispered, and gently touched the side of her face. 'Tye, it's me, Patch. Wake up, yeah? You're never gonna guess what I've found out . . .'

She didn't stir. Something was wrong. He crossed to where Ramez lay and nudged him none-too-gently with his foot. But Ramez didn't react either. Returning to Tye, he used his thumb to open one of her eyelids. Her pupil was barely more than a pinprick.

Patch looked over at the table piled high with booze and grub and swore. 'Drugged.' He stared round the room, trying not to panic. How could he get her out of here now?

The simple answer was – he couldn't.

'I'll be back. I'll get help,' he told Tye softly, taking her hand. 'If you stick with Ramez you'll be safe. They need him, don't they – and he needs you.' He squeezed her fingers. 'We *all* need you, Tye. We really do.'

Suddenly Patch started at a distant round of applause drifting from downstairs. Sounded like the meeting was about ready to break up – which meant it was time for him to break *out*. He'd be no help to anyone if he got himself caught again. Wielding his improvised picks, he blew Tye a kiss and slipped from the room, looking for a back way out of this dump.

It was shaping up to be a really top night, Jonah decided. *First I get beaten to a pulp, then I find out Sixth Sun's whacko plan, and now I'm off to dump a dead body in the great American wilderness.*

There were times when he looked back on his months in the Young Offenders Institution and felt homesick.

Xavier was driving the limo along Highway 24. Still not trusted, Jonah was locked in the back with only Kabacra's corpse for company. The dealer had been wrapped up in black plastic bin liners. Jonah tried not to look at the swaddled figure, glistening in the orange light from the streetlamps that spilled in through the tinted windows.

He leaned forward and banged on the partition between front and back. Xavier slid open a small window. 'What is it now?'

'We're just passing Manitou Springs, right?' he said casually.

'You can read the signs,' Xavier retorted.

'We're heading west though, right? Where are we making for?'

'What's it matter to you?'

'Guess it doesn't.' *Apart from the fact I'm desperately trying to get any clues as to where I am across to Motti and Con, who might still be listening in to this conversation.* 'And it sure as hell don't matter to Kabacra. Doesn't it worry you that Honor had him killed, just like that?'

'He was trying to betray us. Wanted to get his hands on the goddess's treasure.'

'That's all Honor told you?' He supposed the mike's 'ears' were a lot more sensitive than its wearer's. 'How much do you even know about her, anyway?'

'Just shut your mouth,' Xavier growled.

Just open your eyes! he wanted to yell. *Where will you be dropping Traynor's poison? How many people are you going to kill just because your crazy leader tells you to?* But he couldn't give away what he'd found out. That could get him killed right now.

'All right, we're nearly there,' Xavier announced. 'Waldo Canyon. Plenty of side trails we can dump a body. No one'll find him for weeks. Months, maybe.'

Jonah sighed. 'I don't suppose anyone will be calling the cops when he doesn't come home tonight.'

'Just like no one will be calling them if you go missing either,' said Xavier menacingly as he took the exit road from the highway. 'Am I right?'

Jonah didn't reply.

'So no tricks. You try and run, I'll cripple you. Got it?'

'Loud and clear,' Jonah muttered. 'What's your day job, Xavier? I mean, what do you do when you're not running about in a black mask or burying murder victims?'

'I'm studying for a masters in Mesoamerican languages.'

'Bit of a weird fit, isn't it?'

'You could never understand,' Xavier sneered. 'We're only doing what we must. We are the chosen ones whose coming the old priests foretold.'

'Right. 'Course you are.' Jonah rubbed his eyes wearily. 'So, Waldo Canyon, car park six, west side. A limo's not going to stand out here at all in the middle of the night, is it?'

'No one's gonna come looking,' Xavier told him flatly.

He parked the car and Jonah got out. The moon was bright and clear, but its silvery light only seemed to make the tree-busy landscape more sinister. The night was cold, but not as cold as the thick black plastic shrouding Kabacra. Already rigor mortis was setting in, his limbs were getting harder to shift. While Xavier took a couple of shovels from the trunk, Jonah found himself having to carry the body over his shoulder, unaided.

Shining a powerful torch, Xavier soon headed off the main track and pushed through bushes and bracken over uneven ground. Jonah stumbled often, almost dropping the body several times. After fifteen minutes he grew so hot and tired that he started to drag the body behind him, desensitised to the horror of the situation now, just wanting to get this over and done with. All he could think of was how many corpses there'd be when the chemical agents were released into water supplies around the world. And why – just so Traynor could show off to his imaginary friend in the temple?

It was all so insane, obscene, and here he was, caught up at the heart of it. What if he just ran, tried to reach a phone and call Coldhardt? Yeah, and get totally lost and probably die of exposure while Sixth Sun got on with their plans for mass murder – good one. No, if he proved himself, tagged along tomorrow, maybe he'd find the opportunity to do *something* about –

'Hold it,' Xavier announced suddenly behind him, switching off the torch. 'I think I heard something.'

Jonah dumped Kabacra's body and strained to listen. But he couldn't hear anything beyond the rattle of branches in the wind and his own ragged breathing. The sound of the highway had droned distantly in the first part of the hike, but now it felt like they were in the middle of nowhere.

Then the sound of a snapping twig cracked out like a pistol shot.

'Someone's there,' Xavier warned in a low voice. He threw down the shovel and pulled a gun from his pocket.

'Probably an animal,' Jonah suggested, a bone-hard fear forming in his chest. *Please, no more killing.*

But even as he spoke a sudden, explosive rustling sounded close by, like someone had just kicked a pile of leaves.

'Come out!' Xavier flicked on the torch, shining it

into the undergrowth ahead of him. 'Whoever's there, come out *now*.'

'OK.'

Jonah started. The deep, gruff voice had come from *behind* Xavier – and was quickly followed by the clang of metal hitting something hard. With a fleshy thump, Xavier was suddenly on the floor, poleaxed. In the light of the fallen torch, Jonah could see the trickle of blood seeping down from the man's hairline – and a dark figure crouch over his body.

'Geek, is this the guy who trashed your ass in New Mexico?' Motti wondered. 'He's, like, a total pussy. One whack of the shovel and he's down.'

'Mot!' Jonah rushed forwards and grabbed him in a hug. 'You found me.'

'We were able to pick up the radio mike's signal,' Con said, emerging now from the undergrowth behind him. 'And we received your helpful directions.'

'Yeah, geek, how obvious did you feel like being? How this guy never rumbled you . . .' But while Motti's frown was disapproving, he clapped Jonah on the back warmly. 'Nice bruise, man. Between us we got a real good collection.' Then he checked on Xavier. 'His ain't bad either.'

'Is he OK?'

'Sleeping like a baby. Probably gonna cry like one too when he wakes up with the mother of all headaches.'

Jonah smiled at Con, reaching for her hand. 'How long have you been listening in on that mike?'

'We got everything till you left Traynor's place,' she said, and kissed his fingers. 'Then we lost you.'

'We've been driving around for hours,' Motti went on. 'Managed to pick you up again when you were on the highway.'

Con looked pointedly at Motti. 'Good thing I made you stop for that filet-o-fish outside Manitou, yes?'

'So what the hell were you doing out here, man?' asked Motti, looking warily at the black plastic bundle on the ground. 'What's that?'

'One very dead arms dealer,' said Jonah. 'Guys, there is some serious stuff kicking off round here and we are way out of our depth. We've got to get Coldhardt on the case right now.'

'We ain't spoken to him yet,' Motti admitted. 'Figured if he knew that tomorrow was the big day he might drag us back before we could get to you and the others.'

'What is it, Jonah?' Con wondered. 'You look scared.'

'Terrified more like.' He picked up the discarded torch. 'I'll explain on the way back to the car.' He started off through the bracken – then stopped again. 'Uh . . . which way *is* the way back?'

'Jonah Wish, last action hero,' said Motti drily, setting off after Con, who was already sauntering elegantly along a narrow track through the overgrown wilderness. 'Get spilling those guts, geek – and let's move.'

So Jonah told them his story. The cold and claustrophobic woods around them did nothing to ease the mood of fear and unease.

'You think this Honor chick was on the level?'

Motti wondered as they reached the main track at last.

'She's a power-mad bitch,' Jonah told him.

'She doesn't sound so bad,' said Con. 'I could probably learn a trick or two from her.'

'Yeah, she makes you seem totally warm and cuddly. I know Kabacra was no saint, but to poison him just like that –'

'He got what he deserved,' said Con flatly. 'As for the rest of this business, I say we keep out of it.'

'And stick to bottled water,' quipped Motti darkly.

Jonah stared at them. 'But we're the only ones who stand even the slightest chance of stopping this from happening!'

'We are thieves, yes?' Con reminded him. 'Not do-gooders.'

'We're *people*.' Jonah looked at Motti. 'What do you think we should do?'

Motti shrugged as he strode along. 'Maybe Con's right. Sounds like one for the cops, man.'

'What do we do?' said Jonah. 'Call them up and tell them to stake out a temple hidden somewhere in Mexico on the offchance they run into these maniacs? And what about Tye and Patch? How do we get them –?'

Suddenly, Motti stopped mid-stride, yanked his buzzing cell phone from his trouser pocket and flipped up the receiver. 'Lousy coverage out here. Someone called. I gotta message.'

'Coldhardt?' Con wondered.

Jonah saw Motti's eyes widen as he listened. 'Jeez, it's Patch! Calling from a payphone.'

Jonah gripped his arm. 'What's he say?'

'Dunno, it's all garbled. He was panting so damned hard it was more like a phone-sex chatline.' Motti was already working the backlit buttons. 'C'mon, gimme the last number registered. You better not have shifted your skinny ass from there, cyclops, or I'll whup it.'

Jonah waited tensely as Motti called back the payphone on speaker. Someone picked up almost immediately. 'Motti, that you?'

'Patch!' Con cheered.

'Is Tye with you?' Jonah said at the same time.

Motti shushed them both. 'Patch, where are you, man?'

'I dunno. Hiding somewhere off Highway 24. I've been running for ever.'

'We can trace the number of the call box,' Con pointed out practically.

'OK, man, we're coming to get you,' said Motti, stumbling off again down the track. Jonah and Con followed him, picking up the pace. 'Where's Tye?'

'Well out of it. Her and Ramez have been drugged. Guess Traynor wanted to make sure they didn't try nothing ahead of the big day.' Suddenly they heard the roar of a car passing by – then silence.

'Patch?' said Motti urgently, tapping his phone. 'You there?'

'I'm scared to death,' he said quietly. 'Come and get me out of here, will ya? If they find out I've got away, they might not be bothered about bringing me back alive. And you ain't gonna believe what I've got to show you. Pictures of that temple and . . . something *amazing*.'

'Just tell us, OK? We ain't in the mood for games.'

'You know the hidden symbol thing on the statue – the egg with the four trees?'

'What about it?' Con asked, ducking under a low-hanging branch.

'It's not an egg. It's a bloody great big rock.'

Jonah and Con stared at each other. 'What?'

'I've got a photo of it, from one of Sixth Sun's geography surveys,' Patch insisted. 'There's only three trees, but there's the stump of another, it's fallen down. And this rock is enormous, like a giant rugby ball. It's the place in the pictogram!'

'But the other pictograms had encrypted meanings,' protested Jonah, his mind wrestling with the revelation. 'They had to be translated.'

'But the hidden pictogram needed translating too, right?' Motti pointed out. 'All those little lines had to be *visually* translated, rearranged to make the picture.'

'And I'm sure the other two pictures give clues to combined words in Nahuatl,' said Con. '*Secretly cacao.*'

'Then those trees in the hidden pictogram must represent cacao trees,' Jonah breathed. 'And the big rock marks the secret spot where the temple is hidden.'

'There's letters and numbers on the back of the photo,' Patch informed them. 'Might be another code.'

'More likely a map reference,' said Motti. He stopped still and stared in disbelief at Jonah and Con. 'We found the temple. Jeez, guys – we found the god-damned temple!'

'Oi!' Patch complained, his voice sounding tinny

and small over the phone's speakers. 'Come and find *me*, you sods!'

'We'll phone again when we get there,' said Jonah, leading the way now along the track. 'And once we've picked him up and seen what he's got, we must get through to Coldhardt.'

'And get our heads round some kind of plan,' Motti agreed, switching off his cell phone.

'Before the earth shakes the sun from the sky and Coatlicue feasts on the poison in men,' said Con, rubbing at something on her wrist. 'And before I get any more scratches from this stupid bracken – yes?'

CHAPTER NINETEEN

Jonah, Motti, Con and Patch were back in the motel room outside Florissant, gathered round the laptop. Jonah rubbed his eyes and glanced out the window. The dawn was dropping hints it might break soon: slivers of grey scratched the darkness and birds began to sing with sickening cheer.

A digitised image of Coldhardt sat looking out at them from a window on the monitor. Once they'd grabbed Patch and got the hell away they'd come straight back here to talk to the boss man. Patch was holding up his photo of the Mexican landscape to the webcam like a trophy, so Coldhardt could see the resemblance for himself. Taken in conjunction with Con's straightforward translation of the other two symbols, Jonah was definitely convinced.

'Thank you, Patch,' Coldhardt said quietly. 'On several Aztec depictions of the Earth's creation, the cacao tree is shown in a key position. It makes sense that the priests and their architects would bury their temple in soil rich in the roots of cacao – a goddess once gorged with human blood would instead be nurtured with the blood of the earth.'

'"Cacao secretly",' Con murmured, looking pleased

with herself.

'And what about these pix of the temple?' said Patch, holding up some crumpled photocopies. 'Look, this statue's like yours.'

'A much larger effigy of Coatlicue, I should think,' ventured Coldhardt. 'Presumably the focus for the temple rituals.'

'What are those circles round her feet?' Con wondered.

'I don't know.' The gleam in the old man's eyes was clear even over a webcam. 'Perhaps we'll have more of an idea when we see them with our own eyes – inside the temple.'

'What about Honor Albrecht?' Jonah asked quickly. 'Have you got anything on her?'

'I know of her by reputation – specialises in long-term cons with big payoffs. No true allegiance to anyone but herself, prefers to target and infiltrate wealthy extremist groups.'

Jonah nodded gloomily. 'At least she's only after the treasure.'

'Isn't that enough!' Con looked appalled. 'We've got to stop her.'

'And get Tye back,' Patch chipped in.

'I imagine Tye will be going to the temple with Ramez – the boy will want her with him to the end.' Coldhardt considered. 'Traynor is set on doing things properly at all costs. In his mind it's the only way to truly appease Coatlicue. So he presents her with a perfect sacrifice, groomed in the spirit of the old traditions. He brings Cortes's sword along so he can "wipe it clean" before her. And he's ready to poison millions of Western people just as they poisoned the Aztecs by bringing their diseases into Mexico.'

'In other words, Traynor is completely mad,' said Jonah flatly.

Con seemed puzzled. 'But surely the authorities will work out the formula of this biological agent and trace it back to Traynor's weapons plant, no?'

Coldhardt shrugged. 'Perhaps he imagines that Coatlicue's powers will have placed him above human governing by then.'

'Or perhaps in the short term he's covering his tracks,' said Jonah. 'Kabacra said he was getting a weak version of the biological agent as part-payment. Maybe Traynor has been mixing up different versions of the stuff and getting it on the market so it doesn't seem like it came from his labs.'

'S'pose he'd have to,' Patch agreed. 'After all, it's gonna take time to set himself up as the big leader of a whole new age for the human race, innit? Even with a goddess on his side.'

Coldhardt was looking thoughtful. 'Whatever he believes, whatever he and Honor hope to achieve, the fact remains that they now possess the means to raise the Temple of Life from Death from beneath the cacao grove – and that they will do so tomorrow.'

'And now we know where it is,' said Con, her eyes glittering, 'we can get there first.'

'Great,' sighed Patch. 'I always wanted to feel a nuclear bomb go off under my feet.'

Con rolled her eyes. 'Nuclear weapons are tested underground all the time.'

Jonah frowned. 'What, and we're supposed to feel

good about that?'

'This bomb's been prepared by an expert,' Motti pointed out, like this was also in some way reassuring. 'Sixth Sun aren't about to blow themselves up, are they? They gotta know what they're doing.'

'They're about to try and communicate with some ancient spirit they reckon influenced the entire Mesoamerican race,' said Jonah angrily. 'You think that sounds like they know what they're doing?'

'It shall be interesting to see,' said Coldhardt, quietly but in a way that riveted all four of them to his image on the monitor. 'Jonah, I want the four of you to fly out to Mexico as soon as we've confirmed that the map reference given on the back of Patch's picture does indeed mark the location of the cacao grove. I shall charter a plane and make my own way there. Con is correct – if we move quickly we should just reach the area ahead of them.'

'And then what?' said Jonah. 'Try to take control of the situation?'

Coldhardt leaned back in his chair and steepled his fingers. 'Oh, I shall most definitely aim to do that.'

The morning was growing humid, and Tye pulled listlessly at the neck of her blouse. They had been trekking through the Mexican jungle for less than an hour, but already her clothes felt sodden.

Not that she was sweating purely from the heat.

Beside her, Ramez trudged on in compliant silence, his white shirt open to the navel, his dark eyes sunken. He had eaten and drunk way more of the spiked supper than she had last night. And since this morning she was feeling like death warmed up as a result, *he* must be –

No, she thought. *Stop right there with the 'death' stuff.*

Traynor and Honor were leading their priests on the trek – a pasty, motley bunch they looked, without their make-up and costume and sympathetic light. The men who'd guarded her and Patch were coping with the hike pretty well – one of them was carrying Cortes's sword in a mahogany case on his back – and of course the two penthouse bruisers remained as strong and silent as ever, dressed now in light khaki and carrying a heavy-looking flight case between them. But the rest of the Sixth Sun elite – with their baggy shorts, skinny white legs, pot-bellies and huge sweat rings under their arms – looked more like a gang of pensioners off on their holidays than vicious extremists aiming to awaken dark and ancient forces. They'd even come here from the airport in an ancient hire coach, badly driven by one of the professor types. Tye supposed that a couple of swish Chrysler or Merc people carriers could have attracted attention, making their way along the winding roads into the remote jungle wilderness – but who would look twice at yet another coachload of foreigners on vacation?

Ramez grunted as he slipped and lost his footing. He fell, and his bad leg twisted beneath him.

Tye helped him up, ignoring the dull throb from the cut in her side. Luckily it was feeling a lot better. 'You OK?'

'I'll live,' he said dully. 'Well. You know what I mean.'

Tye saw the bitterness in his eyes and looked away.

She wished she had words of comfort to give him. All she could hope was that Jonah had somehow managed to escape. His not being here, the tight-lipped look about Honor this morning, and the gruesome bruise on the side of Xavier's head all gave her hope that he had made his break. As for Patch, she prayed that he was still being held back at the mansion. But no one was giving anything away.

Traynor pulled a portable sat-nav device from the breast pocket of his white cotton shirt and shielded its screen against the glare of the climbing sun. 'All right, everybody, wait up,' he drawled. 'The entrance to the underground shaft is close by. Time to prepare our own personal earthquake.'

Tye stared at him. 'What are you talking about?'

'The temple was designed to be raised up in response to seismic disturbance,' he told her. 'The radioactive waste we stole has been converted into a small, precisely measured nuclear device.'

Now she looked again at the flight case the bodyguards had hauled here. 'You so have to be kidding me,' she breathed.

'The moment our surveys located a natural shaft in the rock, I got moving,' Traynor went on. 'Rungs have been set in the rock face. There are platforms for rest during the descent and the ascent. The materials required to backfill the fissure to prevent radioactive contamination are in place.' He smiled at the penthouse bodyguards. 'My friends here shall carry the device down, and I shall set it myself.'

'That's so comforting,' said Tye, burying her face in both hands.

Jonah wiped the sweat from his face as he followed Coldhardt and the others deeper into the Chicomoztoc rainforest. A guide, hastily picked up by Con from one of the outlying villages, had taken them as far as the outskirts of this near-deserted region. From there they'd been hiking for hours.

The forest was alive with insects and spiders and weird, screeching things. Jonah wondered just how poisonous everything was, how quickly he might die if he was bitten. It helped distract him from the heat and his aching legs, but did little to calm the queasiness he felt inside.

Coldhardt, looking dapper in a pale linen suit, was letting Motti lead the way. Mot was using a relief map and compass to navigate through the jungle and seemed to be in his element; Jonah had never had him down for the orienteering type, but aside from having to stop every few hundred metres so he could wipe moisture from his glasses, so far he had guided them unerringly. And a good job too. Coldhardt was making out that the journey was taking no toll on him, but Jonah could see the sweat beading on his lined and haggard face.

Patch was taking up the rear behind Jonah and Con, chiefly because he kept stopping to fiddle with the portable FM receiver round his neck. The plan was that by listening in on Xavier's radio mike – always assuming he'd recovered in time to go on the expedition – they could be sure not to bump into the Sixth Sun party unexpectedly.

'Anything, Patch?' Jonah wondered.

'Sod all,' Patch admitted. 'Suppose they can't be in range.'

'Perfectly possible. There are many airstrips in this part of Mexico,' Con reminded them. 'And many approaches to this region.'

'By making straight for the site of the temple we should be safe regardless,' Coldhardt reasoned, an unsettling wheeze in his breath. 'Traynor will need to go to the detonation site first so the shockwaves can trigger the temple's lifting mechanism. That site's probably a fair distance away for safety reasons. And once the temple is exhumed, while he and his priests are making their way over, we'll be perfectly placed to get inside first.'

'With the perfect chance to steal the finest treasures for ourselves,' said Con.

Jonah sighed and shook his head.

'Thinking of those millions who may die, Jonah?' she asked coolly.

'Fancy you remembering that.'

'Rest assured, Jonah,' said Coldhardt, dabbing at his forehead with his silk handkerchief, 'that I intend to pay the very closest attention to Traynor's ritual.'

Jonah thought of the cold, empty vault hidden beneath the New Mexican hideout, of the altar it housed, of Coldhardt's fading hopes of redemption. 'Yeah,' he muttered. 'I bet you do.'

'Heads up, people,' called Motti from the lip of a rise, satisfaction in his voice. 'We're getting closer. And whaddya know, I think "eggs" marks the spot.'

Jonah trailed along behind the others to join him. With a tingle of unease mixed with anticipation, he saw that they were overlooking the site in the photo – the grove of ancient cacao trees, with the vast, pitted oval of sandstone squatting in its centre. It had entered his mind as a fragment of some ancient puzzle, and now here it was, an undeniable chunk of reality right there in front of his eyes.

It was an unsettling feeling.

'How far away is it now?' Con wondered.

'Can't be much more than a mile,' Motti reported.

'So, what – we make our way down there and wait for the earth to move?' Patch ventured.

Coldhardt nodded. 'We must be ready. Come on.' Pushing past Motti, he started gamely picking his way down the steep slope towards the temple site.

With a shrug to the others, Jonah began his own descent into the valley, Con, Patch and Motti close behind.

Tye sat with Ramez on an outcrop of rock, guarded by the penthouse meatheads. Ramez didn't want to talk. She tried to hold his hand but he didn't react – it was like squeezing a mannequin's fingers, cold and dead to her touch. He'd been like this all afternoon, retreated into himself, gone some place no one else could reach him.

Tye wished she could just opt out too. But she knew she had to be ready to take advantage of the slightest distraction. She had to try and get Ramez away from there whatever it took – not just to save his life but to stop Traynor's plans from working out.

She had to admit, though, that for all their unlikely appearance, the Sixth Sun priests were proving a formidable workforce, even in the thick plastic hazard suits they'd brought along. They laboured in teams in strict rotation, drinking to keep hydrated and resting often to keep themselves fresh for the next shift. They were moving tons of sand and gypsum and gravel, sealing off the shaft in the rock. Tye supposed that they wouldn't dare to pollute their goddess's homeland.

The fitter ones like Xavier and red-mouth were doing more of course – but unfortunately, they also kept taking turns with the penthouse bruisers to guard Tye and Ramez. If the old professor and pot-bellied Douglas were watching over them it would be child's play to take them and get the hell out. Then again, even if she could get Ramez to help her – with his bad leg, how far would they get?

Her heart sank further as Traynor's triumphant face appeared from out of the fissure. 'The device is in position, and the shaft is almost stemmed,' he reported. 'Soon we shall be ready to detonate.'

Those sitting round launched into spontaneous applause. Traynor climbed out, high-fived Honor and gave her a brief embrace. Tye noted how rigidly the woman held herself.

'She hates you, Traynor,' she called as the clapping died down. 'You knew that, right?'

Honor glanced over blandly, her black hair plastered to her forehead with sweat; she had been working too. 'What are you talking about?'

'It's in the way you stiffen up when he's about. The way you can barely make eye contact with him. The way you cross your arms whenever he talks to you.'

She shrugged. 'I'm useful to Coldhardt because I can read people. And stuff like that will give you away every time.'

Traynor smiled and shook his head. 'Is this the best plan you've been able to come up with? Trying to cause a rift between us?'

'I'm just telling you –'

'Well, let me tell you something. When we've splashed your boyfriend's blood over the sacred stones and smeared his fresh-cut heart over the deity's face, we're going to have some *real* fun with you.' Traynor grinned at her. 'You're going to squeal like a piggy, little girl.'

'We'll see,' Tye said, glaring defiantly. She was good at hiding her fear. But seconds later, as she looked away, unable to bear those staring blue eyes a moment longer, she knew with crushing certainty that she wasn't good enough.

Jonah was slumped in the cacao grove, waiting for something to happen. Coldhardt was pacing slowly up and down, while Con and Motti took turns listening into the radio receiver.

''Course,' Patch reflected, perched up on top of the big oval boulder, 'if Traynor has got his nuclear sums wrong, or if these Aztecs weren't as clever at building as they thought they were, this temple's gonna stay buried below ground and we're all going to feel pretty stupid.'

'I can live with feeling stupid,' said Jonah.

'The mechanism will work,' muttered Coldhardt. He wasn't looking so good now, dabbing at his sweaty face with a wet handkerchief. 'It *must*. We have to get inside.'

And then, just as he spoke, the ground shook like a hundred giants were stamping their feet.

The power of the tremor was incredible. Patch yelled as he was thrown clear of the huge rock and landed face first in the tangled undergrowth. Jonah tried scrambling over to help him up, but it was like the ground itself was billowing in some subterranean gale; he couldn't stay upright. Thrown on to his back, shaken so hard his teeth rattled, he couldn't make sense of the picture perfect blue sky above; he felt it should seem ashen and black, like some terrible storm was breaking over them.

Con was clinging on to one of the cacao trees, and screamed as it started to uproot itself. Motti was rolling helplessly about like a drunk, clutching hold of the radio equipment. Where was Coldhardt?

Then the tremor passed as swiftly as it had begun. Coldhardt was right beside him, helping him up – and Patch was staring round in a daze.

'I can feel something,' Motti said. 'Ground's still shifting.'

Con stared round as if expecting something to jump out of the ground beside her. 'It's different to that last tremor.'

'Get over here,' Coldhardt snapped. 'Now!'

'Uh-oh.' Jonah looked at him. 'The temple mechanism –?'

Then he was shaken to his knees as something huge pierced the overgrown surface of the wild, tangled grove. It was a great stone arrowhead, caked in mud, pushing up through the ground. Motti and Con sprinted away from it, but the ground bucked beneath them and they fell. Jonah staggered forwards, grabbed hold of Con and hauled her back to her feet – in time to be knocked back off his. Together they scrambled away on all fours, clawing at the grass. Jonah saw Motti was making better progress, swearing as fast as he ran for cover.

The temple was still rising up, the noise was growing in volume, a grating, grinding, primeval roar from deep beneath the ground. Jonah cried out as the forest floor began to ripple and fold, like a great, grassy rug being pulled from under him. He was flung forwards, but there was nothing to fall against, the ground had fallen away and he was pitching through empty space . . .

He gasped as he hit a bank of mud heaved up from the colossal split in the earth and found himself tumbling down helplessly in a landslide. Pebbles showered over him, mud filled his mouth and got in his eyes so he couldn't see. Where was Con? *Please God don't let me be smothered*, he thought. He heard the creaking, thundering smash of trees toppling close by – *and don't let me be crushed* – and wiped the dirt from his face.

Just in time to see a tidal wave of mud and vegetation ploughing towards him.

CHAPTER TWENTY

Jonah didn't even have time to shout.

Desperately he ran for the nearest tree still standing, jumped up, grabbed for its thick, gnarled branches, and tried to haul himself up out of range. As the mudslide hit, the tree shook so hard it almost hurled him clear – but just, barely, Jonah managed to hold on.

Finally, with an ear-splitting, bone-grinding crash, the world stopped shaking and the landscape fell abruptly still. Jonah dropped down from his tree into the dry, pebbly mudbank, panting for breath. 'Guys?' he called hoarsely. 'You OK? Anyone?'

There was only silence in answer.

Tye supposed she should've expected as much – Traynor had got it right.

They'd retreated to a designated place of safety, out of range of the immediate area, he'd set off the bomb remotely, and here they were still in one piece. Apparently, the absence of any kind of sunken depression at ground level was good news – it meant the land vaporised in the explosion hadn't reached as far as the surface, that the effect had been contained by all that sand and gravel and stuff. But Honor's binoculars had soon revealed the worst possible news – for Tye and Ramez at any rate. The temple had risen up from the ground.

Ramez didn't react as loud whoops and cheers and applause went up from the rest of the group. Honor just stared, her grin splitting her face wide open. 'Incredible – for the mechanisms to still work after all these centuries . . .'

Traynor flung his arms about her. 'Did you ever doubt it?'

'This can't be happening,' Tye whispered to herself.

'I'm gonna die,' said Ramez dully. 'But 'least my nephews are gonna live. Yeah. They'll be OK.'

Honor looked over, a self-satisfied smile on her pallid face. 'I do hope they don't drink from the tap.'

Tye frowned. 'Meaning?'

'Meaning Coatlicue is going to feast on the poison in men,' said Honor, 'and in women and little children, too.'

Still catching his breath, Jonah stared in awe at the Temple of Life from Death in all its sinister glory, disgorged from deep within the earth. Even half-caked in soil, the dark majesty of the monument remained. Shaped like a pyramid, it stood as tall as a house. Row upon row of gruesome stone skulls had been carved into the base of the pyramid, and above them, steps had been cut into the sloping walls at precise intervals. Each was adorned with stylised stone reliefs of serpents, hummingbirds and jaguars, interspersed with false windows, presumably blocked up to stop the mud getting in.

'Guys!' he called again. *Please let them be all right.* 'You need to see this. Come on out.'

'Remarkable.' Jonah jumped at the sound of Coldhardt's voice behind him. The old man stepped out from behind a broad, twisted cacao tree that stood just clear of the ruptured earth, gazing up in wonder. 'Truly remarkable.'

'One word for it,' Jonah agreed.

Coldhardt gathered up chunks of porous white stone from the mudslide. 'You see? Light, like pumice. Loads of the stuff, packed around the temple with dead branches and plant roots to form a light protective layer – to ensure rainfall drains away swiftly, so that the soil around it isn't weighed down.'

'Easier to push up, I guess,' agreed Jonah, shaking his head in disbelief. 'But that thing's still got to weigh tons! How could a bunch of primitive priests design a mechanism to lift something as big as that?'

Coldhardt's eyes bored into his own. 'Perhaps they had help.'

It felt to Jonah as if a shadow had passed over the sun. 'The presence?'

'It's impressive engineering all right.' Motti had emerged cautiously from the cover of the trees, and Con and Patch were just behind him – muddy and scratched but otherwise unharmed. 'But whoever built it messed up. That boulder they used to mark the spot – it's caved in the south-east corner of the temple.'

Jonah got up to look properly, and saw Motti was right. That corner of the pyramid had risen up right underneath the enormous boulder and, being unable to shift it, the stonework had crazed and collapsed.

'Perhaps it's not a mistake,' said Con slowly. 'Perhaps it was designed that way.'

Coldhardt looked at her expectantly. 'Go on.'

She shrugged. 'Well, the priests must have constructed the temple underground, filling it as they went, yes? And then the temple was sealed up, with no way in – or out. So perhaps the rock wasn't just a marker. Perhaps it was designed to break open the temple as the building rose up.'

'Sort of like a teaspoon cracking open an egg,' said Jonah.

'A giant ten-ton teaspoon cracking an egg shaped like a pyramid,' Motti corrected him.

'Certainly it's been recorded that Coatlicue's attendants sealed themselves inside with their goddess till death,' said Coldhardt, ignoring them both. 'They would doubtless wish to be sure she could leave the temple.'

'Or that the chosen ones the priests thought would come some day could get in,' Jonah suggested.

'Either way, it's an ingenious theory, Con. Let us put it to the test, and see if an opening has appeared.'

Patch hung back, twiddling distractedly with the headphones round his neck. 'Do we have to?'

'Aw, c'mon, cyclops.' Motti affected a bit of a swagger as he led the way over the ridges of mud and debris to get to the temple entrance. 'Where's your sense of adventure?'

Coldhardt turned to Patch. 'Anything on the radio?'

'Don't think it's workin' right. So bleedin' humid

here, I think the circuits have gone a bit funny.' Patch pulled the headphones wonkily on to his head and started twiddling with the muddy radio receiver. 'I dropped it in the mud too, that can't have helped –' Suddenly he jumped and snatched his fingers away as if the dial had bitten him. 'I'm getting something now, though,' he said, his voice high and wavery.

They listened. It was a rustling, crunching sort of noise.

'Footsteps?' ventured Jonah.

'Uh-huh.' Patch nodded. 'Lots of them.'

'Company's on its way,' said Motti grimly.

'How long do we have?' asked Con.

Motti jogged over to the collapsed corner of the temple. 'No way of knowing,' he called back. 'But we're gonna need a while.'

'What's up?' said Patch.

'The designers *did* foul up. That boulder's completely mashed this part of the pyramid.' He pointed to a chunk of broken stonework. 'You can see from the remains of this arch – there *was* an entrance there. But it's totally caved in.'

Coldhardt awkwardly scaled one of the higher furrows in the land to see. 'Can we move the debris ourselves?'

'Don't think so.' Motti gestured towards the jumble of cracked and shattered sandstone. 'Can't see us shifting it without machinery.'

'There has to be another entrance,' said Con desperately.

'What,' Motti retorted, 'you think maybe the priests climbed in through the roof and abseiled down?'

'Check right round the pyramid,' Coldhardt roared, and Jonah and the others hurried to obey. 'I shan't be cheated. I shan't be cheated now!'

Jonah skirted the perimeter, checking for any cracks in the sandstone. The rows of skulls seemed to stare at him as he searched, as if challenging him to find a way inside.

He ran into Con, Patch and Motti at the rear side of the pyramid. From their solemn faces, he didn't even bother to ask if they'd been successful. They trudged back to rejoin Coldhardt.

'No joy,' said Patch. 'How about plastic explosive?'

Coldhardt shook his head. 'Too risky,' he said, a little more controlled now. 'The noise of the explosion would alert Traynor and his followers to our presence here. With the element of surprise, we stand a chance of outwitting them. But if they come in expecting trouble . . .' He flashed a brief, cheerless smile. 'As you may have observed, there are rather more of them than there are of us.'

'Thirteen, minimum,' Jonah agreed.

'Maybe more if they bring the bruisers from the penthouse,' Patch added.

'We've played with worse odds,' said Con defiantly.

Coldhardt dabbed distractedly at his face and neck. 'Of course, so many people stand a far better chance of clearing a way through . . .'

Motti sighed. 'Right. Traynor and his priests will be able to get inside where we can't.'

'Then we can hang back and let them get inside,' Patch said. 'Let them take all the risks –'

'And all the treasure,' Con put in sourly.

'– then follow them inside and sort them all out,' he concluded optimistically.

'What, with three of them for every one of us? We won't stand a chance!' Jonah sank back heavily against the nearest mudpile. 'Maybe we should just face it. Everything we've done, everything we've been through – it's all been for nothing!'

Tye felt an instinctive dread at the sight of the temple, towering over the tops of those few trees left standing. Huge piles of soil, stone and sticks spewed from great gaping wounds in the earth. It looked like a war had been fought here.

Traynor signalled that his followers should hold back, but they had already stopped in silent wonder, even Honor.

'You see?' Traynor breathed. 'It's worked. The temple has been raised.'

'Imagine the power required!' squeaked Douglas, polishing his glasses, impatient to scrutinise the temple properly. 'The foundations must have been built upon special platforms propelled upwards somehow. Some kind of fluid-based system, primitive hydraulics? I don't understand –'

'We *shall* understand, Douglas,' Traynor assured him. 'Coatlicue will be stirring inside.' He turned to address his priests. 'Our faith has been rewarded. We have shaken the earth and reclaimed the temple from the underworld. Already we have wrested life from death.' He walked over to Ramez and placed paternal hands on his shoulders. 'And with the heart and blood of this boy, we shall strengthen and sustain Coatlicue.

We will give her the energy she needs to fully awaken.'

'Please, I . . .' Ramez looked at him, eyes clouded over, like he didn't understand. 'I can't do this.'

Traynor smiled almost kindly. 'Anyone can die, boy. It's easy.' He turned to his bodyguards. 'Sedate him.'

'No!' Tye shouted. She started forwards but Xavier restrained her.

'Her as well,' said Traynor casually. 'For what I have in mind, we'll need her docile.'

One of the bodyguards pushed a pill into Ramez's mouth, clamped one hand about his cheeks and used the other to push a water bottle to his open lips. Ramez swallowed mechanically. 'Thanks,' he said quietly.

'No!' Tye squirmed in Xavier's grip as the same man approached with another pill. His thick fingers pushed into her mouth, and she bit down on them hard. He grunted with pain and cuffed her round the face. For a moment she was stunned – and the pill was pressed into her mouth. The neck of the water bottle bashed against her teeth, dug into her gums as water sloshed out. But she managed to keep the pill beneath her tongue, only pretending she'd swallowed it down.

'In a quarter of an hour or so you'll feel so much more relaxed,' Honor assured her.

Tye discreetly pushed the pill up between her teeth and her cheek, and hoped she could spit it out before too much had dissolved.

'All right, we need to shift the rubble here to get inside,' Traynor told his priests. 'We'll work in rotation again. Proceed slowly and with caution – there may be defences we need to bypass.'

Tye stared at him hatefully. 'This is like one big field trip to you, isn't it?'

'It's the culmination of plans I've been nurturing for almost ten years,' he said. 'Now, here, the dream becomes a reality. I shall speak to Her.'

'Fluent in Aztec, are you?'

He shook his head. 'The Mesoamericans spoke in many tongues – Nahuatl, Tarascan, Mixtec, Zapotec . . . She understood them all.' He smiled smugly. 'Speech is simply the manifestation of thought. She will know the strength and truth of my words.'

The bodyguards were already piling into the rubble, hefting great slabs of sandstone away between them. Tye watched them worriedly. 'Say this presence does exist, say it *can* give you secret knowledge and power – what are you going to do? Dress up your followers as Aztec warriors and attack the White House?'

Traynor's gaze turned on her, hard and unblinking. 'When my biological agents start killing millions in key cities all over the world, then people will listen to me. Then people will respect the old gods.'

Tye felt like she'd been punched in the stomach, and stared at him with disgust. 'You're going to blackmail the world into worshipping Aztec gods? You'll kill them if they don't?'

'I won't have to,' Traynor said triumphantly. 'I'm about to prove that what the Aztecs deemed a deity was something far greater than that. A living entity. A presence.' He half laughed. 'There'll be no need for faith in this world any longer. The presence *exists* – measurable and definable. It tried to give the ancients power, only their minds were too primitive, they had no ears to hear. But I am ready to listen, and when I present absolute proof that the gods exist . . . when I become a *spokesman* for the gods . . . who will not listen? The world shall follow me.'

Tye shook her head. 'You're totally mad, aren't you?'

'No. I am simply *right*. And now I must prepare.'

'Got to put your make-up on? Look your best for the old goddess?'

'I must show respect for the old traditions. Demonstrate that I understand them. That I am truly worthy.'

Worthy of a straitjacket, Tye thought miserably as he walked away. She saw Honor smirking to herself, watching the rest of the priests as they worked.

Tye shivered, and looked around her. She suddenly felt as if she was being watched by someone – or something – from the trees close by. Imagination? Paranoia?

Or waking spirits?

Whatever, she couldn't afford to keep this pill in her mouth a minute longer. She pretended to wipe her mouth, then dropped it on the grass. No one seemed to notice, no one spoke or shouted. She wondered how much she'd ingested.

Maybe it didn't matter. Watching the pitch-black entrance to the temple grow slowly wider as the debris was cleared, like a mouth opening to swallow them all, Tye couldn't imagine ever sleeping again.

CHAPTER TWENTY-ONE

Tye stood beside Ramez just outside the temple entrance. The way inside had been cleared.

Not that Ramez seemed to even notice. He stood swaying slightly, docile, his eyes glassy. An Aztec eagle warrior helmet had been placed over his head – it looked as if his sweaty face was peering out through the bronze beak of an enormous bird – and a tabard had been placed over his shirt, covered with bright blue feathers. He looked weird, beautiful and pathetic, all at once.

Tye's vision kept drifting in and out of focus – the drug they'd tried to give her was clearly strong stuff. While acting dazed and droopy herself, she was secretly pinching the skin on her arms, hoping the pain would help to keep her alert.

Suddenly she jumped as Traynor loomed up in front of her, the strip of ochre make-up smeared across his mouth once more. He wore a loose-fitting jaguar-skin robe that looked stained with blood, and an incredible feathered headdress in turquoise and blue. Behind him the rest of his priests were assembling, all in their own Aztec gear: jewelled wraps, skirts with geometric prints, zigzagged cloaks, sandals laced with gold thread. Honor looked striking in her white knee-length silk skirt and a blouse decorated with suns and birds. On her head she wore a golden crown enhanced with a plume of short, stiff orange feathers. Tye saw how uncomfortable she was feeling, how impatient she was to get on.

'We're going in,' Traynor announced simply. He turned to the bodyguards. 'Take the girl in first – ahead of you.' He smiled across at Honor. 'If there are any traps in there waiting to be sprung, she'll be the one who pays the price.'

Tye blinked sleepily, all the time wishing she could rake her nails down Traynor's face. So this was why they'd kept her alive. As for how long she'd stay that way . . .

The biggest of the two bodyguards shoved her forwards into the temple's entrance. Tye knew she had to pretend to be drugged and drowsy. But the truth was, she was terrified. The darkness inside was absolute, and it was fiercely cold. Her skin was already rising with gooseflesh. No one had set foot in here for centuries. She wanted to turn and run out into the warm sunshine.

But she knew there could be no going back.

'Take a candle,' Traynor instructed, his voice sounding boomy and dead in the freezing passage. 'No flashlights. I want nothing out of place in here.'

An oily yellow light spilled on to the sandstone. In the gloom she saw two bundles of sticks stood in a skull-shaped holder carved into the passage wall.

'Somebody light those torches,' snapped Honor.

The bundles of sticks ignited into pale, smoky flame

as soon as the bodyguards set a candle to them. Now Tye could see more of her surroundings. The passageway was wide and paved with flagstones. A few metres ahead stood a large archway.

Tye was shoved forwards, and stumbled on reluctantly towards the archway, the flickering light making it seem that weird, misshapen shadows were reaching out all around. The shuffling steps of the people coming in behind her sounded like strange creatures woken by the light, shifting about, resentful at the intrusion. The corridor grew danker, the air staler as she reached the archway.

It was the gateway to an inner chamber. The bodyguard with the torch came closer behind her so she could see more clearly.

Not a good thing.

The room was a labyrinth of stone pillars stretching up into the darkness. At least a dozen stone biers were arranged around the chamber, flanking the pillars. A body lay on each, clad in fine regalia. She heard the bodyguard swear under his breath, the first words she had ever heard him say.

'A crypt,' Traynor announced. 'These are the bodies of Coatlicue's attendants.'

'Where will the treasures be stored?' Honor asked.

Cut to the chase, why don't you, thought Tye.

'Perhaps the spirits of Coatlicue's attendants remain here to guard them,' Traynor said reverently. 'Perhaps the treasures are stored in the chamber beyond.'

Tye peered into the inky blackness, trying to see the entrance.

And caught a glimpse of movement.

'There's something there!' she hissed and pointed dumbly into the shadows, starting to shiver.

By the flickering light of the flames, Traynor cautiously explored the area. 'There's a door,' he reported. 'And there are steps leading up. Nothing else.'

'With that pill we gave her, I'm surprised she's not seeing pink elephants,' joked Douglas feebly.

Xavier crossed to join Traynor at the wooden doorway and peered at the pictograms carved there. 'Yes, look. This is where the treasures have been stored. Waiting to be recovered.'

'Can we see?' asked Honor quickly.

Traynor cautiously tried the door, but it did not budge. 'There'll be a secret hinge. It may be booby-trapped.' He nodded to himself. 'We'll leave it for now.'

'Surely, we should –'

'That treasure isn't going anywhere,' said Traynor. 'And anyway – wouldn't you sooner be invited to go inside?'

'Of course.' Tye saw Honor put on her meek act, while Traynor took a torch from the bodyguard and crossed confidently through the sinister mausoleum to the stairway. 'Coatlicue's dwelling place will be on the highest level,' he announced. 'The priests would have wanted as few barriers as possible between temple and sky, so as the Fifth Sun extinguished, the great goddess could escape to the highest heaven.' He looked around at his followers, his smile almost satanic in the red, flickering light. 'My friends, this is what we've all been waiting for. Let's go.'

The other priests pushed past Tye and her body-guard, eagerness overtaking their initial caution now. Ramez was pushed along in the grip of red-mouth and yellow-mouth. Even though he'd been drugged, they were clearly taking no chances.

'Thought I heard something behind us,' said yellow-mouth.

Red-mouth shook his head. 'You're just jumpy.'

Yellow-mouth looked at Tye. 'What about her friends? Both those kids got away.'

Tye blinked sleepily back at him, though her heart started racing. So Jonah *and* Patch had escaped? Could they have somehow followed her, could they be coming to the rescue right now?

'Relax,' said red-mouth, who peered back down the passage towards the daylight. 'There's no one there.'

Tye felt a bitter disappointment – then gasped as she was hauled along up the stone steps by her body-guard, the clatter of shoes and sandals up ahead creating weird echoes all around her.

'Tread softly,' Traynor hissed. 'Have some respect.'

As they reached the next level of the temple, an old, rotting smell caught at Tye's nostrils. In the flickering torchlight she caught phantom flashes of more stone biers, of shields and clubs and swords, of skeletons clothed in animal skins and feathers. Dead warriors, brought here to guard Coatlicue's living spirit. Or maybe to nourish her – wasn't she supposed to feed on the dead?

Whatever, Tye guessed that if there'd been time to linger, she'd find every one of those skeletons' rib cages had been cracked clean open, so the priests could tug out the hot, slithery heart inside. A horrible image of Ramez lying on one of the biers flashed into her mind.

Traynor had already marched on, though Honor was looking nervously back down the stone steps. *Guess she's freaked out too*, thought Tye, traipsing along behind her as they scaled the next flight of stone-flagged steps.

The steps gave on to a long, narrow, claustrophobic landing where Traynor and the others had already gathered in silence. His smoking torch illuminated a cluster of macabre skull-carvings, marking the edges of a dark entrance crafted in the shape of a giant serpent's head.

'This is it,' breathed Traynor. 'The holy place. Where Coatlicue's attendants communed with the Presence.'

Honor turned to Tye's bodyguard. 'They may have left traps for the unwary,' she said. 'Put the girl inside first.'

The other priests made way and Tye was pushed through the dark entrance. It was freezing cold in here. Behind her someone held their torch up, but its light grew pale as the flames waned and flickered. An instinctive feeling of dread enveloped her. The chamber was large and circular. Seven stone pillars formed an inner circle, ranged around a gigantic, terrifying statue.

It was the goddess Coatlicue, but depicted more vividly and nightmarishly than any image Tye had ever seen. The eyes of the two serpents coiling out from the severed neck seemed fixed upon her, as their heads met in profile to form a face. Huge, pointed claws tipped her slab-like hands and feet. The tangle of snakes that formed her skirt seemed to writhe in the flickering light of the torch, and as smoke blew across the chamber it seemed to animate the hands and hearts carved into the statue's broad chest, making them twitch and pulse as if with a power of their own. Tye found herself praying to the voodoo spirits for protection.

Xavier's voice floated eerily out from behind her. 'No traps that I can see.'

'Keep the girl and Ramez at the back for now,' Traynor instructed the bodyguards. 'No unbeliever must be allowed to step inside the inner circle.' One of them walked uncertainly up to her, gripped her arm and steered her towards the shadows in the back of the room. Tye found that his big hand on her arm was actually something of a comfort.

She watched, a sick feeling slowly building in her chest, as the Sixth Sun devotees filed into the dark, smoky chamber. No longer did they seem jokey and out-of-place in their weird get-up. This dank, sinister world was one where they could move freely and in comfort. They did not talk, or smile, or even look at each other. They simply took up places around the temple with the ease of well-rehearsed actors finding their marks.

Two of the priests, Douglas and one other, produced a steel flight case and removed small glass phials from within. Tye shuddered – they had to be the biological agents, Traynor's chemical weapons.

'See? Just as the craftman's drawing showed us.'

Traynor's voice was rapt. 'These indentations ranged round the statue aren't as deep as I'd imagined but . . . Well, thirteen of them, it's *perfect*.'

'Destined to be,' Douglas agreed happily.

'Place one phial in each.' Carefully, the two men began to do so, and Traynor cackled. 'This truly *is* our destiny, my friends.'

'Thought you said nothing out of place in here?' Tye burst out – then bit her lip. She was supposed to be drugged, and hastily added a long, drawn-out yawn.

But Traynor didn't even look round from overseeing the work.

'Coatlicue understands disease only too well. It decimated her people.' His voice fell to a low, reverent whisper. 'The prophecy says she will feed on the poison in men. Well, there is *so much* poison in these phials . . . Thanks to them she can gorge herself on the deaths of her enemies. She must see the phials. She must bless the poison inside . . .'

Tye nodded, sickened. *So you can kid yourself you're doing holy work instead of committing mass murder*. She watched as the phials were neatly lined up in a semi-circle around the statue. It was like she was watching a bunch of kids trying to impress their teacher at some kind of twisted 'show and tell'.

Another of the priests opened the long, mahogany box and carefully removed Cortes's sword from inside. Tye could almost imagine the mass of serpents coiling down from the statue's waist, craning to see as the sword was laid in the centre of the inner circle, its handle presented to the monstrous claws.

Then the priests cleared the inner circle. Averting her eyes from the statue, Tye looked at the sword – and noticed a part of the blade was gleaming. She blinked, but the effect continued. Not a trick of the half-light then, but –

She turned and stared into the inky blackness behind her – and saw a chink of sunshine peeping in through the old, cold stone. She shivered. It was as if the outside world, with all its warmth and light and normality, had been reduced to the faintest glimmer by the darkness of this place. She glanced across at Ramez, who was staring straight ahead. *There has to be a way out of this*, she thought. *I could grab those phials – or kick them over. I could take the sword, threaten to damage it – no, threaten to use it unless they set Ramez free. I could –*

But she felt the strength of the bodyguard's grip on her wrist and knew she'd have to struggle to break free in the first place. That would lose her the advantage of surprise that Coldhardt had taught her was vital when the odds were stacked against you.

'We're ready to begin,' Traynor announced, his words echoing strangely round the cold, dank curves of the chamber. He entered the inner circle and stood astride the sword at its centre while his followers retreated to positions either side of the pillars. Only Honor wasn't attentive; she seemed more resigned than anything else. In one hand she held a long, dark flint knife.

As high priestess, the kill would be hers. And Tye could see from the casual way she held herself, that it meant nothing at all.

'Great goddess Coatlicue!' Traynor began, raising his voice and his arms to the shadows, the folds of his jaguar robe rippling about him like the flames of the sputtering torches. 'You who endure while fragile men fail and die. You who gave shade to those who lived on the Earth, we enter your sacred domain. We are your new attendants. We pray you hear us.'

'*Hear us*,' chanted the priests.

'We know that your rule over men was broken by the invading conquistadores.'

'*Though it be made of jade, it breaks*,' the priests intoned, their voices low and reverent.

'Your great knowledge, your power, was thought lost.'

'*Though it be made of gold, it grows dull.*'

'Your glorious existence was dismissed as primitive myth.'

'*Though it be made of plumes from the quetzal, it shreds apart.*'

Tye bit her lip and shivered. It seemed to be growing colder and colder in here.

'But know this – it is *we* who have awakened you.' A new fervour was creeping into Traynor's voice. 'It is we who have shaken the earth and raised your world from out of the darkness. It is we who bring the sword of your conqueror to break at your feet.'

'*As eagles we fly to you. As jaguars we run to you.*'

All eyes were on Traynor.

Tye knew that now was the time to act.

She elbowed her guard in the stomach with all her strength, wrenching her arm free of his grip at the same time. Whirling round, she swung her fist at the

274

big man – but the blow fell wide, he ducked easily aside, grabbed her wrist and twisted it painfully behind her back. 'No!' she shouted – *I messed up, I blew it* – 'You're crazy, all of you!' The bodyguard's big, clammy hand wedged over her mouth. She saw Ramez was looking at her. For a second he almost looked his old self. Then the glazed look returned to his eyes and his head lolled forwards.

She felt something sharp dig into the cut in her side and gasped with pain. She realised Honor was beside her with the knife. 'Just one more word and I'll be using this twice,' the woman warned her.

Traynor was carrying on as if nothing had happened, his voice ringing out around the temple. 'It is we who arrest the passing of the Suns, we who seek to start a new era where your word will be law. A Sixth Sun, not only in this land, but in all lands.' His voice dropped to an urgent whisper as he stared up at the hideous statue. 'Your mind has touched mine before. Know me again, great goddess . . . as I bring you fresh blood.'

'*As jaguars we kill for you.*'

'I bring you a boy made fit for your feast by the old traditions.' He snapped his fingers without turning round. 'As prophecy demands, we your attendants shall reach into his heart as we reach into our own hearts, and restore you to strength.' He clapped his hands together. 'Bring Ramez to me.'

The guard brought the unresisting Ramez to the outer edge of the inner circle. With a last warning look at Tye, Honor crossed back to the centre of the action. She took one of Ramez's arms and Traynor gripped the other. The bodyguard stepped back.

'You are honoured, Ramez,' said Traynor, forcing him down on the temple floor. 'You never amounted to a thing in this world. But in giving your life to a goddess, she shall in return give eternal life to you. You shall know paradise.'

'Come, little hummingbird.' Honor was pulling open Ramez's shirt, exposing his smooth, toned flesh. 'Let the offering be made.'

CHAPTER TWENTY-TWO

Tye writhed desperately in the bodyguard's grip. She had to break free, had to reach Ramez, struggled harder –

And then the voice rang out.

'*The child is not fit to be sacrificed.*' Harsh, high and terrible, the screech reverberated around the chamber.

The circle erupted in fear and confusion. Priests reeled back, or clutched hold of each other in fear. Shouts and gasps went up, Honor jumped to her feet and rounded on the statue, wielding the knife. Ramez pushed himself up on his elbows, staring round in terror.

'Great goddess?' Traynor's voice was wary and low, he was holding himself completely still. 'This is not how you came to me before.'

'*Bow down to me!*' came the commanding shriek. '*Fall to your knees! All of you!*'

And through a mouthful of thick and trembling fingers, Tye grinned in joyful disbelief.

Because however well disguised, she knew Con's voice when she heard it.

People were falling to their knees all around, and Tye went limp in the bodyguard's grip, making out she'd fainted. But the bodyguard could barely have noticed, he was hurrying to kneel as well.

'*Lower your unworthy eyes from my image!*' Con ranted in full-on goddess mode. '*Or you will be punished, yes?*'

'No!' shouted Traynor suddenly. 'Get up you fools, it's a trick –'

'Now!' came a shout.

It was Jonah's voice – and the cue for all Mictlan to break loose in the temple.

Jonah launched himself through the smoky haze into the inner circle, Motti right beside him. With a bellow, Motti hurled himself at Traynor, bringing him down.

The sound of shouts and fighting filled the temple with hard, noisy echoes. The confusion and chaos was tinted blood red by the flaming torchlight. Jonah made for Honor and knocked the knife from her hand, she snarled with anger – but then someone grabbed Jonah round the waist, yanking him backwards. Jonah spun round, trying to free himself, and managed to crush his attacker against one of the pillars. Another priest appeared instantly to take his place, an old man with a cloak. Jonah ducked a fairly weak blow and then floored the old guy with a punch to the jaw.

But where was Honor now? She'd vanished from view, like Motti and Traynor – was she hiding? Jonah knew just how well you could hide in those thick, freezing shadows. It had been agony, seeing Tye so helpless but with no way of getting to her, as he and the others waited to grab their best chance of taking

Sixth Sun off-guard. Unable to clear the rubble at the entrance, they'd climbed the sides of the pyramid and loosened a slab of plaster from an upper storey. They'd finished up in here, with barely enough time to replace the slab before Traynor led his party crashing out of the jungle. Coldhardt had taken Patch off to explore one of the lower levels, but Jonah had persuaded the others to stay and help him try to save Tye . . .

Staring round at the chaos as the temple filled with smoke from the billowing torches, he decided he was insane for *ever* thinking they could pull this off.

Another priest rushed for Jonah but stumbled over the old man's body and crashed into the statue of Coatlicue. As he tried to right himself, a pair of well-manicured hands reached round from behind the hideous figure, grabbed him by the ears and whacked his head against the carved stone, knocking him out cold.

As the priest collapsed to the floor, Con burst from behind the statue. 'This is madness!' she shouted, high-kicking Xavier under the chin as he rushed for her, sending him sprawling back into the smoke and shadows. 'We should be with Patch stealing that treasure.'

'Did you see where Honor went?' Jonah glanced at the ground and saw the sacrifice had gone – along with Cortes's sword. 'Where's Ramez – did Tye get to him? Where *is* Tye?' He stared round in confusion, but it was too dark and smoky to see far. 'And where's Motti?'

Suddenly Motti loomed up in front of him, glasses smashed and buckled, one eye bloody and black.

'Where's the goddamned exit?' he said weakly, before falling to his knees. Then Con shouted out as a guy with a strip of red across his mouth tackled her and brought her down. She grappled with him on the temple floor.

Before Jonah could go to help her, Traynor came out of the shadows, his feathered headdress discarded, his robe and tunic torn. 'You're gonna pay for this.' He advanced on Jonah, wielding Cortes's sword like a Samurai. 'You're gonna pay with every last pint of your blood.'

With a sudden scream of rage, Traynor hurled himself at Jonah.

In the darkness beside the outer wall, Tye brought her elbow back with a crack against her bodyguard's face then lunged forwards to break his grip. Throwing herself on to her back, she kicked him hard in the chest with both feet. Propelled backwards, he hit the wall with a thunderous crash, knocking out a stone slab from the fake window in the wall. Sunlight peeped timidly inside, filtered by the canopy of trees. But as it turned the smoke opaque, it actually made things harder to see.

Scrambling up, Tye peered through the haze and saw Con trying to drag an injured Motti clear of the fighting, even while red-mouth had hold of her leg. Her stomach twisted as she glimpsed Jonah ducking back behind the statue of Coatlicue, Traynor raising the sword of Cortes above his head.

It was as she was running to help that she realised Ramez was no longer on the ground.

Then suddenly the other bodyguard jumped on top of her, brought her down, his big hands fumbling for her throat. *No time to waste on you*, she thought. She slammed her hands down hard on his ears and twisted his head round with all her strength. He shouted out and rolled off her, clutching at his neck. But then yellow-mouth loomed up, grabbed hold of her arm, and tried to get her in a half-nelson.

'Will you just give up and let me go!' she shouted, anger giving her strength as she twisted her arm clear. She delivered a roundhouse kick to the man's stomach, and when he doubled up, she punched him once – twice – in his stupid yellow mouth, before her final uppercut slammed him into one of the pillars.

Shaking her aching hand, Tye stared through the smoke; in just a few seconds everything seemed to have changed. Motti looked a mess, out of it, slumped on the floor. Con was matching red-mouth blow for blow, but there were others crowding round to deal with her in turn. Jonah was playing cat and mouse with Traynor, who was now lunging wildly with his priceless sword. Honor was still nowhere to be seen and neither was Ramez – he'd been drugged, he would be vulnerable, helpless.

Tye froze, agonised. Her friends all needed her at once. *Who do I help? Who the hell can I help?*

Jonah swung himself round past a pillar and into plain sight. But Traynor had anticipated his move, charged forwards, and swept back the sword ready to strike . . .

Then something knocked against Tye's foot – Ramez's bronze eagle helmet.

'Jonah, down!' she shouted, scooping it up. He looked at her, wild-eyed, as she hurled the heavy helmet with all her strength. It flew through the air and struck Traynor on the shoulder, knocking his sword arm aside; caught off-balance, he staggered and fell.

At the same time Tye sprinted to where Con was now taking on three men at once in unarmed combat. Tye came up behind red-mouth and delivered a karate blow to his back. Xavier spun round. She swiftly struck him in the throat and he staggered backwards into Con. She knocked his legs out from under him, then crouched and rammed her elbow down hard on his sternum. Xavier's whole body jerked, then he lay still.

The third of Con's assailants turned to face Tye – just as she launched herself into a flying jump kick, ignoring the way the wound in her side burned with pain. Her steel toecaps connected with the man's ribs and probably broke a couple. He went down like a sack of sticks.

That was the last of the real muscle, surely – now she could help Jonah. But Tye found her way blocked by still more priests coming out of the smoky gloom to get them. She remembered the way they had worked at the rockshaft, and clearing the temple entrance – working closely together, methodical and precise. Relentless.

Then a shout went up. 'The sacrifice! He's getting away!'

Tye looked over to the exit to see three dark costumed figures vanishing through the doorway in pursuit.

'Go on,' Con snapped. 'Get after Ramez. I'll handle things here.' As if to prove her point she grabbed hold of her nearest opponent and felled him with a single strike to the back of the neck.

Tye choked on a breath of smoke. 'But Jonah –'

'I will help him. If you lose Ramez now . . .'

If I lose him now, what? thought Tye, and as she raced for the gaping serpent's-mouth exit she found she had no idea.

Exhausted, choking on smoke, Jonah pushed himself up from the clammy stone floor. If he could only put some of the Sixth Sunners between him and Traynor, a human shield to stop him swinging that –

'Jonah!' Con yelled.

He looked up at the warning, twisting aside as the rapier blade struck the ground beside him. Traynor was already back on his feet, and looked angrier than ever. He jabbed with the sword like he was trying to skewer Jonah's heart. Jonah threw himself backwards, landing heavily back on the floor, frantically pushing himself away from Traynor with both feet, slithering towards the statue.

'That's right, boy, go to the goddess,' breathed Traynor, seemingly oblivious to the chaos that surrounded him. 'It's time we got you gushing. Coatlicue wants to taste every last spurt of your blood.' His eyes were dark and unblinking in the hazy torchlight. 'What d'you want to lose first, kid – an arm or a leg?'

Jonah cried out as he cracked the back of his skull against one of the statue's huge stone claws, reopening his old head wound. He wouldn't have believed it was possible to feel any more scared, but for a second he was plunged into blind panic. By rights he should just have knocked through the phials of poison ranged in front of Coatlicue. But he'd felt nothing, so where the hell –

Someone darted out from behind the statue.

And suddenly Traynor staggered back, clutching at his face. Jonah saw it was dripping wet.

Coldhardt stood beside Coatlicue, half-hidden by the drifting smoke. In one hand he held an unstoppered phial. It was empty.

'Thanks,' croaked Jonah.

'Sorry to be interfering again, Traynor,' Coldhardt said. 'But I think you've spilled enough blood in this cause.'

'You old bastard!' Traynor wiped frantically at his face with his free hand. 'What have you done?'

'Given you a taste of your own poison.' Coldhardt surveyed him impassively. 'Now, you know better than me how many people that phial could kill if it was poured into a water supply. But I'd imagine that with a concentrated dose, even the tiniest amount on your tongue . . .'

Traynor fell to his knees, spitting desperately, shaking his head like a wet dog trying to dry itself. The sword fell from his shaking hand and clattered to the floor.

'I'll take that.' Coldhardt snatched it up. 'Thank you.'

Jonah could see boils and blisters forming on Traynor's good-looking, square-jawed face. Pus began to run from his eyes like thick tears. His skin began to blacken like burnt toffee. His struggles stopped. Then Coldhardt pressed one foot against Traynor's chest and gently pushed.

Traynor toppled over backwards and lay still in the centre of the inner circle, both arms flung wide so his corpse formed a cross. A counterfeit Christ in a pagan temple.

Tye skidded to a halt on the landing beyond the sacred chamber – the air was clearer but the oily blackness was absolute. She could hear footsteps ringing out on cold stone, and stood on the top step in time to catch the last, indecisive light of a flaming torch as its owner vanished round the turn in the staircase.

The sounds of a struggle floated up to her. Blinking the glare from her eyes, heart pounding, she sprinted down the steps and into the resting place of the dead warriors.

She found three of the priests advancing on Ramez, who had retreated behind a stone bier and was now standing there, slack-jawed. The man with the torch – Tye saw it was pot-bellied Douglas – waved it threateningly in Ramez's direction, while his two friends circled round the bier to catch him in a pincer movement.

But then Ramez burst into unexpected life. He grabbed the man to his left and kneed him in the balls, then shoved him into the path of the cultist circling from the right.

Tye tapped Douglas on the shoulder. As he whirled round she snatched his torch with one hand and punched him hard in the stomach with the other. He collapsed on his back, gasping for breath, flailing about on the flagstones like an upturned beetle.

She gave a low whistle of relief, then raised her eyebrows at Ramez. 'Thought you were drugged?'

'Thought *you* were,' he retorted. 'You don't think they'd get me like that, do you? Hid the pill under my tongue and spat it out when they weren't looking –'

'Me too!' She hurried round the bier to join him, squeezed his arm. 'You son of a bitch, you could have tipped me off.'

He smiled, the smile he always used to flash when he'd promised her the world, and to her annoyance the old swagger about him sent a familiar thrill through her heart. 'Couldn't risk it,' he said. 'I was just kidding 'em, waiting till the last moment so they'd never expect –'

Tye's vision exploded into stars as the blow smacked down on the back of her head. The torch fell from her fingers as she spun round, to see Douglas leering at her, holding one of the dead guard's wooden clubs. She hadn't heard him creep up behind her.

Now all she could hear was the ringing in her ears as she started to black out.

'Don't touch Traynor's body,' warned Coldhardt gravely. He raised his voice as he addressed the whole temple. 'Listen to me. There is nothing to fight for any longer. Your leader is dead. Your dreams are over.'

'Kill them!' snarled the old professor. 'Come on, we can still . . .' But as Con dispatched the cultist beside him with a barrage of blows, he suddenly seemed to realise that he was the last man standing.

Quite casually, Con turned to him, seized him by his stripy cloak and bashed his head against the nearest pillar. He slid down it and lay still in a crumpled heap. She smiled proudly over at Coldhardt, wiping a trickle of blood from her mouth. 'Now that they're sleeping, they may have *sweeter* dreams, no?'

'Where did Tye get to?' Jonah demanded.

Con almost looked awkward. 'She went to help Ramez.'

'But Honor's still around somewhere!'

'She probably just ran out.'

'We don't know that.' Anxiously, Jonah tried to rise but stopped as the temple seemed to spin. 'My stupid head,' he muttered through clenched teeth.

'Con, get after Tye,' Coldhardt instructed, examining the sword in his hands. 'Jonah's right, we can't assume Miss Albrecht has departed. We must secure this site.'

'Secure it?' she questioned.

'I must not be disturbed. Go, quickly. Then join Patch in assessing the treasures on the ground floor.'

Con ran from the circular chamber, and Jonah made a more determined effort to get to his feet. 'I can't believe you used that stuff on Traynor,' he said. 'You could have killed all of us.'

'The agent was designed to be taken orally, in water,' Coldhardt murmured, still concentrating on Cortes's sword. 'It was unlikely the contagion would be airborne.'

'Where are the other phials?'

'I moved them behind the statue so they wouldn't be broken.'

His head pounding, Jonah crossed to check on Motti, who was starting to stir. 'Thought you were still downstairs, anyway,' he called to Coldhardt, 'with Patch.'

'I left him in the attendants' resting place, working on the door to the treasure vaults.' He placed the sword on the ground and crouched in front of the statue. 'There are things I must do here.'

'Sure.' Jonah found he really didn't want to know right now. 'Mot, you OK?' he asked.

Motti nodded, and winced. 'What the hell happened?'

'I think you'll find Traynor made you his bitch.'

'He did too. That bastard can fight.'

'Not any more.' Jonah glanced back at Coldhardt, and caught sight of a glint of gold in the old man's palm. 'What's that?'

'I searched the attendants' bodies, as Traynor should have, Coldhardt explained. 'Remember the prophecy – "*when her attendants reach into their hearts*"?' He held up a circle of gold, like a wide, fat coin etched with a single symbol. 'Where their hearts should have been, one of these had been placed.' He placed a disc into one of the indentations for an exact fit. 'They must have been worn round the neck like the Sixth Sun amulets, part of the ceremony of communion, placed here in a certain order.'

'You seriously imagine you can actually *talk* with this presence thing –?'

'Go to the others. They may need your help.' He looked up angrily at Jonah and Motti. '*Go*.'

'He's right, come on,' said Jonah quietly. Helping

Motti to stand, he led the way to the exit.

Tye was clinging on to consciousness. She fell forwards into Ramez's arms. They felt strong and warm while the world whirled about her. The old, familiar smell of him filled her nostrils, and for those few spinning seconds she was thirteen again and had all she needed.

There was a rustle and clatter of movement close by. 'Aw, Jeez,' Ramez breathed. 'Why don't you suckers stay down?'

'Give it up, Ramez,' said one of the men. 'We've got you cornered.'

No, thought Tye desperately. *There has to be a way out. After all we've been through, I won't let him be dragged away screaming again. If I can only come up with a distraction –*

'You can't run from us, Ramez,' said Douglas sternly. 'We kept our side of the bargain. We've given you everything you ever wanted.'

'That's right, you did. But guess what?' He squeezed Tye protectively to him, his chest crushing against hers. 'You can have it right back.'

And Tye cried out as she was pushed violently away. She fell sprawling into Douglas's arms, knocked him backwards into the other two priests, and they all went down together. Ramez pushed past them in the confusion, ran off and away.

Tye opened her mouth to shout after him, but no words would come. She stayed silent, numb as the men hauled her up. Stared at the staircase he'd fled down, willing him to come back for her.

Then she had to shut her eyes as the flaming torch was pushed up to her face, so close she caught a crackle from her forehead, the acrid smell of burning hair.

'We were going to have power,' came a whining male voice. 'Now everything's ruined.'

'And it's all down to her and her friends,' hissed Douglas. 'Well, she's going to pay . . .'

Then she heard footsteps pounding on the stone steps. Ramez. He had come back for her, of course he had –

'Leave her alone!' Con's shout echoed and re-echoed around the warriors' tomb as she piled into the three men. Tye twisted free from Douglas's grip just as Con knocked him to the ground. The torch fell with him, its heat searing Tye's bare leg.

And as the burn shocked through her, something else ignited.

While Con tackled one of the men, Tye grabbed his friend and threw him to the floor. He landed on his back at the base of a bier. 'Still think you've got power over me?' she hissed. Grabbing one of the warrior's wooden shields, she brought it down on the man's face and he cried out. 'Think I'm yours?' He struggled so she hit him again, split open his nose. 'That I could *ever* be yours?'

'Hey. Hey.' She felt Con pull the shield from her grip and kneel down beside her. 'It's OK, sweets. He's out cold.' Con's arms slipped round her. 'It's over.'

Tye clutched blindly at Con, held her tight.

'We won't let you go,' Con murmured.

CHAPTER TWENTY-THREE

Motti following right behind, Jonah came cautiously down the steps to the creepy warriors' tomb. With a rush of relief he found Con and Tye were the only ones left standing – though from the way they seemed to be holding on to each other for support, only just. He cleared the last few steps and walked up to the girls, ready to hug them both. But Con slipped away at the last moment and it was just him and Tye.

'Where's Ramez?' Motti asked.

'History,' said Con simply.

Jonah and Tye didn't say a word, just held each other in silence.

Motti huffed impatiently. 'Get a room, guys.'

'Get *into* a room,' Con corrected him, as Jonah self-consciously pulled away from Tye. 'Patch has been trying to get to that treasure, we must help him, no?'

Jonah nodded. 'Surely he'll have cracked it by now?'

'Probably peeing his pants, alone down there,' Motti agreed.

'If he *is* alone,' said Tye.

'Honor?' Jonah's headache was getting worse. 'Of course. All she wanted from this whole deal was the poison and the money those relics would bring her.'

Motti nodded. 'And since the poison's out the picture . . .'

'Come on,' said Jonah. He grabbed the torch burning on the floor and led the way down the next flight of steps.

The door to the treasure chamber stood ajar.

'Patch?' Motti called, squinting at the doorway through his one remaining lens. 'Is everything cool?'

'It's freezing!' he shouted back.

Cautiously Jonah pushed open the door. 'Whoa,' he said.

The door opened on to a large, wide chamber, lit dimly by a couple of torches set into the walls. The floor area was square, and the huge step cut into the ceiling above made Jonah feel like he was standing inside part of a giant Tetris puzzle. A pit the size of a swimming pool had been dug in the centre of the room – but instead of water, artefacts in gold and obsidian and jade sparkled in the flickering torchlight. The pit was piled high with treasures.

But there was no sign of Patch.

'Come on, stop playing about,' said Con sharply.

'Excellent advice.' Honor came out from the shadows at the far side of the room, her black hair in disarray. She was holding her sacrificial knife to Patch's throat. 'Now then, Coldhardt's children. You are going to carry these treasures outside.'

'That was kind of the plan,' Motti agreed. 'We're thieves, see.'

'Only now you will be stealing on my behalf, not Coldhardt's.'

'It's no use,' said Jonah. 'Traynor's dead, the poison's been dealt with. It's finished.'

'Finished?' She smiled, almost fondly it seemed. 'But it's never finished, Jonah. I have so many other irons in the fire. So many other plans to fulfill. I've invested a lot of time in this project, and require a return on that investment.' She tightened her grip around Patch's throat. 'No more stalling. You will take as much treasure as you can carry through the jungle to my transport.'

Heart sinking, Jonah looked at Motti, then over at Tye and Con.

'Go on, then!' gasped Patch, as Honor pressed the blade harder against his neck. 'I'm talking to them, not you,' he added.

'Looks like we've got no choice,' said Tye quietly.

Honor nodded. 'So get in that pit and start shifting. Start with the jewellery, it'll be easiest to carry.'

Jonah walked to the edge of the pit, crouched and reached for an intricately cast gold pendant, pulling it out. Tye knelt beside him, rooting through plates and pottery and stuff.

Motti crossed casually round the edge of the pit in Honor's direction. Con took the left-hand side while Motti moved round to the right. Jonah watched as he gingerly flipped over a wide mosaic mask with his foot, as if expecting to find something nasty underneath.

'Did you check this place for traps, cyclops?' asked Motti.

'The door was full of 'em,' he said. 'Took me ages to crack, and I nearly got my hand skewered to the doorframe.' He sighed. 'I'd just got inside when *she* showed up.'

'Speed it up,' Honor ordered. 'You –' she gestured to Motti – 'get into that pit and start sorting through the relics in the middle.' She smiled at Jonah. 'The biggest fish don't swim in the shallows.'

Motti glared at her. 'And if it's booby trapped?'

'Then you'll be maimed or dead and your friends will have to divide your load between them,' she said impatiently. 'Now do it.'

Jonah felt his heart hammering as Motti stepped awkwardly out on to the stockpile of treasures.

'The rest of you, get a move on,' called Honor.

Jonah looked down, and lifted a shield. Underneath was more jewellery, earrings and a necklace lying on a woven mat of some kind. What was a mat doing here? Hardly grade-A treasure . . .

He pulled it away and stared at what lay beneath.

Stone. Stone and broken pottery.

Frowning, he showed Tye, who rummaged a little deeper in her own pile. 'Oh God. It's the same here.'

'This is wrong,' Jonah announced nervously. 'The good stuff's only on top.'

'No tricks,' Honor warned him.

'See for yourself!' Jonah snapped. 'Underneath there's nothing, just landfill.'

By now, Con was sporting four or five dangling gold necklaces. 'I've found plenty.'

Motti knelt awkwardly in the middle of the pit, moving masks and statuettes. 'I got me a throw or something,' he reported. 'And under it . . .' He reached in and picked up a couple of pieces of broken clay. 'Well, whoopee.' He tossed the fragments over to land at Honor's feet. 'So much for the big treasure trove.'

Con looked outraged. 'Someone's already stolen it!'

'And dressed up a pile of rubble with a few baubles to make it seem like the whole lot was still here,' Motti concluded.

'So we take the baubles,' Honor said darkly. 'It'll still be worth a good deal.'

'No,' said Jonah.

'C'mon, Jonah,' Patch croaked.

'No, I mean, something's not right. It would have taken ages to fill this pit with stone and pottery, and the attendants were still alive when the pyramid was buried. They wouldn't have let anyone take the real treasure before it was sealed, so –'

'So this whole goddamned place is a trap.' Motti scrambled back to the side of the pit. 'Jesus Christ, we gotta get out of here, and fast.'

But Honor shook her head. 'That's enough hysterics.'

'Didn't you hear him?' Con stood up and crossed back round to Jonah and Tye, jamming a pair of gold bracelets on to her wrist. 'This place is simply bait, yes? A greed-trap for anyone who might have got inside while Coatlicue was flying up to heaven –'

'Just get on with clearing the good stuff,' Honor ordered. 'We've been in here for ten minutes at least and nothing's happened. Whatever was *supposed* to happen, it's clearly not working.'

The ground shifted and rumbled beneath them. A brutal, grating sound ground out from the walls. Then

Jonah felt a funny sinking feeling in his stomach, like he was in a lift heading for the ground floor.

Or the *underground* floor.

'What's happening?' Honor demanded.

'Whaddya think's happening, you dumb bitch!' Motti bellowed. 'The trap's been sprung – the temple's sinking back into the ground!'

Suddenly Patch twisted his body round and elbowed Honor in the stomach. Caught off guard she overbalanced, and with a short cry of anger fell into the pit. The chamber lurched and Patch staggered, almost joining her in there. But Motti grabbed hold of his hand and yanked him back.

'Thanks for that.' Patch grinned with relief. 'So much for Honor among thieves.'

'Look out!' shouted Con, bustling Jonah and Tye away as a shower of rock dust rained down from above – together with a large chunk of masonry. It crashed into the floor of the chamber, and a large split appeared in the stone, stretching from the pit to the door.

'The temple wasn't designed to survive a journey back underground,' Motti shouted.

'Out of here!' Jonah yelled – needlessly, since everyone was already running for their lives. He reached the doorway and looked back for Honor. But the torches had been extinguished and he could see nothing but thick, dust-choked blackness.

The others were charging up the steps to the next level. 'I don't get it!' Patch shouted. 'What happened to the real treasure?'

'Hidden somewhere else,' Jonah suggested, 'if it

ever really existed.'

'But how do we get out?' Tye yelled over the slow, deafening grind of the temple's shifting foundations, as they emerged into the warriors' tomb and started on the second set of steps.

'We came in through one of the false windows in the side of the shrine,' Con told her. 'It's in the upper storey, it will still be above ground –'

The whole pyramid seemed to lurch sideways. Jonah lost his footing and slipped back down the steps, the hard stone edges biting into his backbone as he tumbled. With a gasp he hit the ground – and found himself staring into the sightless sockets of one of the long-dead warriors. Its remains lay sprawled on the floor, its skull-face grinning up at him as if mocking his efforts to leave. With a shudder, Jonah got shakily to his feet and rescaled the steps in a shower of sandstone shrapnel.

Tye was waiting for him by the serpent's mouth entrance, holding the back of her head and looking woozy. 'You OK?' Jonah asked.

'Not very,' she said, coughing hard. 'Getting dizzy.'

Jonah opened his mouth to reply, but then heard Coldhardt almost screaming from inside. 'Get out! Go on, all of you, get the hell away from here. Leave me!'

He followed Tye inside. Patch was struggling through the window, helped by Motti who was balancing on the narrow ledge the other side. But Con was making no attempt to get out, biting her lip, staring over at Coldhardt.

The old man was kneeling before the statue of Coatlicue, Traynor's corpse still spread-eagled behind him. Some of the temple roof had fallen in, and in the fiery red of the setting sun the goddess looked still more terrifying. As if she were about to pounce on Coldhardt and devour him alive.

'Con, I told you to get out!' the old man roared, staring round. Jonah saw he was clutching the sword in both hands.

Jonah steered Tye over to Con. The ground beneath them lurched again, and the whole temple seemed to scream as it slid lower into its waiting grave. 'Help Tye through the window,' Jonah snapped, and Con nodded. 'Then see if you can help some of those others.'

'What, save Sixth Sun?' She stared at him incredulously. 'Why – so they can try to kill us all over again?'

'We can't just leave them to –' He broke off as another pile of stonework tumbled in from the roof behind them. One of the priests screamed – then the sound choked off.

'*I* can,' Con assured him, and set about helping Tye crawl through the crumbling window.

Jonah turned from her. 'Coldhardt, come on,' he shouted, 'the treasure store was a sham and it's triggered the burglar alarm. We've *all* got to get out!'

'Not yet,' Coldhardt shook his head. 'I can't. Not now I'm so close. A chance of redemption, Jonah. Nothing else matters.'

Jonah rushed over to where he knelt. 'Stay here much longer and you'll be dead! We're a long way from your vault . . .' He frowned as he realised Coldhardt was kneeling in a sticky crimson puddle.

'Is that blood –?'

'Someone attacked me.' Coldhardt gestured impatiently to a body lying beside the statue. Jonah saw it was Xavier, hands still clutched over the fatal gash in his stomach, but couldn't find it within himself to feel much regret. 'Now get the hell out, Jonah. I have to try to commune with –'

'You can't be serious –!'

There was a quick, metallic sliding sound that made them both stare at the statue. In the largest stone heart that hung round Coatlicue's severed neck, a slot had opened – just wide enough for . . .

Coldhardt raised the sword and slammed it into the slot, as the ground rumbled ominously beneath them. The sword blade jammed, three-quarters in. He tried to twist it from side to side, but nothing happened. 'Come on . . . come *on*!' The temple seemed to roar like a creature in pain as the ancient foundations fell in on themselves. 'What must I do?' Coldhardt howled above the cacophony, heaving on the sword. 'To take life from death, *what must I do*?'

Then the blade snapped clean through, not far from the hilt. They both stared as the length of the severed steel blade seemed to be drawn inside the statue, like a key entering a lock.

'The prophecy.' Jonah stared at the statue. 'When the bloodied sword is wiped clean . . .'

'This place is sinking too fast!' yelled Con, swinging herself out through the window. 'Come *on* you two!'

Something was happening to the ground around the statue. It was starting to dissolve. The priests' gold discs that Coldhardt had pressed into the indentations fell through the melting floor – into a shallow cache stuffed full of polychrome cups and precious stones and figurines and codices and –

Jonah reached down automatically, grabbing a handful of Aztec gold. 'The real treasure,' he breathed. 'It's *here*.'

'Left in offering at her feet.' Coldhardt reached inside and groped around the cache. He pulled out a couple of deerskin books and a shell necklace, stuffed them inside his shirt and scrabbled about for more. He looked up at Jonah, eyes shining with naked greed. 'Help me!'

But a deep, splintering scream of stone on stone echoed up from the bowels of the temple and the floor began to tilt. Jonah shifted his weight to keep his balance, then stared in horror as two little glass phials rolled from behind the statue and fell into the cache. One of them broke open on the edge of a mosaic mask.

Jonah backed away automatically. 'The poison! We can't risk touching anything in there now.'

Coldhardt screamed with rage, banging his fist down on the bloody ground in frustration.

Outside Jonah could hear the others urging them to hurry.

'*You're, like, three metres off ground level and sinking fast!*'

'*Move it!*'

'*Get the hell out of there!*'

Jonah looked at Coldhardt. 'If we don't get out now –'

'We never will.'

Jonah turned at the sound of the all-too familiar voice. Honor had followed them up, a thick slither of blood oozing from her forehead. 'Help me carry these treasures,' she said almost drunkenly, 'and I'll share them with you.'

Jonah saw she was clutching a pile of broken pottery together with chunks of slate and sandstone. Determined to salvage something, she must have grabbed for the closest objects to hand, not even realising what they were.

Jonah and Coldhardt ignored her and navigated the shaking floor over to the window. The old man swung himself through with surprising agility. 'Now you.'

'Didn't you hear me?' Honor called. 'I said I'll share it with you!'

'It's worthless!' Jonah shouted, starting to scramble after Coldhardt. 'Drop it and get the hell out while you can.'

Her face twisted with rage as she stumbled towards him. 'Call yourself thieves? Help me!'

The temple lurched downwards again. Jonah was thrown backwards to the cold, crumbling floor. He could see a huge rise of mud rucked up outside, parallel to the window where the others stood waiting. Coldhardt was about to jump for it when the whole of the wall beside him fell away. He lost his balance, mistimed his leap, landed heavily and scrabbled for a purchase in the mud. Motti and Con scrambled down to help him – while the temple went on sinking.

'Jonah!' Tye screamed.

He climbed on to the edge of the broken wall – but Honor ran into him, dropping her pots and cups and lumps of stone as she tried to pull him back. Jonah fought to get free, but a part of him feared it was already too late. It was getting darker as the giant mud banks eclipsed the low sun. He saw Motti and Con helping Coldhardt to the top of the rise – then they slipped from view. *At least they all made it*, he thought numbly. It felt like he was descending into hell in a huge stone elevator that was disintegrating around him.

'Help me, Wish,' Honor snarled, scooping up shards of pottery and pushing them into Jonah's hands. '*Help* me!'

'Help yourself,' he gasped, throwing the pieces back in her face; she recoiled on instinct, fell backwards. 'What else have you ever done?'

Jonah climbed back up on to the wall – and his heart caught in his throat as he saw his chance had gone. The temple had sunk too far back into the split in the earth, the steep muddy bank would be impossible to climb. He felt a terrible coldness, too frightened even for tears.

Then he saw the broken blade and the hilt of Cortes's sword at his feet. He grabbed it, held it in both hands, and quickly backed away into the temple for a run-up.

He'd never been brilliant at the long jump. But then, his life had never depended on it before.

Jonah launched himself from one of the crumbling pillars in the inner circle and sprinted across the rubble-strewn floor. As he neared the broken wall, he saw Honor crawl from the shadows, her face twisted with spite, reaching for his legs to try to trip him.

He knew he couldn't afford to slow for a second. So at the last moment he jumped clear over her head. Her gasp of outrage was sweet in his ears, like a breath of wind at his back pushing him on. He hit his mark on the wall with perfect accuracy and leaped forwards into the void, both hands clamped tight about the hilt of the sword, stretching out with both arms like a diver . . .

The spike of the sword dug into the hard-packed mud. Jonah thudded into the bank a fraction later. He gasped as the air was whumped from his body but clung on to the sword hilt, praying the blade was wedged in deep enough to hold his weight. He shut his eyes tight, ears ringing as Honor screamed, as the doomed temple tore itself apart, deep in its centuries-old hiding place, in the lowest pits of the open grave.

Jonah clung on, but his fingers were already killing him. Any sense of triumph soon dissipated – he had only delayed the inevitable. How was he supposed to scale the wall of the pit? If he had two broken swords, he could use them like a climber used ice picks; maybe then he might stand a chance. As it was . . .

He heard something slap against the mud above his head. Fearfully, he looked up – and blinked in disbelief. Something flopped into view, just a half-metre out of reach. Maybe he'd already fallen. Or maybe he was dreaming, delirious and trapped down in the remnants of the temple.

Whatever, he was staring up at a white lacy bra.

It had been tied to the sleeve of a black polo-neck top. The other sleeve was tied to one leg of a pair of dark jeans.

'Grab a hold, geek,' Motti shouted from somewhere way above.

A rope of laundry, dropped down to his rescue? Jonah figured he had nothing to lose. He reached up, grabbed hold of the bra strap with one hand and wrapped it round his wrist – then, with a muttered prayer to anyone who might be listening, he let go of the sword altogether. He gasped as he actually dropped down further into the pit as the fabrics stretched and knots tightened.

But the makeshift rope held his weight.

Jonah started dragging himself up, digging the heels of his boots into the mudface for extra support. Beyond Patch's jeans was Coldhardt's bloodstained linen jacket, in turn tied to Tye's jeans, in turn tied to Motti's black denim shirt, in turn tied to another bra, padded this time and patterned with little lilac flowers. He found himself smiling as he kept hauling himself up.

'C'mon, Jonah, you can do it!' Motti shouted, closer now.

'I'm just . . . hoping Patch's pants . . . aren't coming up any time soon,' Jonah called to them. The others started whooping, cheering him on. Arms burning, sweating with the effort, he scaled a pair of muddy trousers and Tye's pale blue blouse, and then the mud levelled out enough for him to rest for a moment. Panting for breath, Jonah pushed himself on, crawling up the looser mud until he reached the top of the rise.

A chorus of cheers went up. Motti was in his boxers, covered in bruises, arms raised above his head as he clapped. Con and Tye were dressed only in knickers, Aztec pendants and precarious bikini tops improvised from cacao leaves, so they jumped around a little less. And Patch, though he should have been ashamed for wearing such a vile, flesh-coloured pair of Y-fronts was beaming all over his face.

'Thanks,' Jonah told them simply, giving up to gravity at last and hugging the ground.

'Jonah, mate,' Patch cried, his good eye straying back to the barely-clad girls, 'you gotta fall down these dirty great holes in the ground more often.'

CHAPTER TWENTY-FOUR

Tye changed quickly back into her muddy clothes behind a tree. *We came through it*, she thought. *Somehow, we all made it through*.

Even Ramez.

How far had he run already?

She pushed the thought of him from her mind and rejoined Jonah and the others, who had gone to find Coldhardt. She saw them in the light of the setting sun, crowded round a radio in a small clearing at the edge of the devastated landscape.

'The hidden microphone in the amulet should still be transmitting.' Coldhardt stabbed at the radio's controls. He looked a far cry from his usual debonair self in his grimy, bloodied linen suit. 'I must know if anyone is still alive down there.'

'Hang on.' Jonah frowned. 'Thought I heard something.'

Coldhardt turned up the volume on the built-in speaker, and they all crept in a little closer. Tye heard someone cough. 'Michael? Is that you?' She barely recognised Honor's voice, tinged now with fear. 'My head . . . Why is it so dark?'

A man coughed. One of the Sixth Sun priests.

'What happened?'

'I . . .' Honor paused. 'What was that?'

Tye had been about to ask the same thing. She'd thought she could hear something in the background, a whispering noise. It started to build, like a wind blowing up to a gale. Tye felt a shiver run down her back.

'Who's there?' the man demanded, his voice wavering.

'What is it?' hissed Honor as the noise grew steadily louder. 'What can you see?'

And then the speaker distorted with the sound of screaming. The weird, rushing wind blew louder, all but drowning out Honor's final, bloodcurdling shriek.

The radio fell silent. Then the ambient noise crept back up. They heard a little rock dust fall. No voices. No movement.

For a good half-minute, no one spoke or even looked at each other.

'That could've been me down there,' Jonah said quietly.

Con bit her lip. 'What the hell was that noise?'

'Just interference,' Patch insisted, pale-faced. 'Told you, this humidity sods up the circuits.'

'So it wasn't the spirit of Coatlicue coming to call,' said Jonah darkly, 'feeding on the poison in men – and women – a bit more literally than Traynor thought.'

'Come off it,' Motti snorted. 'That was just air forced out of some vent or something as the foundations fell in on themselves . . .'

'Right,' said Con.

Coldhardt said nothing. The rest of them looked at

each other nervously, trying their hardest to be convinced by the explanation.

'Weird though,' said Jonah, 'how just about everything else in that codex prophecy tallied with something real. There was a kind of mechanism in the statue which needed the blade of a conquistador sword to be pushed in, or "wiped clean", to unlock it. And that showed us the place where the priests had hidden the real treasure.' He reached in his pocket and threw a handful of gold jewellery down at Coldhardt's feet. Con instantly stooped to scoop it up for close study. 'Though I don't understand how the ground in front of the statue dissolved like that.'

Tye frowned. 'Solid stone just dissolved?'

'It wasn't stone,' Coldhardt explained. 'That area with the indentations was a kind of thick, layered paper – designed to *look* like stone. When perfect sacrifice was made – or rather, when enough blood was spilled at the statue's feet – it soaked into the paper, weakened it –'

'And the weight of the gold discs from those dead attendants made it fall away,' said Jonah, 'to reveal the treasure.'

'To those who correctly unravelled the Nahuatl prophecy, yes,' Coldhardt agreed. 'As a result, we have a modest haul of booty.' He retrieved several more pieces of jewellery from inside his shirt, together with two more of the weird Aztec folding books, and handed them over to Con.

'But the rest of the treasure is still down there,' Con said sadly.

'Yeah, soaked with a deadly poison,' said Jonah.

'And there could be a fair few phials of it still intact as well.'

'This whole part of the rainforest is totally screwed,' Motti remarked. 'Ain't gonna be no covering this up.'

Coldhardt nodded. 'Which is why, now I'm satisfied there's no one alive down there to mention my name, I shall make an anonymous call to the government explaining one or two home truths about Michael Traynor, his ambitions, some missing plutonium – and about what they can expect to find in that temple.'

Jonah nodded. 'I guess then at least the authorities will go in prepared.'

'But what about the treasure?' said Con, pouting. 'It's ours by rights. Now it will end up in some dreary museum or something.'

'So?' Patch shrugged. 'They can clean it up for us. Least it'll be easier to steal from there.'

Coldhardt waved one of his Aztec books. 'You never know,' he said, smiling faintly. 'One of these codices could put us on to other secret treasure hauls.'

Tye slumped to the ground heavily. 'Can't wait.'

Jonah looked at Coldhardt. 'Planning on tracking down Coatlicue's presence to another likely spot?'

'Planning on taking whatever I can get.' Coldhardt looked reflective, oddly at peace. 'I asked whatever presence was there in the temple how to wrest life from death – and I was shown riches.' A slow, roguish smile spread over his craggy features. It made him look a good few years younger. 'I take that to be a good omen. I've been a thief from the start, and it looks like I'll die one too.'

Patch shuddered. 'Any more jobs like this one, we probably *all* will.'

'Well, we did manage to stop Traynor's global killing spree,' said Jonah. 'That's kind of wresting life from death, isn't it?'

'Gee, geek,' said Motti, 'd'you think if we write and tell the President we'll get a medal?'

Jonah thumped him in the ribs, and Motti shoved him back. But they were both smiling.

Con started to strip off her bangles and necklaces, adding them to her pile of treasures. 'At least these are worth something.'

Coldhardt considered. 'In total we may have made a couple of million.'

'And with Kabacra dead, we can rip off his place in Guatemala properly, yes?' Her eyes were gleaming.

'And Traynor too,' Patch suggested. 'I mean, his mansion is stacked full of goodies – including that horrible little green statue of yours!'

'I think we have the makings of a plan.' Coldhardt straightened up stiffly, pushing his hands through his grey mane of hair. 'Patch, share your knowledge of the place with Motti. I want the pair of you to come up with a business plan for clearing out Traynor's place by the time we've flown back to New Mexico.'

'Understood, chief,' said Motti.

Patch grinned. 'Gotcha.'

'Coldhardt,' Con asked brightly, showing him a thick gold bracelet. 'May I keep this? It is so pretty.'

He smiled indulgently. 'Who am I to refuse the secret voice of Coatlicue?'

She blushed, clearly delighted. 'You heard!'

'An inspired distraction . . .'

Tye found herself walking away from the noisy, buzzing little group to a quieter spot in a nearby grove, some place she could think. Yes, they had survived; they had blundered through again somehow. But always haunting the back of her mind was the thought of getting caught. The image of herself in place of Ramez, dragged away by police, screaming for all the wrong things while someone scared watched her from the shadows.

She looked out over the cacao trees in the evening light, their branches weighed down with ripening fruit, as someone came up behind her. For a fleeting, frightened moment she thought it was Ramez. It wasn't, though. He had gone, she knew. Gone for good.

'You could really lose yourself in a sunset like that,' Jonah ventured.

'That would be cool,' she murmured.

'You OK?'

Tye didn't turn round. Just took a deep breath and slowly let it out.

'Something's missing,' she said at last.

'What, now *he's* gone?'

'Who?'

'You know who.'

'I didn't mean him.' She turned to face him, smiled to see how serious he looked. 'I was actually talking about my bra.'

He raised his eyebrows. 'Your *bra* is missing?'

'If it's not on the mud bank, then Patch has got it,

the little pervert. Probably sniffing it right now.' She shrugged. 'I'll slap him about a bit and get it back. No problem.'

Jonah sighed. 'I can't bear the thought of someone going down for a crime they didn't commit.' He reached into his jeans pocket and pulled out her bundled-up bra.

She snatched it off him and folded her arms self-consciously. 'Jonah Wish, I hope you can explain yourself.'

He shrugged, smiled his so-not-innocent smile. 'Souvenir?'

'You don't need one,' she told him, turning back round to survey the quiet grove, leaning back against him gently, enjoying the last rays of the sun on her face. 'I'm not going anywhere.'

Jonah seemed to dwell on this a while. Then he slipped his arms around her waist and planted the softest, lightest kiss on the lump on the back of her head.

'Neither am I,' he said.